THE DECISION

"Oh, Freya," Honoria sighed out loud to the goshawk. "How I wish I could trade places with you. Even kept in a mews, you have more freedom than I."

She had never made so fervent a wish, or so sincere. But she hardly expected the gos to reply.

"Are you quite certain you mean that, my dear?"

The voice was female, and entirely unfamiliar; it was with a sense of dislocation and entire disbelief that Honoria turned to look at her goshawk.

"I must be going mad," she said, half to herself.

Freya watched her with her head turned entirely upside down, the position a raptor took when she wanted to get a really good look at something that interested her.

"I assure you, you are as sane as I am." The hawk righted her head. *"You can, you know. Trade places with me, that is. But you'd better be certain that it's what you really want, because you'll be a goshawk for a very long time."*

From "Wide Wings" by Mercedes Lackey

Also available from Mercedes Lackey
and DAW Books:

*Forthcoming in hardcover from DAW Books

FLIGHTS OF FANTASY

EDITED BY

Mercedes Lackey

DAW BOOKS, INC.
__DONALD A. WOLLHEIM, FOUNDER__
375 Hudson Street, New York, NY 10014

ELIZABETH R. WOLLHEIM
SHEILA E. GILBERT
PUBLISHERS
www.dawbooks.com

First Printing, December 1999
1 2 3 4 5 6 7 8 9 10

DAW TRADEMARK REGISTERED
U.S. PAT. OFF. AND FOREIGN COUNTRIES
—MARCA REGISTRADA
HECHO EN U.S.A.

PRINTED IN THE U.S.A.

ACKNOWLEDGMENTS

Introduction © 1999 by Mercedes Lackey
The Tale of Hràfn-Bui © 1999 by Diana L. Paxson
A Question of Faith © 1999 by Josepha Sherman
Taking Freedom © 1999 by S.M. Stirling
A Gathering of Bones © 1999 by Ron Collins
Night Flight © 1999 by Lawrence Watt Evans
A Buzzard Named Rabinowitz © 1999 by Mike Resnick
Tweaked in the Head © 1999 by Samuel C. Conway
One Wing Down © 1999 by Susan Shwartz
Owl Light © 1999 by Nancy Asire
Eagle's Eye © 1999 by Jody Lynn Nye
Wide Wings © 1999 by Mercedes Lackey

CONTENTS

OWL LIGHT
  by Nancy Asire

EAGLE'S EYE
  by Jody Lynn Nye

WIDE WINGS
  by Mercedes Lackey

INTRODUCTION

by Mercedes Lackey

RAPTORS. Birds of prey. Everyone gets a different mental picture when they think of birds of prey—birds who make their livings as predators, the top of the food chain. Some immediately picture the American bald eagle, the symbol of the United States, without realizing that the bald eagle is more often a fisher than a hunter, which is why they are most often found near large bodies of water. Some think of babies being carried off (not in recorded history) or savage golden eagles preying on lambs (unlikely—they are more likely to be taking advantage of a lamb found already dead; birds of prey rarely attack anything too big to carry off). Some imagine noble thoughts going on behind those enormous, keen eyes; others, even in this day and age, see a "varmint," a creature that attacks a farmer's animals and competes for hunting resources, and should be shot on sight.

Most are at least partly or completely wrong in what they imagine.

1

As a licensed raptor rehabber, I know birds of prey personally; sometimes *very* personally, as a great horned owl puts her talon through my Kevlar-lined welding glove and into my hand. . . .

There are no noble thoughts going on in those brains. Real raptors have relatively small brains, most of which is composed of visual cortex with the rest mostly hard-wired with hunting skills. That doesn't leave a lot of room for social behavior. I once read a passage in a romance novel describing a lady's falcon perched in a tree above her, watching protectively over her, and nearly became hysterical with laughter. No falcon in my acquaintance is going to perch in a tree, protectively or otherwise, if left to her own devices. Turn your back on her, and she will be out of there without a backward glance—which is why falconers in this day and age must fit their birds with jesses and bracelets (the leg-restraints) that can be removed by the bird. Nearly every falconer has sad tales of the ones that escaped, and *no* falconer wishes to think of his bird hanging upside down, entangled in her jesses in a tree, to die a slow and horrible death.

As for being "varmints," most birds of prey neither poach on farmers' livestock nor compete with hunters. The single two most common raptors in the US—American kestrels and redtail hawks, which can literally be found anywhere—prey, for the most part, on insects, mice, and sparrows for the former, and field rats, squirrels, and rabbits for the latter. Redtails rarely bother with flying prey—they are built to hunt things that run. As such, they do farmers more service than disservice.

Fascination with birds of prey seems to have been with us for as long as we've walked upright. A recent T-shirt called "Evolution of a Falconer" suggests that the hawk may have been adopted by early man almost as soon as the dog. Certainly there is some justification for saying that there have been falconers as long as there has been the written word. Falconers appear in ancient Persian and Indian miniatures, on the walls of Egyptian tombs, and in medieval manuscripts. There are falconers in every part of the world today, even in places where laws make it incredibly difficult. There are falconers in Japan, where ancient tradition favors the goshawk, and forbids commoners to touch the bird with their bare hands. There are falconers in Mongolia, who carry on *their* traditions of hunting wolves with golden eagles. There are falconers in Africa, in South America, and in virtually every European country. The tradition of falconry goes back so far in Saudi Arabia that the Saudis cannot even recall its beginnings. And needless to say, there are falconers spread all over North America.

There is, in fact, a falconer joke which transcends all boundaries and sends falconers of every nation into snickers. "How can you tell a man who flies a falcon? By the scratches on his

wrist where the bird decided to take a walk."
(Falcons are smaller, by and large, than hawks,
and those who fly falcons use short gloves to
protect their hands from the talons.) "How can
you tell a man who flies a hawk? By the suntan
that stops at his elbow." (Hawks tend to be
larger, heavier, and grip far more tightly with
their feet; only a fool flies a hawk without a *long*
glove.) "How can you tell a man who flies an
eagle? By the eyepatch." (Self-explanatory.)

Kings and emperors have written volumes on
falconry; hawks and falcons figure prominently
in myth. The Romans seem to have been of two
minds about eagles; they topped the standards
of their legions with them, and identified those
standards with the great birds so closely that the
standards themselves were referred to as "The
Eagles." On the other hand, it is from the Romans that we get the myth of eagles carrying
off babies. Zeus and Jupiter were both identified
with the eagle. The Arab world gave us the roc,
a bird of prey so large it carried off elephants.

As for history, New Zealand was once home
to a flightless bird of prey called the moa that
stood over eight feet tall! But more impressive
yet, at one point in prehistory, South America
bred *flighted* raptors the size of small airplanes,
which certainly *were* capable of carrying off, not
just babies, but full-grown adult humans! Could
these birds—or the dim memory of them—have
given rise to the Native American tales of the
Thunderbird? Certainly they would have been

the only birds strong enough to dare the deadly air-currents of tornadic supercell-storms, so that their appearance in the sky would have been heralded by the flash of lightning and the roar of thunder.

But—this anthology is not about real birds of prey. This is about the intersection of fantasy and reality, where raptors and other meat-eating birds are concerned. This is a wonderful collection full of surprises. For Diana Paxton, the "theme" was bent slightly, including ravens (who are, after all, carnivorous). From Mike Resnick comes a little fable that mixes revenge with reincarnation. From Nancy Asire, a spirit bird—

From a dear friend, Dr. Sam Conway, comes his first published story; I had warned him that I would be ruthless with it, and if it did not match the standards of the professionals, it wouldn't make the cut, but to the delight of both of us, it more than qualified.

And my own contribution, which came out of one of those odd cases of serendipity when a character demands more attention than the author is immediately prepared to give her. When I was working on *The Black Swan*, my own version of the tale told in the famous ballet *Swan Lake*, one of Prince Siegfried's bridal candidates suddenly took on a life and personality far beyond that of a mere spear-carrier. The falconer-Princess Honoria *and* her birds absolutely demanded to be center stage. Unfortunately, I had another story to tell than hers. Fortunately, she fit perfectly well into this venue, and I was happy to give her the spotlight on a stage of her own, and a story that proves the adage that what is hell to one may be heaven to another—or at least, an escape.

We all hope you enjoy these highly unusual birds, and their flights of fantasy.

THE TALE OF HRAFN-BUI

by Diana L. Paxson

Diana L. Paxson's novels include her *Chronicles of Westria* series and her more recent *Wodan's Children* series. Her short fiction can be found in the anthologies *Zodiac Fantastic, Grails: Quests of the Dawn, Return to Avalon,* and *The Book of Kings.* Her Arthurian novel, *Hallowed Isle,* is appearing in four volumes in the next two years, with book one, *The Book of the Sword,* in stores now.

THERE was a man called Ketil Olvirson who took up land below Hrafnfjäll in the west part of Iceland. He had two sons, Arnor and Harek. Arnor, who was the elder, liked best to go a-viking to England and Scotland and the isles, while Harek stayed home on the farm. On one of his journeys Arnor took captive a young woman called Groa. His parents were dead by that time, and though his brother said that no good would come of marriage with a woman who had been a thrall, he made her his wife.

She bore him a son whom they called Bui, but they had no other child.

About this time Harek also took a wife, named Hild. They all lived together in this way for some years, until Bui was fourteen years old. It happened then that an old shipmate asked Arnor to go on a trading voyage to Norway. At the end of the summer, when they looked for his return, he did not come. It was not until the next spring that they heard that the ship had gone down with all hands off the Sudhreyar Isles.

When that news came, Harek sat down in his brother's high seat and Hild said that as there were no witnesses to Groa's marriage, she was now their thrall. When Bui tried to defend his mother, Harek told his men to beat the boy with staves and drive him off the farm. They dragged him to the brook that comes down from Hrafn-fjäll, and there they left him.

But Bui did not die.

"Quo-oork!"

Bui opened one eye. Something black moved across his field of vision, paused, quorked again. He raised his head, and it disappeared. In the next moment pain speared through his skull, and he lost consciousness once more.

When he woke again, the light had dimmed. This time the pain was instantly present, a dull, pounding ache localized above his left eye. That eye was swollen shut, but the other was focusing now and he could hear the trickle of water from somewhere nearby. Grass waved gently in the forefront of his vision. Beyond it, he saw the sleek shape of a raven. For a moment its glittering black gaze met his own.

"Kru-uk? Ru-uk-uk?"

The inquiry was answered from above. With a groan, Bui rolled over, and the first raven flapped upward to join its mate in the stunted birch tree. For a moment of distorted vision he saw them as valkyries, waiting to choose the doom-fated men they would carry to Odin's hall.

"I'm not dead, curse you!" he whispered. "You'll have to wait for your meal!"

He closed his eye again in a vain attempt to shut out the images flickering in memory— Harek and Hild in his father's high seat—the malice in the face of the thralls as they closed in. Did the nithings believe they had left him for dead, or did they account a beardless boy of so little worth they did not care?

The movement had awakened the rest of Bui's body to a host of new agonies. He had the woozy, sick feeling that comes from blood loss, but no wet warmth to warn of reopening wounds. He had been hurt badly, but he had spoken truth to the ravens; he was not going to die for a while yet. For a moment, he found himself as disappointed as they.

Beyond the birch tree the fells rose stark against the dimming sky. He set his teeth against the pain and set about the business of learning to live again.

Before Bui lost consciousness he had managed to stagger a fair way up the brook toward the fell. The upper part of the vale was a good refuge, far enough from the farm to keep him from a chance discovery, but sheltered from the winds. For some days he had just enough strength to crawl from the bank to the waterside where the vivid purple fireweed grew. There he quenched his thirst and bathed his wounds.

It was high summer, and the weather held mild, with only a few showers of rain. Once Bui began to move about, the ravens lost interest in him, though he often saw them cruising overhead in search of food. They were clearly a mated pair; he took to calling them Harek and Hild, and threw stones to drive them away.

Three days of nothing but water and the tender inner bark of the birch left him as hungry as the birds. Weak as he was, Bui managed to trap a fish in a circle of stones, which he then filled with more rocks until the water ran out and the fish flopped helplessly. As he tore at the sweet flesh, he could feel strength pouring back into his body.

That night, as he lay curled in a nest of soft grass beneath the trees, he dreamed.

An old man came walking over the fells, wrapped in a dark cloak with a broad hat drawn down over his eyes. As he trudged forward, leaning on his staff, a wind came up, bending the grass and lifting the edges of his mantle so that it billowed like dark wings. And then suddenly it *was* wings, as the cloak separated into a host of ravens that swirled across the sky.

The old man turned, and his figure grew until he towered into the heavens. But now he wore mail and a helmet, and he had only one eye. His staff had become a spear, pointing back toward the farm.

"Look to the ravens. They will be your guides. . . ."

From that time, Bui recovered rapidly, being young and hardened by work on the farm. He followed the vale upstream to the edge of the fell, and found a place where a fissure in the earth had formed a small cave which could be improved with stones and turves until it kept out the rain. He twisted twigs of dwarf willow into a weir to trap fish, and fashioned a sling with which he could bring down birds that came to the lake on the fell. With a fire drill and a great deal of patience he was able to make a fire which he kept smoldering in the cave.

For the moment, Bui was surviving. The reasonable thing would be to make his way to some other farm and take service there before winter came. But he dreamed sometimes that he heard his mother weeping, and could not bring himself to leave Hrafnfjäll.

When he had been on the fell for a moon, he had the fortune to find a strayed ewe caught among the stones. Swiftly he slit its throat with his belt knife and began to butcher it, saving every part of the animal he might be able to use. It was a messy job, and as he finished, it occurred to him that anyone who came searching for the animal would find the remains and him, as well.

A familiar "whoosh" of wings overhead brought his head up. Swearing, he looked for a stone, then paused, frowning, for this raven was a stranger, smaller and scruffier than the territorial pair, with a distinctive white spot upon its tail. It hopped forward and then back again, avid and wary at the same time. Ravens, thought Bui, could pick the sheep's carcass so clean no one would be able to tell how it had died. He sawed off a hunk of fat and tossed it toward the bird.

The raven exploded into the air in a flurry of black wings, circled once, then flew away westward over the fell, emitting a peculiar cry rather like a yell. Bui watched it go in disappointment, then finished bundling the meat into the sheepskin, shouldered it, and made his way back to the cave. He fashioned a rack in the back of the cavern to smoke the meat, and that night he ate cooked mutton for the first time in over a moon.

The next day Bui went back to the carcass, dropping to hands and knees as he approached and taking care to remain unseen. It had occurred to him that the raven he had seen might be a young one, without the insolent confidence of the territorial pair, and he did not want to frighten it away.

He need not have bothered. There were no birds to be seen. Then he looked again and grinned. Raven tracks showed everywhere, and the carcass had been picked clean. On the ground before him lay a black feather. Bui picked it up and stood for a long time, stroking the smooth vane.

* * *

Bui realized that he had decided to stay on the fell the day he found the body of the man. It had been there a long time, and there was little to be scavenged from the clothes. The shaft of the spear had rotted away, but the point, though rusted, was still whole, as was the head of the ax that had been thrust through the man's belt. A disintegrating leather sheath had protected the sword. The metal framework for a leather-covered helmet still shielded the skull. Bui might tell himself that the spear was for the seals that winter would bring to the shore, but the only use for the sword and helm was when you went to kill men.

The Althing had not judged him outlaw, but Bui had heard stories enough to know how to live like one. He turned from the fell, with the pale menace of the glacier on its horizon, to the long dun slopes that stretched toward the sea. The air was so clear he could glimpse the green of the vale. Inner vision supplied the long, turf-roofed shape of the farm, *his* farm, where his mother labored, a thrall once more.

"Odin, hear me! Show me how to take back my land!" He raised the sword to the sky.

As if the action had invoked them, black specks appeared in the sky. One, two, three—Heart pounding, Bui counted as nine ravens plummeted earthward, rolling in the air and pulling up in a long swoop, only to spiral downward, wings half folded once more. Breathless, he watched the aerial display until on some silent signal they all circled above him, and then flapped away across the fell.

"Hrafna-guth, Raven-god," Bui whispered, remembering his dream, "Let your birds show me the way, and they shall never lack for an offering."

As the nights grew longer, the air became clamorous with the cries of migrating waterfowl. Bui spent most of the daylight hours beside the lake, using nets and his sling to bring down ducks of all kinds and geese as well. He built a second structure of turf to smoke the meat, and cured the skins of the eider-duck with the feathers on to serve as bedding.

His activities very quickly attracted the ravens, and he and they began to learn each other's ways. Now, when he set out for a day's hunting a black speck would soon appear, checking at regular intervals until he made a kill. Usually it was one of the pair that "owned" Hrafnfjäll that came first. When there was a carcass, one bird would summon the other. Necks stretched upward, feathers fluffed aggressively and standing up like two ears on either side of the head, they strutted around the meat, and any younger birds that might be present would back away, bowing and bobbing, and waiting patiently to pick over whatever "Harek" and "Hild" might leave.

"Why don't you stick up for yourselves, you stupid birds?" Bui swore at the others. "They don't deserve to get it all."

But it was only when a young raven arrived before its elders, and even then, only if its yelling succeeded in summoning an overwhelming number of its fellows, that it would feed. At such times, Bui would watch in satisfaction as the older pair, coming late to the feast, were forced to take their turn with the rest. He took to hiding carcasses under piles of stones until he saw one of the wanderers, and soon he found that although the mated pair made their patrols no more often than before, wherever he went, one of the young birds always seemed to be near. With time, he was able to distinguish some from among them—one had a bent foot, another was large, with a rough head, and then there was his friend, the bold bird with the white spot on its tail.

The weather grew cooler, and sometimes sleet came mixed with the frequent rains. The migratory flocks departed, and Bui decided that he would have to risk a journey to the shore. He had fashioned a net of sinew for fishing, and with a great deal of luck, he might even get a seal.

He traveled cautiously, moving mostly in the early mornings and hiding during the brightest hours of the day. When he lived on the farm, they had always gone eastward up the coast for fishing, so he made his way to the west. Moving along the edge of the cliffs one morning, he heard a distant barking, and looking down, he saw a scattering of brown-furred bodies basking upon the sands of a small cove.

He stared at the tumble of rock where part of the cliff had slid away, wondering if he could get down. Then a call from overhead brought his gaze upward to the circling black shape in the sky.

"Are you telling me I can make it, or do you just hope for more food?" Despite their companionship, he did not suppose the ravens would care whether they feasted on the carcass of a seal or his own. Nonetheless, he chose to take the bird's arrival as an omen, and with spear strapped to his back, he began the difficult descent to the shore.

By the time he reached the moraine at the bottom of the cliff, Bui was scratched in a dozen places. As he sat down on a rock to catch his breath, he heard a familiar "swoosh" of wings.

The raven braked, banked, and settled on an

outcrop of basalt, where it sat preening its wings and surveying Bui with a distinctly humorous gleam in its black eyes. He saw without surprise that it was the young bird with the white spot on its tail.

In the first days of his exile, Bui had wondered if isolation would lead to madness. It was the ravens that had saved him from it, unless he was crazy to think their response to him the act of an intelligent will. The ravens belonged to Odin; the god was watching over him through their eyes, and he could reassure himself that when he talked to them, he was speaking to the god.

"Are you laughing at this clumsy human?" he asked, inspecting his bruises. "You're right. It would be a lot easier to get down here if I were a bird. But *you* can't kill a seal!"

Bui wondered if he could. Seals were accustomed to human hunters, and wary, but perhaps he no longer smelled like a man after three moons spent in the wild. Nonetheless, he stayed hidden for a day, observing, before he made his move, clambering down to hide among the rocks while the beasts were at sea, and waiting until they had settled down to bask in the autumn sunlight before rising with poised spear.

The seal Bui had selected was young, without so thick a layer of fat to get through. He focused on the spot between the shoulderblades and drove downward with all his strength, knowing, even as the honed blade struck, that his aim was true. Feeling its death, the seal reared up beneath him. Bui hung on with all his strength, knowing he must not allow the wounded animal to reach the sea, and even with the boy's weight to anchor it, the seal managed to reach the edge of the water before it died.

It was fortunate, reflected Bui as the world stopped spinning around him, that it was just past high tide, for he knew he did not have the strength to haul the carcass back up the beach. He slit the animal's throat, and as the blood drained into the sea, the raven spiraled upward, its exultant yelling interspersed by ear-splitting trills.

By the time Bui had the belly open, the rocks behind him were covered with black birds. Cursing, the ravens drove off the yammering guillemots and gulls, then dropped back to their perches, watching his progress with critical gaze. As the boy pulled open the slit flesh, the steaming guts spilled out onto the sand and the entire flock rose in a fluttering mass, calling excitedly.

"Very well—here's your share!" Bui exclaimed. "Now leave me in peace while I get mine!" He scooped up as much of the slippery mass as he could and pulled it to one side, and as he finished extracting it, the ravens swooped down and began to feed.

The gods were kind, and gave him three days of fair weather before the clouds closed in once more. By that time Bui had carved most of the muscle meat away from the bones, sliced it into thin strips and hung them to dry. The ravens picked clean what remained and took to harrying the gulls and stealing their food. The hide he pegged out, scraped clean and scoured with brine. But when the first drops of rain began to fall, he bundled it all into the shelter of the cliff.

He had lived his life mostly inland, and was not prepared for the fury of the storm. When the waves were driven almost to his refuge he was terrified, but better he should die now than abandon the food that might get him through the winter. And presently the waters began to calm. It was when boxes and bundles and the timbers of a wrecked ship began to wash ashore that he realized that the sea had more bounty to bestow.

With them came the corpses of men.

Bui dragged the bodies ashore, swallowing his revulsion at the feel of clammy flesh for the sake of the garments that covered them. Sea-stained though they were, they were better than his own rags. It was a race between him and the ravens, who did not understand why he would not share this windfall as he had always shared his prey with them before.

He finished piling stones over the body of a man whose wool tunic had been clasped with gold, and started toward the next two bodies, which were lying tangled in the seaweed just above the tide. The white-spotted raven had landed on the head of the nearest, but before

Bui could wave it off, it hopped aside with a screech of exasperation and then flapped away. As the boy reached down to grab the neckband of the man's tunic he felt a faint pulse. His own pulse leaped as the other body stirred, and he realized that these two still lived!

They were barely conscious, and the tide was coming in. Trembling, Bui dragged them over the stones to his shelter. It had been so long since he had spoken to anyone he wondered if he could still master human words. He built up the fire, and laid them as close as he dared to its flame, chafing chilled limbs, and presently first one and then the other began to cough and shiver and open his eyes.

It was the next morning before they were able to tell him their story. They were from Norway, nephews to the master of the foundered long-ship, come on their first voyage to trade for wadmal cloth and walrus ivory and the skins of seals. Hogni and Torstein were their names. Younger sons, they had intended to make their way by trading, but all hope of that had drowned when their uncle's ship went down. Did Bui know of a farm that needed laborers?

Bui felt his own features contorting in a twisted grin. "If you are willing to live like thralls, no doubt they will take you on at the farm," he said stiffly. "But if you have the courage to risk a winter in the wilds, you might one day share it with me—" Swiftly he explained how he had been banished by his uncle and aunt, and his plans for revenge.

"You would give us a share in your land?" asked Hogni, the elder of the two.

"I would, or the value of it once it is producing once more."

"And you have not been outlawed?" asked Torstein.

"They do not know what has become of me," Bui gave a mirthless laugh. "I do not offer you safety, but the chance to do deeds that will be remembered. It is up to you. I ask only this. If you do not join me, then say nothing of my presence on the fell. I think you owe me that much for pulling you out of the sea."

Torstein looked at his brother, and then grinned back at him. "It is clear that Ran does not want us. Maybe we can earn a place in Odin's warband with you!"

That seemed likely enough, thought Bui, but he took it as yet another sign from the god.

With two additional pairs of hands and the scavengings from the boat, they were able to take three more seals and a quantity of fish to carry back to Bui's hideaway at the edge of the fell. Once more, the ravens followed. Hogni and Torstein marveled at the birds, and took to calling their rescuer Hrafn-Bui.

"You are laughing at me, but I will claim in earnest the name you give in jest," answered Bui. "The ravens are our allies—you will see."

*   *   *

As the days diminished, the weather worsened, but the warm current that flows past Iceland's shores kept the temperatures on the south coast relatively mild, and the hot springs warmed the fugitives when they did begin to suffer from the chill. They were always hungry, but they never starved, and for this, they thanked Bui's ravens.

As once the birds had followed him, now Bui and his companions followed the ravens to food. In those days, folk used to leave their herds to winter in the woods, for there were no predators large enough to trouble a grown animal, and sometimes the exiles would find a cow or pony that had wandered off in search of the dry grasses that grew on the fell. They preyed on wintering waterbirds and, between the frequent gales, on seals. And leading or following, the ravens hunted with them, just as they did with the polar bears.

During the long hours of darkness the three young men huddled in the light of the seal-fat lamp and told tales.

"I'll help you for a time on the farm," said Hogni, "but the sea is all I ever dreamed of."

"My father loved the sea more than he loved my mother and me," answered Bui, "and it killed him."

Torstein sighed. "You can die anywhere. Our father took a scratch that went bad. His arm swelled up, and he burned with fever until he died. What glory was there in that?"

In his voice was a note that Bui recognized.

Both of them, he thought then, had been abandoned by the fathers who should have protected them.

"Is that what you want? Glory?" he asked.

"Of course. Don't you?"

Bui shook his head. "All I want is my home. . . ."

"Do you really think that the three of us can drive your uncle out?" Torstein asked then.

"I have dreamed that Odin and the ravens will show me the way."

Torstein exchanged glances with his brother, but neither replied.

Either they will keep faith with me, or they will not, thought Bui. He pulled on the rough cape he had cobbled together from sealskin and went outside.

The nights were beginning to grow shorter at last, and though clouds billowed on the horizon, the sleet and snow had ceased. A soft half-light lay over the fell and glittered on the branches of birch and willow where the buds were beginning to swell. Bui let out his breath in a long sigh.

They had survived the worst of the winter. It was colder up here at the head of the vale than it had been at the farm, but there was shelter from the worst of the wind, and the coast took the brunt of the storms. The land here might not be as rich as it was farther down the valley, but the fell provided good grazing. It occurred to him suddenly that if they had been able to live in his crude shelter, in a properly built dwelling one might do quite well.

A whoosh of wings overhead broke his train of thought, and he saw the young raven with the white spot circle and alight upon a stone.

"Have you been hunting through the night, or are you just rising?" Bui asked. Ravens, despite their color, were birds of the daylight. Could they carry enough fat to sleep through the long winter darkness, or like men, were they able to hunt the night when need compelled?

In another moment a second, smaller raven dropped down from the sky. The sleek head turned and dipped as the bird half spread its wings, neck feathers fluffing, and lifted its tail. The first raven watched for a moment, then appeared to expand, rising to its full height, feathers bristling around its head. This was the one, he remembered, that had always taken the lead in calling the other young ones, and challenging the territorial pair for food.

Very imposing, thought Bui in amusement. *Does she appreciate it?* He was almost certain that the smaller bird was a female now.

For a moment she watched the male, then repeated her bobs and bows, murmuring love talk with coos and snaps. Bui was abruptly reminded of the way the servant girls used to flick their aprons to tease the men in the hall.

If these birds were not yet a mated pair, they were certainly courting. *Good luck to you*—Bui thought wistfully. Even if he were to win back the farm, a kinslayer would be a poor marriage prospect for any man's daughter. There was a girl called Asgerd, the daughter of Geiralf Bardson who had a farm over at Langdale, whom he had thought might make a good wife for him when they were both grown. Suddenly her face came clearly to memory.

Since the day he was driven from the farm all Bui's energy had been focused on survival, but in this moment poised between light and darkness while the ravens danced, something long suppressed stirred and shaped itself into a stave of poetry—

> Mournful the man who must go mateless,
> Who lonely lies in the lee of the fell;
> Even Odin's friend, the doom-fated raven,
> the bird of battle, a bride may win. . . .

When the Outmonths had passed, the days began to lengthen swiftly, and the air rang with the cries of returning birds. The green of new grass veiled the sere slopes of the moorland, jeweled with daisy and dandelion and the more delicate blossoms of pinks and saxifrage. The warming air thrummed with urgency, and as the young ravens played upon the wind, Bui and the two Norwegians cut sticks of willow and began to practice their swordplay.

As they sat by their fire on an evening half-way through the Milking Moon, Hogni lifted one foot, wiggling his toes so they stuck out of the holes in his shoe.

"We need to kill a cow."

"What?" The others looked at him.

"I need new shoes, and so do you, not to mention rawhide and sinew to repair our weapons. And I am growing very tired of eating bird-flesh and dried seal."

Torstein laughed, but Bui grew thoughtful. Hogni had a good point, even though, with the warming weather, the people of the farm would be more inclined to come looking if one of their beasts disappeared. Still, he had always known that he could not stay hidden here forever. Perhaps it was time to make his move.

Nonetheless, he insisted on separating the heifer they chose from the herd and driving her up onto the fell before they made the kill.

They had bled out the carcass and were hard at work on the hide when the first raven arrived. Bui looked up, but it was not the white-spotted male he had been expecting. This was a smaller, younger bird. It lit on a boulder, looking around nervously, then extended its wings and flapped away.

"That's right," Bui laughed. "Go call the others. There will be more than enough for all.

They heaved out the guts in a pile for the birds and continued the butchering. Presently a bird quorked from overhead and another answered it. Bui looked up and saw two ravens circling, discussing the carcass with harsh cries. He stiffened, thinking the territorial pair he had encountered the previous year were back, though he would have thought this kill out of their territory. Then the male glided down, emitting three slow "knocking" calls, and he saw the white spot on its tail. After a moment the female followed him.

Now he could see the other birds, half a dozen tattered black shapes fluttering across the sky. They swirled down in the wake of the first two, but as they began to alight, the white-spotted male reared up, head feathers bristling until they stood up on either side like two ears, and began to strut back and forth, warning away the very birds whom the season before he had led against the territorial pair.

For a moment Bui stared, gut twisting as if he himself had been betrayed. Then he ran toward them, waving his arms and yelling until all the birds had risen squawking away. Torstein and Hogni watched open-mouthed, but Bui did not explain.

That night Bui dreamed. He was moving across the moor, and as he looked down he realized that he was flying. A glance to either side showed him black wings. The sensation was sufficiently novel that for some time he gave himself up to the pleasure of exploring the capacities of this body, soaring and diving, performing rolls and twists, dancing with the wind.

His play was so absorbing that it took some time to realize that he was not flying alone. Two larger ravens flew with him, one to either side.

Their feathers shone like polished metal, but the light came from within. They drew closer when they realized he had seen them.

"I am Huginn—" said the first raven. "To know thy way is to know thyself—"

"I am Munnin—" said the second. "Remember. . . ."

Then they soared ahead of him, movements matched until they seemed one being, whose brightness merged, then blinded, so that he floated, without need or volition, in the light. In that blind brilliance it seemed to him that he heard another voice that spoke to him for some time. But when he opened his eyes at last to the thin light of morning filtering into the cave, he could not remember the words.

In the morning, Hogni, who had decided he wanted to make a drinking horn, went back to the carcass for one of the heifer's horns while Torstein and Bui stayed at the shelter to prepare the meat for smoking. But the young Norwegian returned much more quickly than he had gone.

"Douse the fire!" he called, his face pale. "There are men on the moor!"

As they covered the fire and bundled their tools into the shelter, Hogni told his tale. The farmfolk must have tracked the heifer. He had seen two men, circling the carcass and gesturing. As always, the boys had brushed away their tracks, but the carcass would still have shown the marks of their butchering. Bui had frightened the ravens, whose voracious beaks had always obliterated all other evidence, away.

"They're thralls," said Bui when Hogni finished. "They will go back now to the farm to report what they have seen."

"Then we have a little time—enough to get away." Torstein began to bundle up his things.

Bui shook his head. This must be why he had dreamed. Images, half-understood and half-remembered, surged in memory.

"But we can't stay!" exclaimed Hogni. "Now they know someone is up here, they will be combing the fells for us by tomorrow!"

"That's so," answered Bui. "But they don't know that we've been warned—we must attack the farm!"

He straightened, watching the color come and go in their faces, willing them to agree now, before they had time to think about it too much and grow afraid; before he himself lost his nerve. They had all known this moment must come. No doubt they could survive another year living like beasts on the fell, but at the end of it would their hearts still be those of men?

Just when he thought the silence must become unendurable, Hogni gave a little laugh.

"I'm tired of sleeping on a pile of moss and birdskins anyway. Whether I lie tomorrow night in a farmhouse bed or in Odin's hall, it will be an improvement over here."

Torstein grinned back at him. "No doubt Bui will want to carry that sword he's been sharpening, and you're best with the ax, so I guess that leaves me the spear!''

Bui wondered if they could hear his heart pounding in his chest. Wordlessly, he got up and went to the rock-built cupboard where he kept the sword. But Torstein had been right—it was already sharp, fitted with a new hilt of seal-bone and well oiled. With it he kept the frame-work of the helmet. Thoughtfully, he considered it, then cut pieces from the still raw hide of the cow and began to piece them together over the frame.

But it was not enough. The image of the white-spotted raven strutting beside the cow carcass teased at his memory. During the winter he had found a dead raven and saved the wings. Now he bound one to each side of the helm so that they stood up like ears. Then he tried it on. Torstein raised one eyebrow and Hogni laughed, but Bui ignored them.

Now I am the king-raven, he thought grimly, *and I will claim my own!*

When the last light had left the sky Hrafn-Bui led his little war-band down the vale. By the time they came to the wall of the garth, it was near midnight. But it was as well that Bui led cautiously, for as they started to climb over, the door of the long-house swung open and firelight spilled across the ground. A man's figure stood silhouetted against it. Bui's heart fluttered in his breast as he recognized his uncle's heavy shoulders and the foreward thrust of his head.

He reached out to push the others back and found them already crouched behind the wall.

"I thought you said everyone would be asleep by now," whispered Torstein as Harek trudged across the yard to the privy.

"They should be. They're nervous, too—"

"They've been sitting up, planning how to catch you!" Hogni's laugh was stifled as the door to the privy banged open and Harek went back to the hall. The dog stood up as he neared, but Harek kicked it aside and closed the door.

They waited, shivering a little as their bodies began to cool and the stars wheeled overhead through the slow hours of the outtide. When they looked again, the glow around the door had dimmed, and the squat shape of the turf walled long-house bulked dark against the night sky. Bui stood up, feeling excitement fire his blood, and slipped over the wall.

As he moved towards the house, the dog began to growl. Hogni and Torstein hung back, but Bui whistled softly, and the growl became a grunt of delight as the animal caught his scent and leaped toward him. Bui told himself the dog's affection should be no surprise—he was probably the only one on the place who had been kind to it—but his eyes stung with tears all the same.

"Quiet, Ulfr," he whispered, when he could get the beast to calm down. He dragged it by the collar to sniff Hogni and Torstein. "Friend, Ulfr, *friend*. Now be still!"

When he let the dog go, it frisked around them, but made no other sound. He motioned to the others, and they moved around the hall toward the sheds.

"This would be easier in Norway," breathed Torstein. "The houses are made of wood, and we have lots of trees."

"Here we have a woodpile," answered Bui. "And it will do—I only mean to smoke them out, not to burn the whole house down."

The house had two doorways. Moving quietly, they piled firewood in front of each of them, while the dog frisked about, wagging its tail. When Bui smelled the approach of dawn in the damp air, he unstoppered the cowhorn in which he had kept coals smoldering and blew them into flame.

"You two stand at the far door. Ulfr and I will take this one," said Bui, grinning as fire sparked through the kindling and began to bite the logs.

The folk of the farm had slept all the harder for staying up so long. By the time enough smoke had penetrated to wake them, the two fires were blazing merrily. The door slammed open; for a moment they saw Harek, then he recoiled, cursing. From inside the hall came a woman's scream.

"Uncle, uncle—" called Bui. "For a year I

have lived like a raven in the rocks. Will you grudge me a little fire?"

The main door was pulled back again and Harek peered out, breathing through a cloth. His eyes widened as he recognized his nephew beneath the fantastic headgear. At the same moment the far door opened. The flicker of Torstein's spear was followed by a cry of pain.

"My boy, have you gone crazy?" called Harek. "I am your kinsman—"

"Was it the work of a kinsman to drive me from your door? Send out my mother, and men may call me what they will." Bui had always known he risked outlawry as a kinslayer, despite his fine words to Hogni and Torstein. But he could not leave Groa in Harek's power.

He cleared his throat. "She may bring with her the women and all the men except those you set to beat me. But you shall choose whether to face my sword of this fire!" He heard his own voice crack and did not know whether it was with fear or rage.

He waited, shaking with tension, as light grew in the east and the flames paled. What if his uncle decided to hold Groa hostage? No reputation would be left to him, but would he care?

The door was beginning to smolder by the time it opened once more. Bui felt his knees grow weak with relief as he saw his mother hesitate in the opening, coughing, then leap through the flames. Her shawl had caught fire; he slapped at the sparks, then shoved her behind him, sword ready, as the others began to come through. He could hear her sobbing quietly, but she knew better than to speak to him now.

One . . . two . . . three . . . he counted the maids and then the men. There was a pause, then he saw Hild, with another woman muffled in a cloak beside her.

"Oh ho, my aunt, have you got a new maidservant since I've been gone?" As the two women came through the fire, he lunged and sent the cloaked one sprawling. His blade followed his arm, and in the next moment he had the point at Harek's throat.

For a long moment there was no sound but the crackling of the flames. Then, from the direction of the sunrise, he heard a raven's cry.

"You won't get away with this!" snarled Harek. "Kill me, and you'll be outlawed; spare me, and I'll have you killed!"

But Bui was not listening. From the west the raven was answered, and from the direction of the fell, and from the sea. From every direction ravens came flying; the bright air trembled with the sound of their wings. Harek's rolling eyes widened as the black birds settled on the wall of the garth, surrounding them.

Bui began to laugh, and if there was a ring of madness in it, he did not care. "Will you accuse me before the Althing? Here are my witnesses! Or perhaps they are hungry, and think your guts will make a good meal."

A sickly stench began to pervade the air and he realized that Harek had soiled himself. Hild stepped back, the anger in her face giving way to scorn.

Suddenly Bui remembered how the king-raven had faced down an intruder, who cowered and backed away.

I have won! he thought in amazement. *Hild will remember this—they will all remember, and if he tries to attack me, someone is bound to tell the tale.*

He laughed again, but now he was back in control.

"Harek Ketilson, I accuse you of taking a free woman as a thrall and robbing me of my inheritance. Will you acknowledge the wrong and offer me sole-judgment, or must I take you bound in your filth to the Althing and seek an arbitrator there?"

One of the ravens spread its wings to their considerable width and launched itself from the wall in a long glide to land beside his uncle's head. Without surprise, Bui noted the white spot on its tail. Harek paled and closed his eyes. The raven hopped closer, considered for a moment, and yanked out a strand of hair. Harek recoiled with a squeak of anguish.

"I agree—"

"Say it louder," said Bui. "Do you all bear witness to his words?"

"Make your own judgment," cried Harek, "but send that black-feathered troll away!"

"That's no troll, uncle mine, but Odin's bird,

the best witness of all." Bui grinned. The part
of his dream he had forgotten was clear to him
now, and he understood many things. He felt
the invisible weight of Huginn and Munnin on
his shoulders, giving him counsel.

"When he took a mate, he did not drive off
the birds who nest near this farm, but claimed
a territory of his own, and so shall I. This is the
compensation I require—give me the upper part
of the valley and the slopes of Hrafnfjäll. I will
build a house of my own beneath the fells. I will
take my mother, and whichever of the men and
maids she chooses, and the dog Ulfr, and half
of the sheep and cows. You will provide food
and clothing and weapons for me and my men,
and everything we need to begin. But you will
keep this farm."

"Take them—" whimpered Harek, weeping,
"and may Hella take you all."

Bui glanced over at Torstein and Hogni, and
saw wonder, and relief, in their eyes.

"Tie him up—" he pointed at Harek, "and
then put out the fires. And when you have done
that, bring us food. No—" he corrected himself
as the maids began to move. "Before you feed
us, kill a sheep and put the carcass out on the
hill. I am Hrafn-Bui, and I will not forget what
I owe my kin!"

His mother came to him then, and he hugged
her hard. A sudden wind stirred the ashes, and
as the black flakes lifted into the air so did the

ravens, a swirl of bird shapes, black and bright, mounting the morning sky.

Note: For those who are interested in learning more about ravens, I recommend the following.

Bernd Heinrich, *Ravens in Winter,* N.Y.: Vintage, 1989

Lawrence Kilham, *The American Crow and the Common Raven,* Texas A&M University Press, 1989

Candace Savage, *Bird Brains,* San Francisco: Sierra Club, 1995

A QUESTION OF FAITH

by Josepha Sherman

Josepha Sherman is a fantasy writer and folklorist whose latest novels are *Star Trek: Vulcan's Forge* and *Son of Darkness*. Her most recent folklore volume is *Merlin's Kin: World Tales of the Hero Magicians*. Her short fiction has appeared in numerous anthologies, including *Battle Magic*, *Dinosaur Fantastic*, and *The Shimmering Door*. She lives in Riverdale, New York.

ARIKAN, travel-worn and weary, stopped on the narrow way between the cliffs to catch his breath. It had been a long journey, and he was no longer a boy to go tearing along. And . . . it had been a long while since he'd been here. Far too long.

On either side, the jagged gray walls towered over him, with the bright blue desert sky high overhead and the heat of the new day filtering down through the fading chill of the night. Ahead, Arikan thought with a sudden surge of joy so strong that it astonished him, lay the village of the Eagle Spirit People.

His people.

No doubt, Arikan thought, starting forward again, the lookouts somewhere up on those cliffs had already spotted him. And, presumably, since there'd been no attack, they had recognized him first as not of the Owl Spirit People, the enemy, then as one of their own.

They *would* recognize him, would they not? Arikan's mouth quirked up in a wry grin. Maybe not, at that. He had, after all, spent a long time out there in the desert, years alone, seeking a vision, seeking any sign of . . .

Of some reason to still have faith. To still believe in *something*. Arikan couldn't trace the exact moment when he had lost belief, only that it had slipped away from him, leaving him empty.

Ridiculous for a man grown to be hunting a vision. No wonder he'd seen and felt absolutely nothing. Save fatigue. And thirst. And utter boredom.

But the desert's privation had changed him, given him a lean, spare body and a face sharpened by its lack of any extra flesh. His hair was long and ragged, his reddish-tan skin burned a darker brown. A wild thing, he, no doubt about it. Unlikely, Arikan thought wryly, that any would recognize him.

Ah, but there lay the village, the skin lodges of the People spread out in the so-familiar jumble, and Arikan's grin became a true smile. He hurried forward. At least there was this in which to believe, the village and those within it. His people. His home.

A child playing in the dirt saw him first, and let out a shriek that brought everyone running. Arikan found himself facing a wall of warriors with drawn bows, their eyes so wild with alarm that he said hastily, "I am Arikan! You know me, Karik, and you, Lathai—I can't have changed *that* much!"

The warriors stirred, moving aside to let a lean old figure pass: Wenketh, Arikan realized. The shaman's hair had turned pure white, and his face held more lines than before, but he stood as proud and straight-backed as ever.

"This is Arikan," was all he said, then turned away as though no longer concerned. As the bows were lowered, Wenketh called over his shoulder to Arikan, "We meet. Join us. Now."

No choice in the matter, eh? No chance to see if any would give him a place to rest, food or drink in welcome? Granted, the shaman had never been one for idle chatter, but this . . .

Wondering, Arikan took his place among the others, seated on the ground in a circle about the village's central hearth, and acknowledged the stares with polite dips of his head: Yes, he was back.

Courtesy demanded a complicated ritual for one who'd been away from the People so long— particularly, Arikan thought, for one who'd gone off in search of a vision. Of course no one asked if he'd actually found one; that would have been unthinkably improper. But the ritual was little more than the briefest of blessings from old Wenketh, who dusted him with pollen there in the central meeting place, then fixed him with an alarmingly intent stare. And there was such tension radiating from everyone that Arikan burst out, even though it was not his place to speak first, "What has happened?"

"The eagles are gone," the shaman told him, almost accusingly.

For an astonished moment, Arikan could do nothing but stare. There had always been eagles, a mated pair, whether the same or their descendants, living in a cliffside nest overlooking the village; beautiful birds with a vast wingspan and a glint of gold over the brown of their plumage, they were the tangible sign of the People's name!

Even if one no longer believed in the guiding Spirit behind them . . .

"Gone *how*?" Arikan insisted. "There's been no storm so mighty it could tear down the nest, and no one could climb that cliff!"

"No one human," someone said darkly.

"Aie, nonsense!"

But his voice was drowned out by the others. "What does it mean?"

"Has the Eagle Spirit abandoned us? Have all the gods?"

"The village still stands," Arikan pointed out.

"But without the eagles, how can the Eagle Spirit stay?"

Arikan bit back an impatient, There is no such being! "We can hardly pack up and leave. Besides, the water here never fails, and the soil is rich enough—"

"For now!"

"Without the eagles, the land will reject us!"

"We cannot stay!"

Only Shaman Wenketh said nothing, continuing his disconcerting stare at Arikan. Arikan shifted uneasily. "Where would you have us go? To the Wolf Spirit People? They would let us pass, yes, but never settle. And the Owl Spirit People . . ."

"It is their doing," the old shaman said, and Arikan winced, expecting an uproar from the others. But . . . no one said a thing. Wenketh's mouth almost turned up at the corners. "The others cannot hear me. But it *is* the Owl Spirit People who are behind this. Come, Arikan. Walk with me."

They left the circle unnoticed, walked on in silence for a time. Then Wenketh, eyeing Arikan slyly, said, "Speak."

Arikan held up a helpless hand. "What would you have me say? They are only birds."

"You believe that no more than do I. They are *only* birds even as we are *only* people. And we both know that people need their symbols."

"What are you saying?"

"How went your vision quest, Arikan?"

Arikan stopped short. "Forgive me, shaman, but that is a question not even you may ask."

"That badly, eh?"

"I—you—"

"The people need their faith, Arikan, even if you think you have lost your own. They need the Eagle Spirit watching over them. Wait, hear me out. Whether or not you believe in that or any spirit is not the point. The Owl Spirit People have our eagles and are trying to destroy us. And if they succeed in breaking our people's faith, they will succeed in all. I cannot use my powers from afar; the shaman of the Owl Spirit People would know, and kill the eagles. And I no longer have the physical strength for the necessary journey. Someone else must go there and bring them back."

"But why me? Go to the true believers, send them on a—a sacred quest!"

"Send them so blinded by their own beliefs they cannot see reality. Or be sufficiently profane. Besides," Wenketh added dryly, looking Arikan up and down, "no one, not even our enemies, would ever recognize in so ragged a being one of the Eagle Spirit People."

Arikan ceded that with a shrug. "But why should I risk—"

"Why did you return?"

"Because . . ."

"Well?"

"All right, yes, because these are my people! Because, yes, I am part of them, body, heart and mind—Oh, you are manipulating me most beautifully, shaman!"

"One does," Wenketh replied tranquilly, "what one must. But you will survive, Arikan."

"A vision?"

"Knowledge of you. Yes. Still. Even after so long a while. You are a clever man, Arikan, perhaps too clever."

" 'For there is a gap between 'clever' and 'wise,' " Arikan quoted.

"You may yet bridge that gap," the shaman said dryly. "Come, I see you have more to say."

"To ask. One question: How, exactly, did the Owl Spirit People steal away the eagles?"

Wenketh flinched ever so slightly. "By magic. And before you ask: By magic so sudden and overwhelming that I could do nothing."

Arikan stared. "And you want me to go up against *that*?"

"As I say, you are a clever man. If you are clever enough, there will be no need for them to rouse any great and terrible powers."

"Of course not. All they need rouse is some arrow or spear. No need for sorcery at all."

"There is always risk," the shaman retorted. "But there is reward as well. At the very least, you will, if all is well, find your home anew, and know you have preserved it. Is that not reason enough?"

"I . . ." But Arikan suddenly could find no useful argument at all.

* * *

"If all is well." If. *And I believed him,* Arikan thought. *Hah.*

He was standing before the Owl Spirit People's village, which was, like his own home, sheltered between cliffs, with its skin lodges looking so alarmingly like his people's own— alarmingly, because there should be *something* different, something to mark this as Enemy Territory.

I let Wenketh overwhelm me with thoughts of home *and* family.

Arikan stiffened. Grim-faced warriors armed with bows and spears were swarming out of the village to block his way. *I let him talk me into this. Now, if only I can talk my way out again!*

There was a trading language held in common by many of the Peoples. In it, Arikan said, keeping his voice carefully neutral and his hands outspread, "Greetings. I come in peace."

"Who are you?" a warrior asked coldly.

"A wanderer, no more, seeking only a fire by which to rest for the night."

"We have no space for wanderers."

"Have you not? How strange! I have heard tales of the kindness of the Owl Spirit People toward those alone and in need." Arikan paused, as though mildly disturbed by children's rudeness, then added, just as mildly, "A shame were the tales disproved."

Oh, that struck the mark! He saw the warriors stir uneasily, wondering, as anyone might, if this

stranger might not be more than he seemed,
Other than he seemed.

"Wait," one said. "We will speak with our
shaman."

I can imagine you shall! But Arikan kept his
face innocent. "Do as you must, of course."

He waited, seemingly doing nothing at all.
But Arikan was seeing signs of tension, of a people who were not at peace. Why? The rains fell
here as they did elsewhere; the hunting should
be just as good. He saw children . . .

But not that many. Not as many, surely, as
should be in a healthy village.

*Ah, is that it? Was there disease here that slew
the young, or prevented the young from being born
at all?*

*And do they think Wenketh and, through him, all
the Eagle Spirit People to blame? Wenketh does not
deal in such dark magics!*

But these folk might not accept that. And if
their shaman had then stolen away the eagles in
retaliation—

No, Arikan realized suddenly. For sacrifice.

*Have they already been slain? Have I come here,
risked my life, for nothing?*

A bit late to worry about that, he answered himself dryly. For here came the warrior again, and
with him, a tall, lean figure that must surely be
this People's shaman.

No. No, he wasn't. "The shaman cannot speak
with you now," the man said portentously.

Ah, of course not! Any magic powerful

enough to catch Wenketh off-guard must certainly need a great deal of recovery time. "I would not wish to disturb him," Arikan said piously. "If I may just rest a while?"

He held out his hands again in the universal gesture of: *See? No weapons.*

"What's in the pack?" the lean man countered.

"Oh, this. Nothing much, see?" Kneeling, Arikan unwrapped it: A worn, stained hide such as a poor man might carry, and within it, the bits and pieces someone not quite . . . right might carry—a shard of flint, a coil of twine, some bright pebbles, and a shred of dried meat. "Would you like some meat? A pretty pebble? No?"

"No."

"Oh." Arikan wrapped everything back up and slung the makeshift pack over his shoulder again. "May I . . . ?"

After a moment, the lean man grunted and waved him on. Arikan wandered through the village, then sat down in the shade of a lodge, cross-legged, and pretended to be nothing more than a footweary nobody.

All around him, life went on. And for all the underlying tension, this was still the ordinary life of ordinary people, women carrying water, gossiping, men tending weapons, everyone doing their best to ignore the stranger in their midst. The children, though . . . they must have been warned to stay away from him, but that didn't mean that they wouldn't stare, curious as the young ones of his own people. Too few of them, definitely, for a village this size, but looking healthy enough. They also looked like the children of his own people, and Arikan reminded himself sharply again, *No. They are the enemy. These are all the enemy.*

Where were the eagles? They must surely be kept near the center of the village, near where he sat . . .

They were.

Had been. Arikan fought a fierce battle with himself: He must show no emotion at the sight of the cage and the charred bones within, even though the shock of horror that raced through him was almost beyond bearing.

They can't be dead. They can't all be dead—

Not quite. One bird remained alive, trapped in a cage far too small for it . . . a fledgling eagle, its brown plumage still mottled with white, its gaping beak evidence of shock and exhaustion.

It will die before they can even sacrifice it!

No, it would not. Not if he had any say about this. Amazed at the intensity of his emotion, Arikan forced himself to continue pretending to do nothing but resting. But his sly, subtle glances took in every detail about his surroundings, about the eagle . . .

Maybe, Arikan decided at last, then altered that to, *no "maybe" about it.* Now that he'd committed to this, it was simply succeed or die: basic choices.

Assuming that poor bird lives long enough. Till

nightfall, youngling, he pleaded with it, *at least till then.*

Had the eagle somehow heard him? The beautiful, wild head turned to him, the savage, desperate eyes seemed to stare directly at him.

Then the moment passed. The eagle was but a bird, no more than that.

And I? I am a fool.

Oh, indeed. And a fool wouldn't sit here all day. Arikan got to his feet, forcing an amiable, almost idiotic smile onto his face, and ambled about the village, projecting *I'm not quite right in the head* with all his might. He let warriors shove him roughly out of the way, helped the women carry their water skins as though unaware that it *was* women's work, wearing his torn and badly stained hide as a cloak—and all the while continued to subtly study the village and the way it fit into the landscape.

The cliffs here were barely more than half the height of those shielding his village. A determined man could scale them if need be.

A man burdened by a fledgling eagle? *And,* Arikan added with a sudden start, *only if those owls I see dreaming in those niches aren't trained to attack.*

Could owls be trained?

No, Arikan scolded himself, he wasn't going to worry about what might or might not be.

Enough of this. If he hadn't established his slow-witted harmlessness by now, he never would. Arikan returned to his resting place, sitting back down with the air of a man prepared to stay the night.

It would seem to be working. A woman threw him some scraps of meat, another dropped a small watersack at his side, and Arikan, shrugging mentally, ate and drank. This wariness of strangers, the lack of genuine hospitality . . . yes, these people had been hurt by something. Disease, he thought again, gone now but not without having taken its toll on the young.

Why blame us?

Why? Because we are the enemy. Because, were the situation reversed, we would surely blame them.

And he, Arikan reminded himself sharply, was not there to solve the problems of feud or enmity. He was there to rescue that eagle—and keep his life at the same time.

The day faded into twilight, the twilight into night. Arikan, wrapped in the dirty hide, trying to ignore its sour smell, settled down as best he could, wondering if he was really going to be left unchallenged.

Not quite. One warrior gave him a not too rough kick, and a harsh, "Are you staying there all night?"

Arikan blinked up at him, trying to look utterly innocent, utterly weary. "If it is not inconvenient, yes, I was hoping to do just that. I will be off in the morning."

The warrior paused, then shrugged. "See that you are."

Oh, I will, I will, indeed.

And still the night darkened. Little by little, the village grew quiet beneath the heavy blanket of stars. Arikan waited. No sign of human life now, though he didn't doubt that guards had been set: That was the way of his people, too. But they would be bordering the village, looking out to potential danger. No one seemed to be watching him, so Arikan folded up the hide, slipped the roll of twine on one arm, and stood, picking out his path, shadow to shadow to shadow, then moved forward as silently as ever he had in the desert. The fledgling eagle woke, staring at him from its cage, and for a heart-stopping moment, Arikan was sure it was going to start shrieking. Could it know why he was here? Was that possible?

It is a bird. No more than that.

And it wasn't going to know he was a friend, or that he was trying to rescue it. The cage was sturdy wood, too sturdy for an eagle's beak or talons, and it was held together by thickly woven reed rope. Arikan studied the knots, as much by touch as sight in the dimness, and warily began to untie them, keeping a cautious eye on the eagle.

He had it. Arikan took a deep breath, bracing himself. Then he hurled open the cage, enveloped the eagle in the folds of the hide—and instantly had his arms full of terrified, furious chaos. The fledgling was heavier than he'd expected, not that he could tell accurate weight from the frantic struggle the creature was putting up. At least he didn't have to worry about those sharp talons raking him; they had clamped shut on the hide with alarming strength. The eagle was trying its best to get him with its beak, and Arikan got another fold of the hide over its head, praying that he wasn't going to smother the creature, or kill it from the sheer shock of being handled so roughly. But no, if it was going to die of shock, it probably would have done so already.

Don't die, Arikan told it silently, repeating it like a prayer, *don't die*.

Amazingly, no one had heard, or else was so used to the sound of frantic flappings not to notice. And the hide was muffling the eagle's attempts at shrieks.

Now, Arikan thought breathlessly, *to get out of here*.

Oh, indeed. Just walk right out of the village with a squirming bundle about the size—and, he thought, the weight—of a child. No problem at all.

Well? Didn't really think this part through, did you, clever one? That the eagle might not want to be carried out like a package. There really is a gap between "clever" and "wise."

Never mind self-mockery. Arikan wrapped the eagle-bundle about with a few loops of twine, just for security's sake. No need to worry about airholes—that sharp, wickedly curved beak had already stabbed a few in the hide. Gingerly, trying to keep the beak pointed away from him, Arikan shouldered what now looked, at least in this darkness, like his pack, and— walked, keeping to the shadows since he wasn't suicidal.

Too easy, his mind kept whispering, *far too easy*.

Never mind, he snapped back at himself. *I'll gladly take the "easy."*

At least the eagle had stopped its wild thrashing. It must be exhausted. It . . . *was* only exhausted?

Don't die, Arikan repeated yet again.

"Hai. Where are you going?"

One of the warriors. Arikan, heart pounding, smiled his most innocent smile and told him, "Out there. The stars, you know. They talk to me."

"Of . . . course they do." The warrior hesitated, then shrugged. "Who am I to deny the stars? If you want to spend a night out there, so be it."

Arikan walked on, willing to the eagle, *Keep still. Keep quiet.*

They'd be in utter darkness soon enough, the heavy shadows cast by the cliffs—

Just then, the eagle decided it was unhappy enough, and began a shrill series of furious *yeep-yeep-yeeps*. And that, of course, was a sound that had to be familiar to its captors.

Arikan didn't hesitate. He broke into a run, the eagle a shrieking, bouncing weight on his back, hearing shouts behind him of:

"Stop!"

"After him!"

Arikan kept going, stubbing his toe on rocks unseen in the darkness, staggering, stumbling, but refusing to stop.

"The shaman!" someone yelped. "Rouse the shaman!"

No need. The shaman must already be awake and aware, because suddenly a cliff was blocking Arikan's escape, looming out of the darkness where there'd been open space before. And even though he knew it must be illusion—it *was*, wasn't it?—even so, the sheer rock face looked utterly real, so very solid that Arikan stopped, whirling to face the village, the eagle protesting on his back—

But that way was blocked, too, warriors rushing toward him. A quick glance forward again: the shaman's cliff was still there, still seemingly solid. If he charged through it—no! Who knew what sorcerous traps lay hidden there? Still, he was rapidly running out of choices—

Hah, no, not quite.

You said *that the cliffs, the real ones, looked scalable. Now's your chance to prove it!*

No way to see the easiest route up. No time to be fussy about it. Arikan all but threw himself at the nearest cliff, finding hand- and footholds through sheer desperation, almost totally blind in the darkness, frantic to get himself and the eagle out of range of spear or arrow, sure he was going to be struck down or simply fall. The eagle wasn't helping, one heavy, squirming bundle on his back, nearly pulling him off-balance. At least it couldn't get its beak or talons into him, but it was *yeeping* and *yeeping* in his ear.

"Will you . . . please just . . . shut up?" Arikan hissed breathlessly. "I'm doing . . . the best . . . I . . . can!"

An arrow clicked sharply against stone, alarmingly close, and Arikan clenched his teeth and continued his grab-blindly-at-handholds nightmare of a climb.

The cliff's not that high. I can do this. Hah, I'd better!

But what if this, too, was the shaman's work? What if there wasn't a top, and he went on climbing and climbing till—

All right, Spirits in whom I really don't believe, if you want this eagle alive and, not incidentally, me as well, give me strength!

But he—yes! He was at the top of the cliff, and pulling himself clumsily up onto the blessedly flat surface of the mesa.

For a time, Arikan lay flat on his stomach, panting, the eagle a weight on his back. But then a knife-sharp stab at a shoulder brought him staggering to his feet, cursing breathlessly. The eagle had managed to get him with the tip of its beak.

At least it was still alive, Arikan told himself, and grimly set out across the mesa, hoping he wouldn't fall into a hole in the darkness. But was the darkness quite as dense as it had been?

True dawn wouldn't be here for some time, but when it came, when the sun rose, he'd be a clear target. Arikan groaned and forced himself on, determined to put as much terrain between himself and the Owl Spirit People as possible.

Not too possible. He was just too worn out, mentally and physically, and the eagle's weight wasn't helping. Couldn't be helping the eagle, either, being wrapped up like that. No one seemed to be coming after him; presumably no one was crazed enough to try a midnight climb after him.

But the shaman . . . ?

He'd deal with that problem when it happened. The eagle had stopped struggling, and its *yeeps* were getting alarmingly faint.

"So be it," Arikan said.

He wormed his way out of the pack, then began very carefully to untie the hide. The moment the fledgling was free, it was going to try escaping. Could it fly yet? He wasn't sure, but didn't dare risk . . . a foot, now . . . where . . . ha, got it!

There was a brief, frantic, flapping struggle. Arikan, buffeted by wings, bleeding from a dozen not-quite misses from beak and talons, got a loop of the rope firmly about the fledgling's leg and anchored the other end to . . . ah, yes, a good, sturdy little tree. He scrambled back, out of the reach of the eagle as it tried to claw him, lost his balance, and sat down, hard. The eagle, perched on a rock, sat, too, glaring at him in the darkness as though blaming him for the whole situation.

"You could show a *little* gratitude," Arikan told it dryly.

But the eagle, with a dazzlingly quick pounce, landed on some small creature, a mouse or ground squirrel startled out of hiding. The brown-and-white wings spread wide, the fledgling began devouring its small kill.

"Well, that's something. Guess that means you aren't ready to die."

The eagle glared at him again, then returned to its meal.

"That's not going to hold you for very long," Arikan said to it. "Ah, and what do I do with you now? How do I get you back home?"

Yes, and what of the shaman? It seemed very strange that all he'd done so far was create one convincing but not all that useful cliff-illusion.

Not so strange at that. Something was all at once there, Something great and gray-brown-white, Something terrible, looming up over him. The eagle screamed, then huddled against the ground, staring, terrified, and furious in one.

Arikan wanted to huddle, too, because what was forming he realized now was a great Owl— an Owl with eyes that were only empty blackness.

"Oh, now this is impossible," he heard himself say. "You don't exist."

"Don't we?"

The voice had not come from that Owl beak,

but from all around him, but Arikan persisted, "If no vision came to me when I sought one—"

"And do we come when we are bid?"

"You came at the shaman's bidding, didn't you?"

Was that a vast sense of . . . amusement? "Brave small one!"

"Not so brave," Arikan retorted. "Just too stunned to be wise!"

That was definitely a sense of amusement radiating from all about. "Wise enough, it seems. We heard the shaman, ah, yes, but *chose* to appear here and now."

We? "You are . . . uh . . . the Owl Spirit?"

"In a fashion. Come, fight me."

The suddenness of it almost overcame Arikan. As the Owl lunged for him, Arikan desperately threw himself sideways, rolling, hearing a huge talon scrape the ground where he'd just been, coming back to his feet—aie, here came the Owl again, *diving at the eagle*!

"For there is a gap between 'clever' and 'wise.' "

Why should he be thinking that now? There wasn't any time for adages—

Wait! Yes!

"Owls don't stoop at eagles!" Airkan cried. "Nor could a mortal man ever fight a— This is a trick!"

"A test, rather," the Owl replied, swooping up again.

But one long talon neatly sliced the rope holding the eagle. And the fledgling proved that it could, indeed, fly, taking to wing before the horrified Arikan could move.

"No," he murmured as the young eagle disappeared into the graying sky, "ah, no . . ."

It was all for nothing, then. The last of his people's eagles was gone.

"Why did you—"

The Owl was gone, too, dissipated by the first rays of the sun.

If, Arikan, thought, it had even been there. But when he bent to study the rope, it had not frayed loose; it had been severed as cleanly as though by a knife.

Wearily, heartsick, Arikan started for home.

The people came running to greet him, with cries of "Hero!" and "Rescuer!"

Arikan stopped. "I didn't . . ."

But they were pointing up, to the cliff where the eagle nest—

Was occupied by a bird with the mottled white of a not-quite-grown fledgling.

He . . . couldn't have found his way back here on his own. Could he?

"How went your vision quest?" a voice murmured.

Arikan turned to see Wenketh smiling slyly at him. "You knew."

"Did I?"

"What was that, Wenketh? Did I really see and speak with a . . ."

"With a god? With an aspect of the Great Divine? What do you think?"

"I . . . don't know. I don't know how the eagle got back either. I only know, well, that I *don't* know!"

The old shaman chuckled and turned away. "There," he said, his voice trailing back to Arikan, "is at last the beginning of wisdom. Welcome home, Arikan."

TAKING FREEDOM

by S.M. Stirling

Stephen Michael Stirling has been writing science fiction and fantasy for the past decade, collaborating with such authors as Jerry Pournelle, Judith Tarr, David Drake, and Harry Turtledove, as well as producing excellent novels by himself, such as *Marching Through Georgia, Snowbrother,* and, most recently, *Against the Tide of Years.* Born in Metz, Alsace, France, and educated at the Carleton University in Canada, he currently lives in Santa Fe, New Mexico, with his wife Janet.

ADELIA the sorceress was an uncommonly proud woman. This was obvious from her fine dress, a king's ransom of green satin, tucked and ruched, bright with ribbons and glittering with gold lace. Her thick brown hair, beautifully coiffed, was held in place by a gold net glittering with jewels, and in one richly gloved hand she bore a delicate little peacock feather fan.

She was certainly pretty enough to carry off these fripperies without looking ridiculous, which couldn't be said of every finely dressed lady at the fair. But it wasn't merely her appearance that made Adelia vain. The lady was a sorceress of note; an accomplishment which made her a person greatly to be feared as well as admired.

Adelia wore the signal of her achievement upon her smooth white brow, an illusion which the uninitiated saw only as a spot of flame. But the adept could read her capabilities there and know that she was both capable and very powerful indeed.

The sorceress moved through the fair with her glossy head held high, ignoring the wary, often unfriendly stares of the folk around her. Ignoring as well the embarrassing meeping and cringing of her servant Wren, whose shyness had the wretched girl well on the way to panic. Wren had dropped the parcels she carried into the dust and the mud twice after a meaningless sight or sound had startled her; once, a cat sleeping on a window sill, then a dog barking in the street.

Listening to the sniveling and the whimpering behind her, Adelia rolled her eyes. *I should never have made her from such a pathetic creature in the first place! What was I thinking? A wren is the very essence of shyness. If I'd made her from a nightingale, she'd still be shy, but at least she could sing.*

Suddenly she turned on her servant, glaring

at the small, brown-haired girl in her plain dress. Wren froze, her mouth agape, panting in unabashed terror.

"Return to our room at the inn, Wren," Adelia commanded. "I shall come when the sun is there," the sorceress indicated a spot just above the western horizon. "Have a hot . . . have a *warm* bath prepared for me."

The last time she'd ordered a "hot" bath, Adelia had raised a blister on the foot she'd so incautiously plunged into the near boiling water.

Wren gaped and panted.

"Do you understand me?"

Wren nodded.

"Then go!" Adelia pointed in the direction of the inn.

The little servant girl turned and bolted through the crush of people, trying to go in a straight line and calling out in little shrill peeps when she couldn't.

Some of the surrounding crowd cast a surreptitious glare in Adelia's direction, and she couldn't blame them. There was every appearance of a girl broken by ill treatment. But the truth was that Adelia never abused Wren; there would be no point.

Existing is punishment enough for that poor creature. With a tsk of disgust she continued on her way alone. It might be best to simply unmake the girl. Adelia was not quite ready to take that step just yet. Though admittedly, after this afternoon she was much closer to it than she had been.

Perhaps, she mused, *I would have better luck if I began with a bolder creature.* Adelia paced on. *A stallion?* The thought brought a smile to her face as she walked along. Then, with a sigh, she dismissed the idea. A stallion's size and aggression would be as difficult to manage in their own way as poor little Wren's terror. *Pity.*

At last her walking had taken her to the far end of the fair, where the animals were kept. Here at the leading edge of the animal market were smaller, less offensive creatures, and she passed by cages of dogs and ferrets and even monkeys.

Adelia paused to examine the capuchin monkey in its little velvet vest and fringed cap, sitting on its master's shoulder. But something almost human in its hands turned her away with a shudder.

That won't do, she thought with a grimace. *If I wanted something almost human, I could pick up any urchin off the streets.* And she moved on.

At last the sorceress came to the sellers of birds, and her steps slowed. Her experiment with Wren had been an almost total failure. The girl that had resulted from her spells ate worms, feared everything and had to be constantly coaxed down from the rafters. But some part of Adelia resisted giving up.

Here, she knew in her heart, was the answer.

Birds. They pleased her so, their beauty, their grace, their freedom.

She longed to possess that freedom, or at least to take it; on the theory that if you could take something from an entity, then in some measure what you had taken became yours.

She passed the song birds, lingered by the rare parrots. They were far more intelligent than the finches, she could see, but none of these had the fire she sought.

At last she came upon the hunting birds; some in cages glaring boldly out between the bars, some, hooded, sat upon their perches.

Yes! Adelia thought triumphantly. *A predator! Just like herself. This is what I need.*

"You there," she called imperiously. "Are these yours?" A gesture encompassed all the falcons of every variety.

The man she'd called looked up from his bargaining to note the lady sorceress. He bowed, and the man he'd been speaking with murmured that he'd return later and made off.

"Tell me about these," Adelia demanded.

The man was tall and hazel-eyed, with a shaggy beard streaked with gray. His craggy face fought a frown and Adelia wondered at it. Did the creature dare to think of denying her whatever she asked for?

"My Lady Sorceress," he said at last in a voice deep and quiet. "Is it your pleasure to hunt with hawks?"

"My pleasure," she said stiffly, "is to know

about these birds. Instruct me in their character."

It seemed to the hawk seller that the flame on her brow burned brighter for a moment, and he bowed his head, leading her over to the cages.

"Their character, Lady?" He pursed his lips. "It varies from one to the other, just as character varies in people," he said at last. "Here," he said, pointing to a tiny kestrel, bright as a song-bird, "this little lass, perfect for a lady . . ."

"No!" Adelia exclaimed contemptuously. "Nothing so small will do. And I want a male," she added on impulse.

"Females are preferred in falconry, Lady Sorceress," the man assured her. "The males are smaller, you see."

"Hmm," Adelia murmured. As she looked around, she spied a handsome blue-gray bird perched on a block, a curious leather mask over its head. Its color pleased her, and the size was just about what she wanted. "Tell me about this one," she said eagerly.

"He . . ."

"Ah!" she said approvingly. "He!"

"Yes, my Lady Sorceress. He is a goshawk. And," the hawk seller paused. "And if the Lady Sorceress is unfamiliar with falconry, he would be a very poor choice to begin with."

Adelia leaned in close to the bird, studying its plumage, it had a clean, spicy fragrance. Suddenly she blew hard against its breast and the bird started with a sharp cry, then settled.

"I like him," she said decisively. "How much?"

The hawk seller's mouth dropped open. He looked at her, then at the bird, then drew himself up, like a man facing an angry mob.

"I cannot sell him to you, my Lady Sorceress. Unless, of course, you have some servant skilled in the ways of hawks."

She was utterly astonished at his audacity. Fortunately for the hawk seller, Adelia chose to find his response interesting.

With narrowed eyes she asked him, "Do you imagine that anyone in this whole fair will so much as touch this bird when I have expressed an interest in him?"

With a bow, the hawk seller replied, "The Lady is undoubtedly correct. If I do not sell him to you, he will not be sold."

Adelia studied him; he would not meet her eyes, and she detected a fine sheen of sweat forming on his brow. Clearly, he feared her.

"Then why will you not sell me this bird?" she said at last.

"Goshawks are the most difficult of hunting birds to bond with, my Lady. They are sensitive and wild and are considered utterly indifferent to the falconer. Some think them quite mad. And this fellow is not even fully trained, my Lady Sorceress. Let him fly, and he will leave you. And . . . in panic, to which goshawks are inclined, he may harm you."

"Then *why* is he here for sale?" Adelia demanded in exasperation.

"Because, my Lady, many falconers prefer to train their own birds."

She frowned. All this talk of training was unexpected, and indeed was useless since she never intended to hunt with the bird. Still, as a predator, it might need specialized care. Certainly it would need more than a seed cup and a little water. With a deep sigh, she resolved to pay heed to the hawk seller's concerns. Besides, she would need a male slave on hand, she might as well get some use out of him.

"Where might I find a servant skilled in the ways of hawks?" she inquired.

The hawk seller gave her directions and she tsked in disgust. The slave mongers were on the opposite side of the fair from the animal sellers.

One would think that they would keep all the livestock together, Adelia growled within her mind.

In less than two hours she returned with her purchase. The man she had bought was in his mid twenties, only a little taller than herself, but with a muscular warrior's build. He had a thick head of rough-cut black hair and a short, curly beard. It was his shrewd, narrow, sherry-wine eyes that had decided her to buy him, though, over the older fellow the slave dealer told her was also familiar with hawks. Around his neck hung a relsk stone, the spell that rendered him obedient despite the pride with which he carried himself.

"My name," he murmured to her as they approached the hawk seller, "is Naim."

His name is Naim, she thought, amused. Naim was a word in the ancient tongue meaning an amount so small as to be nothing at all.

She walked up to the hawk seller and, ignoring the customer he'd been speaking with, the one she'd interrupted twice now, announced, "I believe that this person should satisfy you. Ask him what you will of caring for hawks." She glanced at Naim. "And he'd better satisfy you." She deliberately left it unclear as to whether this was a threat against Naim or the hawk seller.

She wandered idly around, examining the little kestrel that had first been shown to her. A pretty thing, but, she sniffed, female. Adelia listened without much interest as the two men talked, exchanging terms like "creance" and "tiercel." At last they settled down to dicker on price. Adelia crossed her arms beneath her breasts and raised one brow. Still, though she had not given him permission to do so, she allowed Naim to speak for her in obtaining the bird.

At last the two men shook hands. Naim turned to her to obtain money, while the hawk seller went into his little booth and returned with a heavy glove, a perch, and what looked like a leash.

Naim put on the glove and touched the back

of the hooded hawk's ankles. The bird stepped
back automatically, caught his balance and settled on this temporary perch.

"I wanted to carry him," Adelia complained,
chagrined.

"Of course, my lady," Naim said soothingly.
"But he's heavy, perhaps two pounds in weight,
and he *is* a bird. I should hate to see him soil
your beautiful gown."

She smiled slightly at the manipulative courtesy of his response and wondered where he'd
learned it.

"No matter," she said with a shrug and led
the way to the inn proud as a queen at the head
of a procession. Being followed by a handsome
young man carrying a hawk was far more in
keeping with her vanity than the attendance of
the wretched Wren. *I shall definitely have to do
something about her,* the sorceress thought.

Wren began to scream the moment they
brought the hawk into the room. To scream and
to leap from chair to bed to table to chair. Had
it been open, she'd have gone straight out the
window. As it was, she bounced off the shutters
more than once. And she kept up the cacophony
until Adelia threw the bedquilt over her, whereupon Wren dropped to the floor and lay silent
and panting.

"Obviously someone will have to sleep in the
barn tonight," Adelia snarled.

Naim bowed.

"Not you! That's a valuable bird," she said. "I won't risk its being stolen. "And don't get any ideas," Adelia warned him as she noted a flicker of interest spark in those sherry-brown eyes. "You will only be here to see that this bird is well tended."

The sorceress turned and contemplated Wren where she lay quietly beneath the blanket, then the gently steaming tub of scented water, and finally she turned back to look into the interested eyes of her falconer.

"Put that down," she said, indicating the goshawk. "Then go and tell the landlord that I'll need a curtain set up to run across the room. If we can keep Wren from seeing the bird, she should keep quiet."

She could have created some sort of barrier magically, but Adelia never wasted *power* if there was a more mundane way of doing things. Particularly if the doing required no effort on her part.

Naim settled the hawk on its perch, bowed, and left the room. Adelia smiled, pleased with her purchases. She could hardly wait to see what he and the hawk combined would become.

Now I think on it, the girl I combined with Wren was a coward. She remembered the pale, tear-stained face with disgust. The spell had been designed to put the bird personality uppermost, but the shy little bird and the cowardly girl had only accentuated each other's defects. *This time,* she thought happily, *I should have* much *better results*.

Adelia carried her hawk on her wrist for the first few miles of the journey home, wearing the too large gauntlet over her own exquisitely embroidered glove.

Wren, blindfolded, rode behind her, clutching the high rim of the sidesaddle and trying not to slide off. Every now and again, Naim, walking beside them, put a hand beneath the girl's foot and hoisted her back up.

"Should we feed him?" Adelia asked Naim.

"Nay, my lady. From the look of his crop, he'll be all right for a while. And the hawk seller told me he hadn't been trained. While I'm sure he could find himself some dinner with no problem, getting him back to hand would be impossible."

She looked down on him and allowed herself a very small smile.

"I can do many things that others consider impossible, Naim. You would do well to remember that."

He bowed, and she laughed at his ridiculous courtly manners. Then she pulled up her horse.

"You were right, the bird grows heavy. Take him." She lowered her arm, and raised her brows when Naim sought to remove the glove with the bird. "Take him, I said," Adelia commanded.

The relsk stone did its work and Naim

brought his bare hand up immediately and touched the hawk behind the ankles. As soon as its talons clamped down on the man's arm, blood began to flow.

"Ah," she said, stripping off the glove and dropping it. Immediately it filled as though an arm were wearing it and it floated into position behind the hawk. When the bird had stepped onto it, she said, "Now put your arm inside the glove."

Wincing, Naim did so. She rode on, unconcerned.

"Have you a shed where we can keep the bird, my lady?" he asked, his voice thick with pain.

"Yes, but why can we not keep him in the house?"

"He is still half wild and would be frightened to be among us. The dark and quiet of the shed will be soothing for him, and he will learn that when I come, there will be food and something to relieve his boredom. These are the first steps to forming a bond." The hawk shifted, and Naim drew in a rasping breath.

Adelia frowned. "I do not like it that he should be fearful."

"It is his nature, my lady. Those creatures that do not fear humans don't live to breed."

She laughed at that, then fell silent for awhile. "When we return home," she said at last, "I will have Wren tend to your hand." She couldn't use wounded flesh in her experiments. Still, by the time she'd gathered the needed ingredients, these slight punctures should be healed.

A week later Adelia flung down Naim's hand in disgust.

"Why are these wounds not healed?" she demanded.

"They're very deep," Naim answered. "One of the punctures went right to the bone, I'm sure."

She glared at him, hands on her hips. "Well, this is very inconvenient!" He bowed and she spun away from him with an impatient tsk!. "I detest delay," she snapped. "Absolutely detest it!"

Naim opened his mouth to speak, closed it, frowned, then licked his lips. "My lady," he said at last, "I must speak to you on a matter of some concern to me."

Adelia cast a disdainful glance over her shoulder and asked, "Of what matter could a *matter* of concern to you, be to me?"

He bowed, and her brows snapped down into a frown. She decided that she didn't like all this bowing. *A mere nervous tic*, she thought contemptuously. A habit, like clearing one's throat before speaking or always saying, "therefore." *It is an imperfection. And I do not like it that my subject should have an imperfection.* Working with imperfect material had created the disaster that was Wren.

"I am the son of Baron Tharus of Arpen. If

you will but send to him, he will ransom me, I know. Whatever price you ask, he will pay it." Naim gazed at her most earnestly.

"Hmph," she said, turning to look at him. "You are the son of a baron?" '

"Yes, my lady."

"*Don't* bow," she cautioned him. "So you are familiar with the use of a sword and lance?"

"Yes, my lady."

Oh, excellent! she thought, hugging the information to her. *I must translate those skills to my new creature. I knew I'd made the right choice in this slave!*

"And how did the son of a baron come to be in a slavepen?" she asked in idle curiosity.

"I was kidnapped," he replied, "and carried over the border."

"Oh, really? Well," she said and brought her hand to her face, "I don't imagine your father wants you back, then."

"I promise you that he does," Naim insisted, somewhat piqued. "I am his only son and his heir."

"Then don't you find it odd that your kidnappers never applied to your doting papa for this ransom you so confidently promise. I doubt the slave dealer gave them as much as I paid for you, and I assure you, Naim, you weren't very expensive." She smiled, knowing by the look in his eyes that she'd shaken him, at least for a moment, and it amused her tremendously.

"I gave an enemy who may have paid them to do it," he said slowly.

In a sudden shift of mood Adelia became bored by the subject, and she cut him off with a graceful gesture.

"It doesn't matter!" she said dismissively. "I don't need your pathetic *ransom*. I can provide for myself very well. And have I not said that I detest delay? I don't need gold, I need you. So put any thought of leaving here out of your head." Adelia spun on her heel and moved toward the door of the parlor.

"Wren told me what you did to her," Naim shouted.

Adelia stopped like one struck in the back by a dagger, and looked toward the kitchen as though she could see through the wall. Then slowly, she turned toward him.

"Wren speaks?' she said in astonishment.

"Aye," he said defiantly. "Just not to you."

"Huh," she said, and quirked her lips downward. "And your point is?"

"My point is that I am a nobleman! It cannot be that I am meant to be destroyed by your evil magic!" he cried. "There are standards in the treatment of nobleman that every right thinking king or duke will acknowledge. You have no right to do this to me!"

"But, Naim," she said gently, taking a step toward him, "you aren't a nobleman. You are a slave. And I have every right to do with my property whatever I wish. As every *right* thinking king or duke would agree." Adelia gave him a taunting smile. "Did you not have slaves in your father's house, Naim?"

He glared at her, breathing hard.

Adelia enjoyed his obvious anger, and his helplessness to act upon it.

"No doubt you embraced them as your brothers, treated them as equals. What a paradise your father's house must have been," she sneered, spreading her arms wide, "with everyone living in perfect harmony."

Naim lowered his eyes, his cheeks flushed with fury or shame.

"Oh, no?" Adelia stepped closer, lowered her head in an attempt to look into his eyes. "Did you beat them? Humiliate them? Let them go hungry?"

"Yes," he whispered.

"And yet you expect better." Adelia quirked the corners of her mouth downward. "I fear you will be disappointed, Naim."

He merely glared at her from under lowered eyebrows.

"Go," she said. "Tend my hawk. Feed it, make friends with it, do whatever you must to keep it alive and healthy."

Naim gave her a surly glance, then stomped out of the room. Ruefully, she watched him go.

So Wren can speak, Adelia thought. *And she knows and understands, at least a little, what's happened to her. Hmph. Well, that's useful to know, but somewhat annoying, too.* Naim might well prove a handful over the next few days if he believed she intended to destroy him. *I would rather he had remained ignorant of his fate.*

Not that knowing it would change anything. Adelia gave a little huff of annoyance. Then decided that she would keep Wren a little longer. The girl was hopeless at most things. *But she does my hair so beautifully.* Doubtless a carryover of her nest-building abilities.

Well, there were worse reasons to keep someone alive.

She contemplated the necessary delay while Naim continued healing and sighed. *A few days shouldn't make that much difference,* she thought. Adelia calculated planetary influences in her head and frowned, not greatly liking the results. There would be ample power to draw on, but nothing that especially favored *her;* ever the most important part of the equation where the sorceress was concerned.

"I want you to show me my hawk," Adelia said, coming up behind Naim.

He started and turned, frowning, made a slight move as though to bow, thought better of it and did not.

"He has only seen me for days now, my lady," Naim said. "It would not be good for his training to introduce a new person into his life just now."

Adelia smiled brightly and nodded.

"I don't care," she said. "I have never seen

my hawk without that stupid looking *thing* on
its head, and I want to look at it."

"It would cause delay, my lady."

She stepped close to him and held his gaze
with her own. "Are you trying to manipulate
me, Naim?"

"No, my lady." He seemed genuinely confused.

*Ha, so it really would affect the hawk's training.
How very fortunate that it doesn't matter.*

She gestured for Naim to take her to the shed,
and they moved off.

"Have you given any further thought to what
I told you, my lady?" he asked as they walked
along.

"Of course not, Naim. And we will not speak
of it again."

Naim compressed his lips and walked on. He
opened the door and stood aside for her.

"Oh!" Adelia gasped in astonished dismay.

At her entrance the tethered hawk had flat-
tened the feathers on its body, but those that
framed its head flared in a sunburst around its
staring, blood-red eyes. The hawk's beak gaped
half open as though eager to rip at her flesh.

She took a step backward and looked at Naim
in horror.

"Its eyes are *red*? The other hawks didn't have
red eyes! This is most unexpected." *That rotten-
hearted hawk seller never mentioned those freakish
eyes.* "What's wrong with it?" she demanded of
Naim. *I'll give that hairy fool red eyes if he's sold*

me a sick bird! I'll pluck them out and feed them to him!

"The bird is perfectly normal, my lady. His eyes will darken as he ages, but all goshawks have red eyes." Naim couldn't help the superior little smile that twitched at the corners of his mouth. The lady sorceress was so very startled.

Adelia looked up at him, gazing into his eyes intently as though searching for some great meaning there. Pleased, he turned the full force of his very charming smile upon her.

I'll have to keep Naim's eye color, she thought. *Size. Size will be a consideration as well. Hmm. Perhaps I'll import Naim's eyes entirely, just as they are.* But she was not pleased. She'd hoped to use the hawk's vastly superior vision, but . . . the hideous color and freakishly large orbs would be impossible to live with.

Adelia sighed, and Naim closed his eyes and lowered his head, seeking her lips.

"*Back!*" she snapped, her voice like a whip crack.

Naim almost leaped away from her, his eyes wide.

"What *is* the matter with you?" She looked at him as if he'd gone mad. "Is this some ploy to get me to send you back to your papa?"

"No, no," he stammered. "It's . . . when you looked into my eyes like that . . ."

"By all that lives," she said in wonder, "you are a vain and foolish little man." Then she laughed. *Oh, dear,* she thought. *I do hope he'll be as amusing when I've changed him.*

And laughing, she walked back to the house, where Wren stared in wonder at her as she came through the door.

"Ah. So you're here," Adelia said, smiling. "The time has come at last."

Naim stood in the door of her spell-casting chamber, his face somewhat pale.

"Go away, Wren."

The servant girl, who'd summoned Naim at Adelia's command, gave him one last, desperate look and flitted off. Adelia grinned conspiratorially at him.

"She spoke to me, you know. On your behalf." She was genuinely delighted to have heard Wren's voice, which was high and sweet. "She wished me to spare you. And I'm so pleased that she dared to speak up that I've decided I shall. Come in," she gestured him forward.

"Do . . . do you mean it?" he asked, looking very young in his relief.

"Yes," she said, bustling about. "Sit there." She indicated a chair set within a complicated design. "Step through the break I've left in the pattern."

He looked nervously at the chair and then back at her where she mixed something in a cup. The hawk, hooded, sat on it's perch inside an identical design.

"You're going to let me go?" he asked.

"No, of course not." Adelia glanced over her shoulder at him. "I told you to sit down."

Naim simply stood and stared at her. He swallowed visibly, looking stunned.

"Sit!" she told him in a voice of command.

Naim took a deep breath and then reluctantly, fighting the compulsion of the relsk stone around his neck, moved to the chair.

"I don't understand," he whispered, his voice thick with tears.

"You have been well fed, you have enjoyed Wren." She grinned at his shock. "Don't look so surprised. I know everything that happens in my house or on my land. It accorded with my wishes, and so I've allowed it." She moved toward him, cup in hand.

"You said that you would spare me." His eyes were pleading.

"And I will." Adelia held out the cup. "There is no reason for you to be awake while the transformation takes place. Apparently that was the worst of it for Wren, and so I shall spare you that." She smiled. "Drink."

"I do not want to be transformed!" Naim shouted. "I merely wish to go home," he said softly.

The sorceress closed her eyes and took a very deep breath.

"By the same token," she said crisply, after a moment's pause to hold onto her temper, "there is no need for you to be asleep either. You can sit here screaming your head off, totally aware the whole time of what is happening to you, or you can sleep through it." She held the cup out to him. "It's entirely up to you."

"Can I say nothing that will change your mind?" he pleaded.

"This is your last chance," Adelia said through clenched teeth.

Looking her straight in the eye, he took the cup. Then he flung back his head and drank it all in three great swallows.

"Excellent," Adelia said with a nod, taking back the cup.

She knelt and completed the open space in the pattern around his chair. Then placing the cup outside her circle, she completed all the spaces left undrawn, picked up her wand, and began to work the spell she'd labored over so long.

Adelia called upon forces and elements and gods so old they barely knew themselves that they existed. Her long hair belled out around her head with the discharge of power, and the words she spoke made no sound though she shouted them. She gestured with her wand and the words that she wrote on the air hung there, palpable, but invisible, yet squirming with a life of their own.

Naim's head dropped to his breast, his breathing the slow, regular rhythm of deep sleep; even as the goshawk screamed and bated, beating its wings frantically as it sought to escape whatever *thing* crawled insidiously beneath its feathers.

At the appointed moment Adelia spoke a word, and the air boomed like a thunderclap. The man and the bird began to stream toward each other in thin ribbons, meeting and mixing over a complex pattern in the center of the design. Faster and faster the elements of their being mingled and solidified into one mass, until the jesses hung empty and the man's clothes collapsed with a small sound like a sigh.

When the shape that hung over the design was complete, the sorceress called out again and silence fell so sharply it stung like a slap.

Adelia fell to her hands and knees, drooling with exhaustion and nausea. She fell onto her side, panting, and stared up at what she'd created.

The man who stood over her had hair of a curious gray-blue shade, and proud, imperious features. His chest was broad and muscular as were his arms. His legs, though, were thin and his feet curiously bony. But the eyes were Naim's.

We can do something to build up his legs, Adelia thought. *I am pleased.*

"There are clothes for you, there," she croaked, gesturing at a table in the corner.

The man looked down at her, then went to the table and began to dress.

She'd chosen black for him, trimmed in blue. It went very well with his odd hair color.

He picked up the sword, drew it partway from its sheath, and smiled at the quality of the blade. Then he wrapped the swordbelt around his slim hips as he walked back to where she lay.

With difficulty Adelia hoisted herself onto one elbow and reached up to him.

"Help me up," she commanded.

"I think not," he said, his voice a sharp tenor. "There is no relsk stone on me to bind me, nor am I blindfolded." He smiled down at her, flashing white teeth. "And you are far too weak to command me, sorceress."

Adelia blinked.

"As Naim, I would have done anything you asked to stay as I was. I'd have done twice that for my freedom. As a hawk, all I knew was that I wanted to fly free. And you would have taken that hope from both of us. You meant to meld us into one earthbound creature tied to your will. Didn't you, sorceress?"

She dropped onto her back and licked dry lips.

"You are bound to me," she said.

He smiled again.

"No, I am not." He looked down at her, examining her with cold but interested eyes. "I am my own. More than I have ever been."

He drew his sword and stroked the flat of it over her cheek.

"What you have made of me, sorceress, is a better predator than I have ever been. The hawk

in me thanks you for that. And the man in me,"
he drew the sword down her neck and across
her breast to her heart, "he sees great possibili-
ties. The man in me knows that he doesn't need
to fear the sorceress; your powers are spent. The
hawk in me knows that I need not fear the
stranger; you lie there panting like a rabbit broken in the hunt."

He grinned, most joyfully, and pressed the
point of his sword onto its target.

"Good-bye, Adelia."

A GATHERING OF BONES

by Ron Collins

Ron Collins' short fiction has appeared in several magazines and anthologies, including *Dragon, Return of the Dinosaurs, Mob Magic*, and *Writers of the Future*. He lives in Columbus, Indiana.

I HAD fallen asleep last night without making a fire, and the stone walls now stood with cold permanence in the overcast morning light. The sound of the ocean echoed inside the hollow of my room. Odors of salt and seaweed hung in the air like new ghosts. Damp fog thickened the sky outside my arched window, and waves rolled in the distance, steel-colored swells capped with streaks of white foam that broke relentlessly against the rocky beach.

I cleared my lungs with a deep breath, remembering the chore that awaited me.

My father is dead now.

The ache of loss returned in a rush, filling me physically as if my nighttime dreams had served to keep this reality away. He had been working in our open-air laboratory, concocting another spell that he would someday pass on to me if he found time. Something went wrong. The explosion rattled the whole of Castle Talon, the small stone building my father and I have lived in for as long as I can remember.

He probably never knew what happened.

Fitting. My father had always been a man whose focus was intense, who could set aside distractions in order to concentrate on what he found important. And as one of the distractions he oftentimes placed aside, I knew how firm the walls around those compartments had been.

So today I was alone inside this place he named after the hawks, the place where the two of us have lived for so long, alone to deal with him as I have always been.

And for the last time, deal with him I will.

I tightened the drawstring on my trousers and slipped summer sandals onto my feet. The morning was cool and overcast, but the sun would soon burn through the morning mist. Building Father's pyre would be hot work, and there was no one else here to share the labor.

Kiva chose that moment to land heavily on my stone windowsill. Her golden-brown feathers beat against the air as she navigated the tight quarters. Once settled, she stood proudly on the sill and stared at me with her intent black eyes, her gaze unwavering but nervous, the feathers of her chest ruffled and full.

At her feet lay a bone, the small curved rib of perhaps a mouse, bare and smooth, its surface gray in the morning gloam.

Her call pierced the room.

"Fly, Kiva," I said while making a sweep of my flat hand, the motion that meant she should return whence she came.

But she did not. Instead she cocked her head and continued to stare intently at me.

Confused and angry, I strode to the windowsill. The sound of the ocean was stronger here. The wind blew cold against my face, moving my dark hair away from my eyes. The bone lay pitched up at one end. I twisted it around in my fingertips. It was dry and brittle, its surface slightly roughened like the finest of all sandpaper.

But it was just a bone.

I let it drop outside the window, knowing it would be lost amid the shale rock that lined the beach.

Kiva called again, and she leaped off the sill, swooping downward to catch the bone in midair just before it disappeared into the jagged rock. In a moment she had perched back on my windowsill, and the bone lay again in its spot.

"Damnation," I said to myself, wondering if she had lost the common sense that the gods gave all creatures. "All right, Kiva. I'll keep it." I slipped the bone into a small pouch that was clipped to my belt, then turned and walked out the door.

I had more things to worry about than a deranged hawk.

For as long as I can remember, we have kept hawks at Castle Talon. As of this past breeding season there are fifty-eight of them. We leave them free to come and go as they please.

And yet, they stay.

They always stay.

My father studied them intently, casting sorcery amidst them on more occasions than I could possibly count. They fascinated him, and drew every ounce of his attention. While he loved them all, he had been particularly fond of Lissa, a huge hawk with golden feathers and a wingspan as wide as my father was tall. He doted over her, speaking to her in quiet moments, and watching her glide over the land, flying majestically in the blue sky while he remained locked to the ground.

His eyes would mist sometimes.

And after these times he would increase his efforts in the laboratory, feverishly studying magic and incantations at the expense of his own physical health.

He wanted to get closer to the hawks, I know. He wanted a deeper connection.

I remember a night in a distant tavern where Father and I had traveled to fill a contract for his sorcery. Father, as he always did, had brought Lissa with him. A woman with thick, red lips and wearing strings of gold so false that even a boy my age could see them for such, asked if I was jealous of the birds.

I didn't know what to say then.

Certainly I was jealous. I knew *that* to the core of my being. I never understood my father's single-minded fixation on these creatures while I stayed outside his circle of concern. But at the same time, the hawks were as much a part of my life as they were of my father's. I fed them in the winters. I cleaned after them as they needed cleaning after, and I tended their wounds and sicknesses as they arose.

The hawks were a part of my life, and if truth is told, I had in some ephemeral fashion always felt attached to them. I asked my father about them once, though.

"Why do we have so many hawks?" I said.

His face grew troubled and distant, and he pursed his lips. For just an instant, his eyes softened, losing the edge that his glance always carried when he looked at me. He tried to speak, then stopped. He breathed deeply and hesitated longer.

"You will understand when you are older."

Father's smoke was gray and black. It curled upward in thick streams that twisted like drunken snakes and smelled of driftwood and salt. The hawks, all of them, glided in the sky above, riding drafts and twirling downward in a dance that seemed almost ritualistic.

The fire baked my face and prickled my bare

chest with heat that made my skin ache. Sweat I had given in the preparation of the pyre boiled away.

When the burning was done, I cast a spell over the embers. Fire can hide, and, no matter the castle's dilapidated condition, I had no intention of waking to find my newly inherited manor burned to the ground. It was an easy spell, among the first my father had taught me.

I sighed, watching the last of the flames snuffed.

When my father was alive, there was always a goal—always a plan, a new spell to try, or a fresh experiment to run.

But he was gone now. And yet I felt his presence stronger than ever before. His gaze seemed to come from each direction, expectation riding upon it as thick as the morning mist. The familiar hills reminded me of him; he had been like these hills to me, always here. How could they still spread from the oceanfront and he be gone? I thought of the creases in his forehead that I, too, would likely have someday, and he seemed even more real. I turned to the castle, expecting at any moment that he would step from the laboratory doorway and announce he had discovered some new facet of his magic.

He was not there, of course.

I had watched his body burn and the smoke that carried his soul waft up into the hawk-filled sky.

Now I felt like a lifeboat freed from a ship, adrift and loose on a windless sea.

Drained and hungry, I returned to the castle.

Kiva swooped down to land gracefully on a perch beside the doorway. Another bone slipped from her hooked beak, falling to the ground at my feet. She called again and stared at me insistently. I picked it up. This bone was similar to the last, but a bit larger.

It was certainly not from a mouse.

Kiva had been borne of Lissa, as had been the rest of the hawks that wheeled in the air above. But Kiva had been the first. She stood in much the same way as her mother had, held her head in a similar fashion and moved on a perch likewise. Strange, I thought. Or perhaps appropriate. Lissa had died a fortnight ago, sending my father into the laboratory for his last feverishly pitched efforts at developing new magics.

Now both Lissa and my father were dead. And it was Kiva, Lissa's first daughter, who brought me these gifts.

My muscles ached from my day's efforts. My stomach growled and my thoughts wandered. Without questioning her this time, I slipped the bone into my pouch with the other.

Given a hawk's eyesight, nothing alive can move so much as a hair's breadth in the territory around Castle Talon without the knowledge of one of our—my—birds. So it was no surprise when several days later, the hawks roused my attention.

Men were coming.

As always, I set the precautionary wardings, magical traps that would protect me if I needed to retreat into the castle. Men had often come here seeking sorcery, and my father was nothing if not cautious.

Nervous energy played inside me as I waited. This was the first time I would handle business on my own, and I worried about the encounter. I used the time to play conversations in my head until the words became a jumbled mess that was more confusing than helpful.

Five men arrived an hour later, riding horses that jangled with metal and leather harnesses, and whose hooves beat heavy patterns on the earth. The men wore brown and dark green. They carried weapons, but not in any outwardly aggressive fashion. I stood before them in tanned breeches and a billowing blue tunic. Leather talon guards were strapped around both of my forearms, their rawhide cords tied with comfortable pressure.

Hawks glided through the air above me.

"We've come to see your father," the leader said. He was a rugged man with sun-blond hair and a face chiseled from years on the trail.

"He is dead," I answered, the words coming oddly to my lips.

"That's damned unfortunate," the leader replied.

I ignored his comment. "I am Cullen. I run Castle Talon now. My father passed what he knew to me. If you require the aid of a sorcerer, I will listen to your situation."

The leader considered my statement, confusion written on his face. "I am Parr, from Ellingsworth," he finally said. "The king's daughter has taken a sudden illness, and he has need of a sorcerer's aid."

I could not help but frown. My father had been born in, and had lived in, Ellingsworth for many years before my birth. Yet while men from all across the continent had from time to time come to barter for my father's sorcery, none had ever arrived from that city. And now, scant days after my father's passing, here stood five riders asking me to travel to that place with them.

"Ellingsworth has a strong clergy. Isn't such a problem better handled by them?" I asked.

Parr's face darkened. "King's already tried that. The high priest prayed for days but nothing worked. Now the church says she's been cursed by sorcery too strong for them to break."

Lines crossed Parr's face. He was anxious dealing with sorcery, as many are. It was a prejudice my father suffered often in his life. Sorcery is wild and confusing to people who do not understand it. It is powerful beyond their ability to comprehend.

"I will go to Ellingsworth with you," I said. "Assuming the price is acceptable."

"Princess Terisa is the king's only daughter,"

Parr said angrily. "The queen died years ago. Rest assured he'll pay you more than you're worth."

I snorted, surprised at the man's bluntness. "Fair enough. I'll travel with you. But let me tell you I don't take kindly to such pointed comments, and *you* can rest assured that an upset sorcerer will cost your king more than a comfortable one will."

Wheeling in the sky, Kiva called and swooped down. I held out my arm, and she landed lightly on it.

"We are going on a trip, Kiva."

The men looked at her, obviously distrustful of the bird and uncertain of its tie to me.

"Tell the others," I said, motioning her to the sky once again.

She took to the air then, calling loudly with high-pitched screams. The rest of the hawks flew around her, responding and gliding out over the prairie that stretched away from the rolling ocean.

The men remained quiet, but I could see the display had done nothing to reduce my stature in their eyes.

My father had taught me well.

I offered to put the men up overnight in Castle Talon, but they decided to make a campground in the hills to the east, explaining that they had not been near the ocean before and wanted to be in the open while they were here.

I smiled and pretended to accept their words, all the while sensing their anxiety.

So I slept alone in the castle, the physical separation of the men from Ellingsworth speaking volumes, telling me that I was not like them, that I was dangerous.

I suppose I could not help but dream about my father. As the night passed around me, I asked him questions that he would not answer. I requested advice he would not give. Despite these rebuffs, or perhaps because of them, the conversation felt warm and familiar. His voice rumbled, and his breathing rasped nasally like it always had. When the beam of his concentration would fall fully on me, he was gentle and easy to talk to, a natural teacher with a calm demeanor and a lighthearted approach.

I woke fresh and oddly confident, feeling close to my father, a sensation that fought with my ingrained fears and doubts to make a mixture of emotions that was not completely pleasurable.

By the time we left, Kiva had placed three more bones on my windowsill—one a round vertebra the size of a pea, one the curved needle of a rib cage, and the last a small pelvic segment. I placed each into my pouch, still no farther along in puzzling out why she was leaving them.

But my collection had now grown to a firm handful.

*   *   *

The city was large and sprawling. It smelled of baked bread and fried meats.

Buildings of white stone and yellowed brick towered over the landscape. A large river ran past to the east, glittering with the silver-gold reflection of the setting sun as we entered the main gates. Men pulled carts through rutted streets. Women carried ceramic bowls and woven baskets on their shoulders. I caught a whiff of cinnamon, and my stomach growled.

Parr had no time for my hunger, however, and directed us toward the king's castle.

This was the city my father had grown up in. I stared at it as we moved, dwelling over the buildings, imagining him as a boy playing tag or kicking rocks, and wondering with each moment if he had ever stood in the exact spot where I was now.

I glanced at Kiva.

She rode anxiously on my arm. At first I attributed her demeanor to her distaste for the city's closed space. But as we progressed she grew more agitated, ruffling her feathers and stretching her wings often. A hawk's silhouette graced the sky above, another of our birds following at a cautious distance.

I had never previously known any of the birds to follow my father and me when we traveled, and the novelty of its appearance in conjunction with Kiva's odd discomfort made me feel uneasy.

As we neared the king's castle, the gates opened and an armored guard approached.

"How is the princess?" Parr said as he slid from his mount.

The guard grunted and pulled at his well-trimmed beard. "Worse off, from what I hear," he said, his expression grave.

Parr gave a deflated sigh. "The king?" he asked.

"With the princess."

"Come on," Parr said to me. "There is no time to spare."

I swung my leg over my horse's saddle, glad for the opportunity to stretch.

The guard pointed at Kiva. "We can put the bird in the aviary," he said.

Kiva had not calmed any, and I would not leave her alone for fear of adding to her anxiety.

"Thank you," I responded. "But I will keep her with me."

The guard glanced at Kiva, then looked to Parr with a question in his gaze.

Parr merely shrugged and motioned me to follow him.

"It's all right," I cooed as I went, noting Kiva's heightened nervousness with each of my steps and hoping my assertion was correct.

Kiva opened her wingspan, then settled in a little.

We walked across the manor yard. It was a large, rolling field that seemed to absorb sound. Crows strutted across the green grass, scattering as I drew near, their shoulders shimmering with blue-sheened lurching motions. The fragrance of corn and beans and tomatoes came from the king's garden.

Members of the manor stopped as we passed them by. The weight of their awkward stares burned on my back. I felt the presence of my father then, so close I could smell the bitter reek of sorcery that had always hung around him. I had watched him handle this situation time and time again, walking into a place where people around him feared what he was, feared the whole of what he stood for.

In an unusual burst of verbosity, he had once talked to me about it.

"You must go into a new city as if you own it, Cullen. Or else it will own you."

Remembering his words, I threw back my shoulders and set my face with the same firm countenance that had once been his. We are very similar in features, my father and I. I know this. And now I cast myself as him, twenty years younger and walking into Ellingsworth with all the confidence in the world.

A doorman opened the gates.

We entered the castle, our footsteps muffled by plush rugs that lined the floor. Clean-burning candles lit the expansive hallway of gray stone. Paintings and heavy tapestries lined the walls. Kiva grew suddenly subdued.

"Come," Parr said anxiously.

He led me through the hallway and up a set

of wide, sweeping stairs. A long corridor led past several doors before we stopped at a guarded chamber.

Nurses stood anxiously around the bed. The king sat in an upholstered chair by the princess's side, his eyes worn and hollow, ringed by dark circles. Age had lined his face and tinted his hair with gray streaks. He wore simple, unkingly clothes—a yellow tunic and cloth breeches. But he held himself with the firm posture of someone accustomed to obedience.

"Parr," he said, rising.

"The mage is dead," Parr said quickly, not taking the care to soften his language for me. "So I brought his son."

The king stepped before me, glancing once at Kiva with a strange expression of dread. His eyes took me in from top to bottom, his face an odd mixture of hardness and pain, and something else, too, something seething underneath, angry and cold but hidden under layers of restraint.

He did not *want* a sorcerer here, yet had asked for one.

"You are your father's boy. No mistaking that," he said with a sword's edge to his voice.

"Thank you," I said, trying not to furrow my brow. My father had never mentioned his association with the king before, which, of course, was so like him as to not need thought. "Let me see the princess," I continued, trying to divert the conversation into a place more comfortable.

He escorted me to her side.

I placed Kiva onto the sill of the open window by the bed, then bent to examine the princess. Kiva opened her beak as if to call out, but then settled into place, staring now at the princess with intense concentration.

Terisa was dark, like her father. Her face, however, was gaunt and sickly; her skin pulled over cheekbones like dry leather. She was about my age, I saw, maybe a year or two older.

I placed my hand over her forehead and spoke a quick magic. Her body radiated the pale crimson light that only sorcerers can see. Her form glowed through the sheets with cold magic that echoed through my mind.

At my side, Kiva spread her wings and gave a shrill screech, a sound that reverberated with a yearning for freedom so universal as to be unmistakable.

My eyes narrowed.

Burning heat grew against my thigh. I looked down to find light radiating from my pouch. This glow was blue, however, and it met with the crimson sorcery over Princess Terisa to bathe the room in lavender and black shadows.

The bones, I thought, this new magic sprang from the bones Kiva had been laying at my feet since the day my father had died.

Kiva called out again, and urgency came to my spell work.

Something new grew inside me, burrowing out of my understanding like a rodent emerging

from the ground. The birds have magic, I
thought, remembering my father's words when
I had asked of the hawks' presence.

Sorcery whirled around Kiva, and she fed my
spell with magic of her own. I felt her heartbeat
swishing rapidly through her body. I saw into
the magical realm of my spell work with the
clarity of her vision. And what I saw shook me.

The link that enveloped us grew, closing a
loop that included the princess. The three of
us—Kiva, the princess, and I—were all linked,
bonded in some fashion seemingly inseparable,
and that bond *was*, in some way, my magic.

"What is it?" the king asked breathlessly.

Ignoring his question, I bent further over the
princess. Yes, her complexion was dark like her
father's. And she had the severe curve of his
nose. But the shape of her face was familiar,
rounded at the cheekbone and tapering at the
jawline. Her hair had bronze highlights.

Similar features to those I saw every time I
looked into the reflection of my father's mirror.

Kiva called, a shrill scream that made everyone in the chamber jump.

"Get the damned bird out of here," the king
said.

The guard moved toward her.

"No!" I called. "Kiva must stay."

She stood in the open window, her wings par-
tially unfurled, their curve graceful and fluid.
Her heartbeat still fluttered against mine, and
her gaze was still intense. Magic flowed from

her. Another heartbeat joined ours then, slow and methodical, so familiar it could have been my own.

The princess.

With that sound, with the throbbing beat of Terisa's heart so very much like my own, I knew the truth with such startling clarity I found it hard to breathe.

I clutched the bedclothes and turned my gaze to the king. Blood drained from my face.

"She is my sister," I said accusingly.

The king looked crestfallen. "Yes," he admitted, his head nodding almost absently.

The gasp from those in the room was audible.

"But my father?"

"Was once my own wizard," the king said. His eyes grew sharp and he set his jaw. "I sent him away."

"But only after I was born and it became obvious who my father was," I said, making it a statement rather than a question.

Kiva cried again as if prodding the king. For an instant I pondered the power of her magic, the sway she might hold over him as well as over me. But there was not time enough to consider this fully.

"Yes," the king finally said, speaking as much to Kiva as to me. "I was angry. I was jealous and embarrassed. So I sent him away, and I sent your mother, the queen, away, too."

"But, sir," Parr broke in. "The queen died

with her stillborn son. The entire land mourned her for months."

Movement stopped in the room. The king chewed his bottom lip. Kiva spread her wings farther and stared into the king's gaze.

The king shook his head. "No, Parr. Lissa did not die."

Lissa.

The name rolled off the king's lips and rang through my head with a peal as clear as a church bell. Lissa. Lissa. The name of the queen. The name of the hawk my father had kept beside him his entire life. Lissa. Lissa.

The link between the princess and Kiva and me still burned. I thought for a moment, knowing now with certainty that just as Terisa and I were siblings, so, too, somehow were Kiva and I.

"She became a hawk," I said in a stupefied monotone. "My mother, the queen. She was a hawk."

The king nearly broke down. Tears formed in his eyes. "Yes. She had always kept a raptor in the castle, and it was her falconry that drew your father and her together. So I felt it fitting punishment. I paid dearly for the spell that made her a hawk and tied his magic to her soul. Then I sent them away."

The king drew a chest-wracked breath.

"But now my daughter is dying, and I don't know why. Please save her. She is all I have left."

Fire burned along the top of my thigh. The pouch glowed with blue waves.

The bones.

I touched their magic flame and felt what I for the first time in my life knew to be my mother. She was warm and she was kind. Through her eyes I saw my father, their awkward early meetings, the love that grew between them that both fought against, and the fervor with which he had worked in his later years.

He had spent his life trying to free her, but the binding had been too great.

And with both of their deaths, the bond had passed to her next generation—including her daughters, Terisa and Kiva. Kiva and I were together throughout the past weeks, but Terisa was alone. And bound as we were, none of us could live apart.

But the magic was weak, now. I could feel it, see the cracks in its casting.

And I could break it if I wanted to.

If I wanted to.

I shuddered with the thought.

"You will understand when you are older," my father had said. And now I did. The king had tied my father's magic to the hawks. I knew this to be true. All of my magic was founded on the birds, fueled by their existence and the link I had to them.

If I broke this binding, I would no longer have magic of my own.

The thought rang in my heart and sent ice

through my veins. I had been raised since a boy to be a sorcerer. I knew nothing else. The truth of the moment sat before me like a starved lioness.

Terisa lay on her bed. She had been apart from us for too long. If I did not cast the final spell, she would die. Kiva folded her wings and sat calmly on the sill, awaiting my decision. She, too, was caught in this web of deceit spun by the king and queen and their wizard. If I did not cast the final spell, we would be bound for the rest of our lives.

And if I did cast the final spell, I would lose my sorcery, the only thing my father had left me.

The king looked at me with deep, watery eyes.

He had lost his wife and his friend years ago. When news of his deceit was released, he would likely lose his rule. And now he stood to lose his daughter no matter what I did.

Outside the window, the sky was dark with circling hawks.

I reached into the pouch and withdrew the bones of my mother. They were weightless, shimmering with magical heat. I clasped my fingers around them, holding on to her for a moment that seemed to last forever and to be gone at the same time.

She smelled of orchids, my mother.

And her smile was playful.

The spell came to me unbidden, the words

flowing easily, the fullness of courage and justice expanding my chest and making my heart feel as if it would burst.

This was the right thing to do.

I cast the bones down on my half sister's bed, speaking the final phrases of the spell work.

"Will you stay?" my sister said to me with pleading eyes. She had recovered rapidly, and now we sat on a pair of iron lounges in the king's gardens, perhaps as our mother and my father once had. A light wind blew dogwood and apple tree scents from the west.

I wanted to stay. That I could not deny. We had much in common, having both grown up without a mother.

And I wanted to know my sister. There was procedure to follow, but her father was stepping down from his rule and soon she would be queen. I wanted to see her grow through this moment in her life.

But I shook my head instead. "No," I said. "I have a whole life to discover again, Terisa. And I'm not ready to stay here. I will return, though."

She smiled. "I understand. This is your home, though. Do *you* understand?"

I matched her smile and nodded. "Yes," I said. "This is my home." And suddenly it was. I felt it in the way Terisa smiled, and at the way we had grown comfortable with each other's presence in such rapid fashion.

We stood then, and I gave her a hug.

Terisa smelled of orchids, and I of my now dead sorcery.

"Will you go back to Castle Talon?" she asked.

I stared into the birdless sky. The hawks had left after the spell had been cast, scattering into the hills and the mountains to live in the high rock as all hawks should. Even Kiva had left. I had given them back to the gods, to whom they rightfully belonged. I was alone now, truly alone.

"No. I'll travel for a while. Father used to tell me of his wanderings as a boy. Perhaps I'll follow his path."

"Good luck," she said with a playful smile. "I'll look forward to your return."

"As will I," I replied. "As will I."

I left the next morning.

The king offered me a horse, but I decided I wanted to walk. I felt like a week's-dry sponge, empty and waiting. I wanted to know the land and see it up close. And the closer I was to the ground, the more real it would be, the more I would learn from it.

I strode alone past Ellingsworth's tall buildings and out of the main gates. The soil smelled of clay. The grass had the cold edge of the approaching fall season. I set off to the east, toward the Ridge Mountains.

The sun rose higher in the sky, and the day

became warm. I eventually stopped to make my lunch.

My father was a good man. I knew that now. He loved my mother, and she loved him. He was caught up in his magic, and he was caught up in his efforts to find his love. Maybe that was enough for me to forgive his lack of attention.

I planned to think about it often in the next weeks.

A shadow flashed silently over the sun-drenched grass.

I glanced up at the same time Kiva called out.

Her feathers golden brown in the sunlight, she swooped down from the sky, gliding on unseen currents to land on a branch above me.

She sat silently, her magic now as dead as my own. Her glance was nervous and self-conscious, or perhaps I was just applying my own understanding to her actions. The other birds were gone, their tie to Castle Talon rent with the tearing of my inheritance. Kiva and I were no longer bonded by sorcery.

But I felt close to her in a way stronger than ever before, and I think somewhere deep inside her eyes I saw this same connection. I reached to my side and pulled out the pouch of our mother's bones.

They were still there, light as air. Kiva watched me, her curved beak seeming to cut into the afternoon.

I untied the drawstrings and emptied the pouch onto the ground before me. The bones fell, crumbling at the touch of soil, spreading and melting into the earth as if they were made of water. A whiff of orchids twisted in the breeze, then the scent was gone.

Kiva cried a mournful sound, full of sadness and emptiness, yet carrying undertones of understanding. I had been born of two human beings. Kiva had been born of my mother's body and my father's magic.

Now the souls of both had been joined.

Their lives were done.

Ours was about to begin.

I stood up, wiping my lips with the back of my hand. "You're welcome to travel with me, sister," I said to Kiva, strapping a leather guard over my forearm.

And Kiva, bound to me in a different fashion than I had ever felt before, flew to my hand.

NIGHT FLIGHT

by *Lawrence Watt-Evans*

Lawrence Watt-Evans is the author of more
than two dozen books and over a hundred
short stories including several set, like this
one, in the World of Ethahar. His latest
novel is *Dragon Weather*.

PRINCESS Kirna of Quonmor sat upon her bed
and frowned at the barred window. The sun
was down, and daylight was fading rapidly; she
would be spending another night here in the
wizard's tower, and once again, she would be
spending it locked in this room, all alone. This
was not working out at all as she had expected.

Running off with a wizard had seemed like
such a very romantic idea! She had thought she
could entice him to either marry her, whereupon
they would travel all over the world having
wonderful adventures together, or to take her
on as his apprentice, whereupon she would
spend years learning all the secrets of magic and
then someday return to Quonmor to find a

usurper on the throne, whom she, as the rightful heir, would then depose and punish horribly for his effrontery. Her subjects would cheer as she crowned herself queen in her father's throne room, and she would use her magic to transform Quonmor into a paradise, and to reconquer Dennamor, which her great-grandfather had lost.

And then perhaps she would reunite all the Small Kingdoms into an empire—after all, if that warlock Vond could conquer a dozen of them, without having even a trace of royal blood, why couldn't a wizard-queen rule them all?

But this had all depended on this Gar of Uramor falling in love with her, or at least taking her seriously, and so far he hadn't. He hadn't objected to her company on the walk home, but when she had tried to flirt with him, he had laughed and said she was too young, and when she had asked about an apprenticeship, he had said she was too old.

And then when she had explained that she was a princess, so the ordinary rules didn't apply to her, he had gotten angry and locked her up here, in this room with the thick iron-bound door and the distressingly solid iron bars in the window.

And then when he came back—well, it had been downright embarrassing. He had treated her as if she were little more than a baby, and hadn't agreed to *anything*. What was the good of being a princess if you couldn't have what you wanted?

She pouted, and bounced on the bed—it wasn't as soft as her featherbed at home, but it was pleasantly springy and fun to bounce on.

"Princess Kirna?" a breathy voice asked.

Startled, she stopped bouncing and smoothed out her face—her father had always told her a princess mustn't pout. The voice hadn't been Gar's. It had sounded as if it were right beside her, but of course there wasn't anyone else in the room; she turned toward the door and called, "Who is it?"

"Hush!" She jumped; the voice was right in her ear.

"Who's there?" she whispered.

A vague blue shape shimmered in the air before her, and the voice said, in a slightly accented Quonmoric, "I am Deru of the Nimble Fingers. I've come to help you." The blue shape raised a hand, and she glimpsed a blurry face.

"A ghost!" she gasped. "A real ghost!"

"No, I'm not a ghost," Deru said. "I'm a wizard under a spell."

She flung a hand to cover her mouth. "You're under a *curse*? That terrible Gar did this to you, and is keeping you prisoner here?"

"No, no," Deru assured her. "I did it to myself, so I could get in here to talk to you. It's called the Cloak of Ethereality. It'll wear off soon."

"Oh," she said disappointed. "You just came to talk to me?"

"I was sent to find out why you're here."

Kirna stared at the misty blue outline for a moment. Who *was* this person? Who had sent him? Was he really here at all?

He said he was a wizard—had the Wizards' Guild sent him?

Might Gar be in trouble? Kirna had heard stories about the dreadful things the Wizards' Guild did to people who broke its rules. . . .

Maybe he wasn't in trouble yet, but he *could* be, and it would serve him right for mistreating her.

"He kidnapped me!" she said. "He dragged me here and locked me up, and he *tortured* me!" She held up her left hand, where Gar had nicked her with a knife to draw a vial of blood.

The apparition stooped to stare at her hand, and she snatched it away before he could see just how small the cut really was.

"He took my blood," she said. "I'm sure he's going to do something *terrible* with it."

"He took your blood," Deru said thoughtfully. "Anything else? Hair? Tears?"

She blinked at him, startled; this wasn't the reaction she had expected. She decided she had better tell the truth—more or less.

"Yes," she said. "He tortured me until I cried, then caught my tears with a cloth and a little jar." The "torture" had just been shouting and teasing, but she didn't see any need to admit that.

The misty figure nodded.

"Well, that'll be *some* relief to your father anyway."

"That I was *tortured*?" Then she realized what he had said. "My father?"

Deru nodded. "Your parents sent me," he said "Didn't I say that?"

"No, you didn't!" Kirna felt cheated; this ghostly figure hadn't come from the Wizards' Guild after all. Then she remembered the rest of the conversation. "You think they'll be relieved that I was *tortured*?"

"No, they'll be relieved that Gar was collecting your tears," he said. "Normal tears aren't worth anything, but a virgin's tears are used in at least half a dozen different spells; if Gar was collecting yours, then he didn't rape you."

Somehow Kirna found that annoying. "Yet," she said. "He still might, now that he's filled that jar!

"I suppose he might, at that," Deru agreed. "Virgin's blood and hair and tears are all valuable, but so are various parts of unborn children."

Kirna's eyes widened in horror. "He wouldn't."

"Well, people do," Deru said. "And if he kidnapped a princess, who knows what he might do? On the other hand, he might just keep you here and murder your parents—there are a few very powerful spells that call for the tears of a

virgin *queen*, rather than just any virgin. Those
spells are beyond my abilities, but maybe Gar
knows them."

Kirna shrieked. *"Murder* my *parents?"*

"The Guild wouldn't approve, but . . ."

"No! You need to stop him!"

"The easiest way for me to do that would be
to take you home," Deru said. "I'm sure that if
you were safely back at Quonmor Keep, with
guards all around you, that he wouldn't
bother—he'd find an easier target."

"Take me home!" Kirna said.

"I'd be glad to," Deru said. "The question is,
how do we get you out of here? Do you think
Gar would just let you go, if you asked?"

Kirna stared at him. "Haven't you heard anything I've told you?" she said. "He *kidnapped*
me and *dragged* me here and locked me up and
tortured me!"

Deru sighed. "But he might have just wanted
the blood and tears. He's got those now, so
maybe he'll let you go."

"You're crazy!" Kirna said. "He intends to
keep me here forever, I'm *sure* of it!"

Actually, Gar had said something about sending her home in the morning, but she wasn't
about to admit that. She had failed to impress
Gar, but perhaps this other wizard, this Deru,
might be more amenable. Perhaps, once they
were out of this awful tower, she could convince
him to run away with her, so they could marry

and have adventures and he could teach her all
his magic.

Maybe she could even get him to *kill* Gar! A
wizards' duel, fought over her— She shivered
with excitement at the thought.

Deru sighed. "Well, you're probably right. I'll
just have to get you out of here without him
knowing it."

"Oh." Her excitement dimmed. That meant
no duel.

But still, it would be a dramatic rescue that
might lead to romance.

"How?" she asked.

"Leave that to me," he said.

Then he vanished.

"*Hai!*" she called. "Where are you?"

No one answered.

Deru stepped out through the locked door of
the third-floor chamber, back out into the stair-
well, ignoring Kirna's calls.

He suspected the princess was embellishing
her story somewhat; he still didn't think Gar
had brutally kidnapped her and dragged her
away, as she alleged. The Wizards' Guild for-
bade its members to interfere with any sort of
royal succession, and kidnapping a princess
would qualify; Deru had trouble believing Gar
would openly defy that rule. To do so was suicidal, and Gar didn't appear to be sufficiently
deranged.

Besides, how could he have done it without

being noticed—and without putting a single mark on her face? Deru had studied her briefly before becoming visible. He was in no hurry, since the Cloak of Ethereality lasted a predetermined length of time and he could not remove it for hours yet, so he had taken a few minutes to explore the tower and look over the princess. He hadn't seen a bruise or scratch anywhere on her, except for the one little incision on her hand.

But Gar *had* locked her in, and collected blood and tears and hair—and besides, it would make a much better story to carry out a magical rescue than to simply walk her home, and it would be easier to collect a huge fee if he had a good story to tell.

Deru drifted invisibly up the stairs to Gar's workshop, and peered in at his fellow wizard.

There was no need to do anything to Gar; he appeared to be settled in for the evening, and if Kirna disappeared, he probably wouldn't notice anything until morning.

And when he *did* notice, he probably wouldn't do anything about it. After all, Kirna was Crown Princess of Quonmor, and the Wizards' Guild had rules against meddling with royalty. If Deru could just get the girl out of the tower, that should be the end of Gar's involvement. And after that, it was only twelve miles back to Quonmor Keep; that wouldn't be a difficult walk.

Deru looked past Gar at the open window;

the cool outside air was stirring the curtains slightly, and the light of the greater moon tinted the white muslin orange. Somewhere in the forest outside the tower an owl hooted.

It all seemed peaceful enough. There was no point in being unnecessarily complicated; all he had to do was get Kirna out of the tower. He had come prepared for that. He had brought the materials he needed for Riyal's Transformation, and had even prepared the oakleaf-tea countercharm in advance.

He allowed himself to sink through the floor, back to Kirna's room, to wait for the Cloak's spell to break.

There was no flash or bang; one moment Kirna was lying in bed, half-asleep but kept awake by wondering about her mysterious ghostly visitor, alone in her candle-lit room, and the next instant a curly-haired young man in a blue silk cloak was standing next to her, holding a finger to his lips.

Her eyes opened wide; she flung off the blanket and sat up. "You're back!" she said.

"Yes, I am," he said, his voice low. "And in a few hours we'll be out of here and on our way back to Quonmor."

"A few hours?"

"Yes," he said. "We'll be going out that window." He pointed.

"But it's barred," Kirna said. "Are you going to turn me into a ghost like you?"

He shook his head. "No, that spell only works on wizards—but I brought another that can affect us both. It will shrink us down until we can easily walk between those bars, and then I can levitate us safely down to the ground."

"*Shrink* us?"

He nodded. "We'll be not much larger than mice. It takes about three hours to prepare."

She hesitated. "Is it safe?"

"Oh, yes," Deru assured her. "It won't harm you, and the countercharm is very easy—just a drink of a special tea." He slipped a battered leather pack off his shoulder, opened the top flap, and pulled out a brown glass flask. "This is the cure right here. A sip of this will break the spell and restore you instantly to your normal size. Once we're well away from the tower we'll drink it, and then it's just a matter of walking you home."

"Oh," Kirna said.

This was exciting, in its way—the idea of being shrunk down to the size of a mouse was strange, certainly—but it wasn't quite what she had hoped for. Walking home? Not flying, or vanishing in a puff of smoke from one place and appearing with a flash in another? Shrunk down, but not turned into birds?

Well, it would do, and perhaps it would be more interesting than it sounded.

"Now, I need you to stay close, and stay quiet, while I prepare the spell," Deru said. "Oh,

and you'll need to open the shutter and case-
ment, so we can get out once we're small.''

"All right," Kirna said. Rather than wait, she
rose and opened the window immediately,
while Deru removed and folded up his silken
cloak and fished more items out of his pack.

Beneath the rather dramatic cloak he was
wearing a disappointingly ordinary brown-and-
cream tunic and suede breeches. Kirna had
hoped for something more wizardly.

A moment later, as she sat on the bed and
watched, Deru began the ritual. He drew lines
on the floor with something white and waxy,
then positioned three candles on the resulting
design before seating himself cross-legged at
the center.

He lit the candles one by one while mumbling
something Kirna could not make out, then set
out a dagger, two scraps of fur, and two tiny,
bright-red objects Kirna did not recognize. The
mumbling turned into a rhythmic chanting, and
his hands moved through the air in curious
patterns.

Every so often he would lean over and move
one of the objects, and sometimes he was holding a lump of the white stuff, sometimes he
wasn't.

It was all very mysterious and magical—and
after the first few minutes, boring. Kirna
watched, waiting for something to happen, but
the chant droned on endlessly. . . .

She awoke with a start to find Deru standing

over her, shaking her gently. "Your Highness!" he said. "Wake up!"

"I'm awake!" she said irritably, sitting up and looking at the room.

The air was thick and hot, and she had trouble seeing clearly, whether from sleep or smoke she was not sure. All the candles had burned out but one, which was down to a smoking stub; the design on the floor had vanished, but an identical design of white smoke hung in the air a foot above where it had been drawn. The dagger was sheathed and on Deru's belt, and the other things were gone.

Her head seemed to be buzzing, and she suddenly was unsure whether she was awake or dreaming or somewhere in between.

"Stick out your tongue," Deru said.

"What?" The unexpected order halfway convinced her she was dreaming.

"Stick out your tongue! Quickly! We need to do this before the candle goes out!"

Confused, Kirna stuck out her tongue, and Deru quickly pressed something onto it, a tiny something that tickled and scratched, and stuck.

"Wha . . . ?" She tried to talk, but the object on her tongue made it difficult; she gagged.

Deru was holding out a piece of fur; he reached over her shoulders with it, then stretched it out. She could feel it on her back, and it seemed to be stretching out forever.

"What's that?" she asked, and discovered that the thing on her tongue had dissolved away into nothingness. She looked up at Deru, who seemed to be taller suddenly. The ceiling was rising up away from her, as well.

"It's the skin of a field mouse," Deru said as he wrapped it around her.

She tumbled from the bed, and it was a much longer fall than it should have been; she landed on her hands and knees, her palms stinging with the impact. Her vision blurred.

When it cleared again, she clambered to her feet and looked up.

Deru stood before her, unspeakably huge, the pack on his shoulder the size of Quonmor Keep; between the gigantic pillars of his legs she could see the smoking stub of candle, taller than she was. The pattern of smoke hung over her, out of reach. She looked up, and up, and up.

Deru was putting a tiny red thing on his own tongue; that done, he took a scrap of gray fur and lifted his hands up over his head.

And then he began shrinking. The mouse-pelt didn't stretch; Deru shrank.

And moment later he stood before her at his normal height, a few inches taller than herself, as the candle flared up and went out and the pattern of smoke dissipated. Darkness descended, broken only by the orange glow of the greater moon outside the open window.

The little bedchamber stretched out before them in the dimness, an immensity of space.

"There," Deru said. "It worked."

"Oh," Kirna said, looking around.

The world was strange and different, with ordinary furniture becoming looming monstrosities, but she no longer suspected she was dreaming; everything was quite solid and real. She looked up at the window, impossibly far above them, and asked, "How do we get out?"

"We levitate. Or rather, I do. I'll have to carry you, I'm afraid; I don't have a levitation spell that will work on both of us."

She frowned, but could hardly argue. She was no wizard.

At least, not yet.

Deru knelt and opened his pack. He pulled out a small lantern, a gray feather, and a silver bit; he lit the lantern, set the coin inside it, then drew his dagger again and did something Kirna could not see. Then he straightened up, the lantern in his hand and the dagger back in his belt; the feather seemed to have vanished.

"Come here," he said.

Cautiously, Kirna approached—and then shrieked as Deru grabbed her and hoisted her over his shoulder, her head and arms dangling down his back, her legs pinned to his chest. She raised her head and turned to look around.

Deru was walking, one hand holding her legs and the other carrying the lantern—but he was not walking across the floor; instead he was walking up into the air, as if climbing an invisible staircase.

"Varen's Levitation," he said.

Kirna made a wordless strangled noise. She

had wanted to learn magic and have adventures, but being shrunk to the size of a mouse, flung over someone's shoulder, and carried up into the air, with nothing at all holding them up, all in quick succession, was a little more than she had been ready for.

But, she told herself, she was being silly. This *was* a magical adventure! She should appreciate it.

She thought she could appreciate it much more easily if she weren't draped over Deru's shoulder, though. She tried to twist around for a better view.

"You don't want me to drop you," Deru cautioned. "The spell only works on me."

Kirna ignored that and watched. Deru was marching up higher and higher above the floor, and had now turned toward the window. Kirna could see the sky and the surrounding treetops, lit by the orange light of the greater moon. The feeble glow of the tiny lantern didn't reach more than a few inches.

Fitting between the bars would be no problem at all at their present size—but how would they get *down*?

"Shouldn't you have a rope?" she asked.

"We don't need one," Deru said, panting slightly. "Varen's Levitation goes down just as well as up."

"Oh," Kirna said.

That sounded well enough, but she had noticed the panting—this fellow Deru was already getting tired, and they weren't even out the window yet.

Well, he had been working magic for hours, which must be tiring, and while Kirna certainly would never have said she was fat, or even stout, she knew she wasn't a frail little twig like some girls—princesses were well-fed. Carrying her might get tiring eventually even for a bigger, stronger man than Deru.

"You're sure you'll be all right?" she asked.

"I'll be fine," he said, and the panting was more obvious this time.

Kirna was hardly in a position to protest, though, so she shut her mouth and watched as they mounted up over the windowsill.

Deru leveled off just a foot or so—no, Kirna corrected herself, perhaps half an inch—above the sill, and walked straight forward, placing each foot solidly on empty air.

The bars were as big as oaks as they passed, great oaks of black iron—and then they were out in the night air, cool and sharp after the hot, stuffy bedchamber. Kirna felt her hair dancing in the breeze, and she squirmed, trying to keep it where it belonged.

"Stop it!" Deru hissed. "You do *not* want me to drop you from here!"

Kirna looked down the side of the tower—and down, and down, and down—and decided that Deru was right. She knew it was only about thirty feet to the ground, at most, but in her shrunken state it looked more like a thousand,

and besides, thirty feet was enough to kill someone. She stopped squirming.

Deru marched forward, just as if he were
walking on solid stone rather than empty air;
then he started descending, step by step, as if
he had arrived at another invisible stair.

Kirna, tired of looking down, looked up—and
shrieked, "Look out!" She pointed and began
struggling desperately.

Deru turned, trying to hold onto his burdens
and see what she was talking about. "What is
it?" he started to say, but before the words had
left his lips, he knew what had caused Kirna's
panic.

It all happened incredibly fast for Deru; he
had been looking down at his feet, watching his
descent and staying well clear of tree branches
or whatever seeds might be drifting on the
wind, since Varen's Levitation would end instantly if either the wizard stopped paying attention, or his booted feet touched solid matter,
when Kirna had shouted and begun thrashing.
He had turned his attention to the sky and seen
nothing but a night-flying bird.

Then it registered that the bird was approaching rapidly, that it was an owl swooping
silently toward them.

And then, finally, it registered that this was a
threat, that in their shrunken state an owl could
eat them both.

He instinctively flung up his arms to ward the
huge predator off, whereupon Kirna tumbled off

his shoulder and plummeted into the darkness beneath.

And at that instant Deru forgot all about Varen's Levitation and dropped the lantern, and he, too, fell into the night. The owl, wings muffled and talons spread, swept harmlessly through the space where the wizard had stood half a second before.

Kirna sat up, dazed, trying to remember where she was and what had happened to bring her here. She was sitting on a gigantic leaf, surrounded by a thick tangle of wood; it was dark, though the orange light of the greater moon alleviated the worst of the gloom. To one side she glimpsed an impossibly tall stone tower; everywhere else she saw only forest.

Everything seemed distorted.

Then she remembered why; she was only about two inches tall. That clumsy young wizard had shrunk her, carried her out the window . . . and then what? Had he carried her off somewhere and abandoned her?

No, he had *dropped* her, when that owl had attacked. She remembered the vast rush of air as she fell, and the utter helpless terror she had felt, and the crunch as she had hit a bush.

The bush must have broken her fall, though, because she was still alive, albeit somewhat bruised and battered.

And she was, she realized, under that same bush, a few feet from Gar's tower.

But where was Deru? Had the owl gotten him?

She scanned the sky overhead as best she could through the tangle of bush, but saw no trace of Deru. She did spot the owl, however, drifting far overhead.

She tried to remember what she knew about owls. Her father, King Tolthar, had insisted she receive a proper education, and while that had mostly meant politics, geography, history, and etiquette, several lessons about her natural surroundings had been included.

She thought the owl up there was a big one, even allowing for her own diminished stature, perhaps even what Tharn the Stablemaster had called a great horned owl, though of course owls didn't actually have horns.

At least, she didn't think they did.

Owls *did* have exceptional eyesight, even for birds, since they preferred to hunt at night. They also had special fringes on their wings that let them fly silently, with none of the audible flapping and rustling of other avians, and they generally gave no cry in flight—hooting was for when they were safely at home, not for when they were out hunting.

That one up there looked very much as if it were hunting.

If it had eaten Deru, she asked herself, wouldn't it be done hunting? She tried to take encouragement from that, to convince herself that this meant Deru was still alive; the possibility that he was simply too small to satisfy so large a bird was too uncomfortable to consider.

For one thing, if the owl had swallowed him, she doubted it had managed to remove his pack first, and that was where the antidote to the shrinking spell was. The idea of spending her entire life able to meet chipmunks and large spiders face-to-face did not appeal to her.

Of course, when the owl spat out a pellet of Deru's bones and hair, the pack and bottle might still be in it, but that was really too gross to think about. And besides, how would she *find* it?

So she would assume he was still alive, and that he still had that flask in his pack. All she had to do was find him and take a sip, and she would be herself again, and the owl would be no problem at all.

She got to her feet and brushed bits of dry leaf from her gown. She was safe enough here inside this bush, she was sure.

"Deru!" she called, as loudly as she could.

No one answered; she glanced up to see that the owl had wheeled about and was soaring overhead again.

"Deru!" she shouted again.

The owl wavered slightly in its flight, veering toward her.

"Hush!" Deru's voice called back from somewhere a good way off. He sounded strained.

That was an immense relief; she let her breath out in a rush. He was still alive.

She wouldn't have to stay tiny the rest of her life.

"It can't get me here," she called back. "Where *are* you?"

"Over here; in another bush," Deru called back. "And are you *sure* it can't tear its way right through to you?"

Kirna swallowed her reply, suddenly not sure at all. She ducked under one of the larger branches and looked around for better shelter, just in case.

There was a hole in the ground, half-hidden in the darkness; if the owl came for her she could duck in there. . . .

She stopped in mid-thought. *Why* was there a hole in the ground? Presumably something lived in it.

That might be worse than the owl. She had a sudden vision of meeting a snake while still her present size.

"Do something!" she shrieked. "Grow back to normal size and get me out of here!"

"I can't!" Deru called back. "I dropped my pack. It's out there in the open somewhere—if I go after it, the owl will get me."

"Can't you do *something*?" She was starting to go hoarse from shouting.

"The countercharm needs oak leaves from the very top of a tree ten times the height of a man," Deru called back, his voice sounding weaker. "That's what the tea is made from. Even if these trees are oaks, I can't climb that high when I'm this size!"

"Can't you levitate?"

"Where the owl can see me? Besides, I lost my lantern."

"So what do we *do*?" Her voice cracked on the final word.

"We wait until the owl goes looking for easier prey, and then I fetch my pack from the clearing."

That didn't sound so very difficult, but what if the owl was stubborn? What if Gar noticed her absence and came looking for them? What if whatever lived in that hole came out? Kirna eyed the black opening fearfully.

She didn't really have much choice, though. She looked up.

The owl was still up there. It seemed quite persistent. She wondered if perhaps Gar had put a spell on it so that it would guard the tower.

She waited for what seemed like hours, but which the motion of the greater moon told her was only minutes; then Deru's voice called, "Your Highness?"

"What is it?" she snapped. She was afraid that their conversation was keeping the owl interested, and that it might wake whatever was in that hole.

"I didn't want to worry you, but I think I had better warn you—I hurt myself in the fall. I landed on a thorn. I bandaged it, but I'm still bleeding pretty badly, and I'm not sure I can walk."

"What am *I* supposed to do about it?" Kirna shrieked.

"I thought you should know," Deru called back weakly.

"Idiot!" Kirna shouted. She rammed her fist against a branch of the bush.

This was a nightmare. Everything had gone wrong. When she had followed Gar from Quonmor, she had thought she was bound for love and adventure and a life of magic, and now . . . well, she had gotten some magic, anyway, but she was alone in the dark, dirty and bruised, stuck between a monstrous great bird and a mysterious hole-dweller, with the only one who could help her probably bleeding to death a few feet away.

It wasn't *fair*! She was a princess. These things weren't supposed to happen to her. People were supposed to obey her and protect her, not lock her up or steal her blood and tears or shrink her down to nothing or carry her around like a sack of onions—and *drop* her!

It just wasn't fair at all. The World was not treating her properly.

If she could just find Deru's pack and get the antidote, she would be fine. She could go home to her parents and pretend this was all just some grand lark—but that owl was out there, and she didn't know where the pack had fallen. If the owl would just go away. . . .

But it was hungry.

And whatever lived in that hole might be hungry, too. It might come leaping out at her at any moment.

She frowned and looked at the hole. She had had quite enough unpleasant surprises. At least if she knew what lived in there she'd know whether it was dangerous. Whatever it was, it was probably asleep; she could creep down and take a look, then slip back out.

She picked up a big stick—a tiny twig, actually, but to her it was a thick as her arm and somewhat longer than she was tall. Thus armed, she crept across the dead leaves and down the sloping earth into the hole.

She had only gone a few steps when she stopped; ahead of her, the hole was utterly black. The moonlight did not reach that far. Going farther suddenly didn't seem like a good idea.

She wanted to cry. Here she was trying her best to do something useful, something to improve her situation, and it wasn't working. She sniffled.

Then she sniffled again.

There was a smell here, a smell she recognized.

Rabbit.

She suddenly relaxed. This was a rabbit hole! Rabbits wouldn't hurt her, even at this size— they were harmless vegetarians. All she had to worry about was the owl.

That was quite enough, though, if it wouldn't give up and go away. Then a thought struck her.

The owl was staying around because it was hungry, and knew there was prey here. All she had to do was feed it, and it would leave.

She gathered her courage, raised her stick—she was trembling, she realized—and charged forward into the blackness, shouting. "*Hai;* rabbits! Come out, come out! Get out of here!"

There was a sudden stirring in the warm darkness, a rush of air, and she found herself knocked flat against the tunnel wall as something huge and furry pushed past. She flailed wildly with her stick, but whatever it was was gone.

After a moment the racket subsided. She hoped that at least one of the furry idiots had fled out into the open.

She turned and headed out of the tunnel—or started to. At the mouth of the hole she abruptly found herself face to face with a rabbit that had apparently decided its departure had been too hasty.

"Yah!" she shouted, jabbing her stick at the rabbit.

It turned and fled, kicking dirt and bits of leaf at her; she blinked, trying to shield her eyes. Then she pursued.

When she emerged into moonlight, she saw that the rabbit was still under the bush; she ran at it, screaming and waving her stick.

The rabbit fled again, hopping out into the clearing. . . .

And then, without a sound, the owl struck.

The rabbit let out a brief squeal, and then bird and prey were both gone, vanished into the night.

For a moment Kirna stared at nothing; the strike had been so fast, so silent, and so sudden that at first she had trouble realizing it had happened.

And when she did, she also realized how close she had come to following the rabbit out of the bush, trying to herd it further. She flung away her stick and let out a strangled gasp.

For a moment she stood there, looking out into the night—first at the clearing, then up at the sky.

The owl was gone. The rabbit was gone. Everything was still.

And Deru's pack was out there somewhere.

It was several minutes before she could work up her nerve to go find it.

She was still searching when Deru staggered out to join her. His face and bare chest were deathly pale, and one leg was wrapped in a bloody bandage made from the tunic he had doffed.

"There," he said, pointing.

She hurried to the spot he indicated, and a moment later she held the precious flask. She turned to Deru.

"Is there any ritual? Anything special we have to do?"

He opened up a palm. "Just drink it. One sip."

She opened the flask and sipped, then handed the rest to Deru—barely in time, as she began growing the instant she swallowed.

The oak-leaf tree had a harsh, slightly nutty taste, but she hardly noticed as she watched the world around her shrink back to normal. The bush she had sheltered beneath, which had seemed as big as a castle, barely reached her waist; the tower wall, while still massive, was no longer the vast World-girdling thing it had been a moment before.

It was also far closer than she had realized.

She looked up at the barred window of her room, and saw that their entire adventure had only taken them a yard or so beyond the bars.

Then Deru, who had been nowhere to be seen, shot up to his old height beside her; she stepped back to avoid catching his elbow in her chest. He staggered.

He looked awful—and, she realized, it was her fault. He had come here to save her. And it had been her own fault she needed saving in the first place.

She hadn't meant for anyone to get hurt. And no one had really meant her any harm either. She had thrown herself at Gar, and he had taken some advantage of that, but he hadn't tried to hurt her. Even the owl, which would gladly have eaten her, had just been hungry.

Deru had been trying to help, but *he* was the one who got hurt. It wasn't fair.

"Do you have any healing magic in there?" she asked, as he swayed unsteadily on his feet.

"No," he said, "but I've been thinking about it. The Cloak of Ethereality should stop the bleeding and take the weight off my injured leg—I won't weigh anything when I'm ethereal. You start walking; I'll catch up."

"How long will it take?"

"Just a few minutes."

"Then I'll wait," she said.

It was still early in the morning of the following day when Princess Kirna, escorted by what appeared to be a crippled wizard's ghost, arrived safely back at Quonmor Keep.

Judging by the expression on her father's face, her arrival was not half as surprising as the first thing she said when shown in the audience chamber.

"I'm sorry, Daddy," she said. "I won't do it again."

He snorted. "We should hope not." he said.

"On the way home Deru explained to me about wizards not being allowed to get involved with royalty," she said. "I need to tell you that Gar didn't really kidnap me; I followed him. I don't want the Wizards' Guild to punish him." In fact, Deru had gone on at some length about how ruthless the Wizards' Guild could be—information that Kirna knew she had heard before, but had never paid the attention it deserved.

Tolthar frowned, clearly puzzled. "We have nothing to do with the Wizards' Guild." He looked at the rather insubstantial presence standing just behind his daughter. "Is this the wizard we hired? He looks . . . different."

"He's under a spell. He got hurt, and needed to enchant himself until he can get home. You'll still pay him, even though I wasn't kidnapped, won't you?" Deru hadn't said anything about his fee; mentioning it was entirely Kirna's own idea.

Tolthar looked at Deru, who definitely did not look human just now. "Of course," he said, with a rather forced-looking smile. "We wouldn't want to anger a wizard. If we did, the Wizards' Guild you mentioned might decide to show us the error of our ways."

Kirna nodded, very seriously. That was exactly what she had been thinking on the way home. Wizardry was powerful stuff. The Wizards' Guild, given a reason, might well swoop down on them.

Just like an owl, she thought.

A BUZZARD NAMED RABINOWITZ

by Mike Resnick

Mike Resnick is the multiple award-winning author of such novels as *Stalking the Unicorn, Ivory, Purgatory, Kirinyaga,* and *A Miracle of Rare Design*. His novella "Seven Views of Olduvai Gorge" won both the Hugo and Nebula Awards in 1995. He is also an accomplished editor, having edited such anthologies as *Alternate Presidents*, *Sherlock Holmes in Orbit*, and *Return of the Dinosaurs*.

JUSTIN O'Toole had it made.

It took him a while. He'd started by illustrating the *Continental Lingerie* catalog ("for the oomph girl!"). Then he'd worked on the daily *War King Sky Killers* strip. From there he'd jumped to the editorial page in Hackensack, then to Dayton, and finally, the big time—chief editorial cartoonist for the Chicago *Beacon*.

He had wit, he had talent, and now that he was in Chicago, he had more subject matter than he could use in half a dozen lifetimes.

At first he'd gone the normal route, caricaturing everyone from the President to the Mayor, but then a fan sent him one of Walt Kelly's old *Pogo* books, the one in which Senator Joe McCarthy had been drawn as a wildcat (and which subsequently made Kelly's reputation as a political satirist), and he realized that no one had done anything like that for years.

So the President became a bellicose rhino, and the Mayor became a sly weasel, and Alderman Berlinski became a skunk, and Senator Neiderman became a cockroach, and Police Commissioner Ryan became a sloth, and within two years O'Toole had won a Pulitzer Prize and published his first book of political cartoons, which became an instant bestseller, not just locally but nationally.

Of course, not everyone was pleased with his approach. The President was above it all (or at least pretended to be), but the Mayor actually took a swing at him when they met outside the opera. Commissioner Ryan kept a 24-hour watch on him, and if he went one mile over the speed limit, he could count on a ticket. Alderman Berlinski actually sued him for defamation, though the case was laughed out of court. As for Senator Neiderman, he mailed O'Toole a box of dead cockroaches on his birthday.

But no one—repeat: no one—was more out-raged than Saul Rabinowitz.

Saul lived in Glencoe on Chicago's posh North Shore. He wasn't a politican himself, but he owned more than his share of them. He had no party affiliation; he'd buy any politician of any political stripe. And suddenly farms would be condemned, to be replaced by Saul Rabino-witz Developments, complete with golf courses and recreation centers. Public parks would van-ish, to be replaced by modern new Saul Rabi-nowitz Office Buildings. Old city blocks would be replaced by brand-new improved Saul Rabi-nowitz City Blocks.

It wasn't long before O'Toole began looking into Rabinowitz's dealings, and found, to his surprise, that the Catholic Church was no longer the biggest landowner in Chicago. Rabinowitz was. He owned 3,016 apartment buildings, 82 office buildings, 3 shopping malls, 4 local air-ports, and the word was that he was the real reason the Chicago Bulls had been able to afford Michael Jordan's salary.

It was when O'Toole discovered that in addi-tion to his real estate empire, Rabinowitz also controlled most of the prostitution and drug traffic in the Chicago area, that he began incor-porating him into the editorial cartoons—as a buzzard, an ugly eater of the city's carrion.

Rabinowitz was on the phone the next morn-ing, the soul of reason, suggesting they have dinner and discuss the situation before his lawyers were forced to sue. O'Toole agreed, met Rabinowitz at an upscale steak house on the Gold Coast, started listing what he had found out about the drugs and the prostitutes and the bought politicians, and left before desert when Rabinowitz threw his main course against a wall in a fit of rage and began threatening O'Toole's life.

The subpoena arrived after the third cartoon appeared. A black Lincoln tried to run him down after the fifth. A wild shot came through his bedroom window after the eighth.

O'Toole kept drawing, and the people kept reading, and before long the Mayor was serving 15 years for fraud, and Commissioner Ryan had been fired for incompetence, and Alderman Berlinski was sitting in the cell right next to the Mayor, and Senator Neiderman was censured by a vote of 92-7 in the Senate (the only abstention was Illinois' other Senator)—and Saul Rabinowitz was serving six consecutive 30-year terms with no hope of parole.

O'Toole soon accepted an offer, at double his current salary, from the New York *Globe*, and spent the next couple of years happily turning the New York city government into a new batch of animals. Then one day he got a phone call form the Cook County Jail.

"Yes?" said O'Toole.

"Do you know who this is?" demanded a familiar voice.

"Hi, Saul. How are you doing?"

"I'm dying, that's how I'm doing!" grated Rabinowitz. "And it's all your fault!"

"I'm not responsible for your bleeding ulcer or whatever the hell you've got," said O'Toole calmly.

"It's your fault," repeated Rabinowitz, "and I'm going to get you for it!"

"I thought you were dying."

"I'll come back from the grave if I have to."

"Give my regards to Hitler and Caligula and that whole crowd," said O'Toole, hanging up the phone.

And that was that. He saw on the wire that Rabinowitz had died the next week, and a few weeks later the Mayor committed suicide and Alderman Berlinski contracted cancer, and within a year everyone he'd gone after back in Chicago was dead.

He didn't give it another thought, until one fall day when he was walking through Central Park on his lunch hour. There was a flash of motion off to his left, and he turned and saw a weasel, which was passing strange, since there aren't any weasels in Central Park.

This wasn't just any ordinary weasel either. It looked exactly like his rendering of the Mayor in the Chicago *Beacon*. Curious, he approached it. It snarled and bared its teeth.

He walked a little farther and suddenly came to a skunk. Not any skunk, but an Alderman Berlinski skunk. It glared at him with red little eyes.

Frowning, he passed under a tree, and suddenly felt a heavy weight fall onto the back of his neck. Claws dug into the flesh, and as he reached up and tried to disengage whatever it was, his foot hit something and he fell heavily to the ground.

It was a sloth—the very image of Commissioner Ryan—that was tearing at his neck, and as he tried to get to his feet he found the weasel holding one and the skunk gripping the other.

Then he heard a rustling sound above him and looked up. It was a buzzard, a huge black creature with Saul Rabinowitz's face, diving down toward him, claws extended to rip out his eyes, beak razor-sharp to tear open his belly, hooded eyes filled with hatred.

Just before the raptor reached him, Justin O'Toole heard a familiar voice say, "I *told* you there was nothing funny about a buzzard!"

In the moment of life remaining to him, O'Toole found himself agreeing.

.

TWEAKED IN THE HEAD

by *Samuel C. Conway*

Samuel Conway holds a doctorate in organic chemistry and is a pharmaceutical researcher when he is not busy writing. He has worked closely with birds of prey as a hobby since 1989, both in Vermont and in Pennsylvania, where he now resides. He has written several stories on the theme of anthropomorphic animals, bringing together his love of nature and his scientific background. "Tweaked in the Head" is his first published story.

ACROSS the chess board sat a hawk, its feet gripping a padded perch, its keen eyes fixed attentively ahead. Dr. Pollard sat facing it, chin resting on his hands. An analog timer clicked monotonously on the table. It was the only sound in the room.

"Aren't you going to make a move?" Dr. Pollard said at last.

Red's gaze never shifted. "Shut up," he rasped. "The second quarter is starting."

Pollard sighed and looked over his shoulder. Through the window he could barely make out the tiny speck of a television screen glowing on the other side of the complex.

"Goddamn Philly," Red muttered. He fluffed his feathers up and shook them out, head first, then body, then tail. "They pay these guys enough. You'd think they'd actually make an effort once in a while."

"What is it with you and football?"

Red shifted his weight and tucked one foot relaxedly up into his breast feathers. "What is it with you and chess? Maybe I just like watching humans beat the snot out of each other." The feathers on his head suddenly stood up in an angry crown. "Oh, you stupid son of a bitch! You were wide open. Jeez . . ."

Pollard closed his eyes. "Why do you keep paying attention if you don't like how they're playing?"

"I got a bundle riding on this game."

"You bet on Philadelphia?"

"Yeah. Figured you'd have made me smarter than that, huh?"

"Mm." Pollard stood up resignedly, stretched, and watched as Red shifted his cigar to the other side of his beak and took a long drag. The tip glowed merrily, and twin jets of blue smoke shot upward from the bird's nostrils. "I wish you wouldn't smoke those things in here."

"Kiss my cloaca."

"I've told you before, they're bad for your lungs."

"They're my lungs."

"No, they're not. They belong to the government."

Red grunted and glared at him. After a moment he leaped from his perch and flew to the windowsill. Bending, he ground the cigar out against the smudged and sooty paint and then spat the butt out through the wire mesh. "Stuff your government," he croaked, settling down on the sill with his back to Pollard. "I can see the game better from here anyway."

Pollard watched the hawk for a long time, and then sank down dejectedly on the sofa, wondering where it had all gone wrong.

Dr. B. Philip Pollard had been the first scientist with the courage to announce the conclusive identification of a genetic sequence that determined the level of intellect in higher animals. "Courage" is perhaps the wrong word; Dr. Pollard was rarely accused of possessing such a trait. It was more a case of unchecked scientific zeal that caused him to blurt out his findings in an eager paper to an international journal. Sadly, his colleagues had not yet recovered from the devastating public outrage over the few tentative experiments aimed at combining human and animal chromosomes. Somewhere along the line, someone had decided that this meant that Science was out to create some grotesque hybrid. Spurred by breathless news reports, some of which were almost accurate, mobs of terrified citizens all over the country had descended upon any institution involved with genetic research, forced their way into the laboratories, and proceeded to smash everything in sight. With the dust from those uncomfortable months still settling, it is perhaps understandable that Dr. Pollard's peers did not take his report well. With cries of "intellectual discrimination" and "eugenics" echoing at his heels, Dr. Pollard was driven into hiding.

That is where the government found him.

Dr. Pollard listened unhappily to their proposal. They had followed his earlier work in the field of gene therapy, and were particularly intrigued by his talent for overcoming the body's annoying habit of destroying damaged or altered DNA. This handy mechanism is nature's way of avoiding genetic mutations, but creates a dreadful conundrum when it is the mutations one wishes to preserve. Dr. Pollard had made tremendous strides in the use of viruses as delivery vectors for what he called "tweaked" DNA. Dull and mindless and tiny, viruses had nonetheless perfected the art of injecting genetic material into living cells and successfully altering the DNA therein, all for the singular purpose of replicating themselves. By removing the contents of a viral particle and replacing it with genetic material of his choosing, Dr. Pollard could introduce that genetic material into whatever part of the body the virus would normally infect.

At first, Dr. Pollard thought that the government men were trying to recruit him for biological warfare experiments, and he tried to flee through a window. They caught him, though, and gently explained that they wanted no such thing from him. Would it be possible, they asked, to "tweak" the intellect-coding sequence he had discovered in order to enhance a living creature's mental capacity?

Dr. Pollard reluctantly admitted that it was possible. This was the sort of thing that had nearly gotten him strung up on the nearest light pole, though, and he wanted no part of it. Once more he tried to make good his escape.

After calming him down again, the visitors patiently explained that they wished to implement a program in which animals—not humans, they assured him—would be intellectually enhanced and used for purely peaceful military missions. They evoked dazzling images of thinking creatures with keen ears and noses who could help find lost children or disaster victims buried in rubble, who could locate unexploded land mines or chemical weaponry facilities and thus save thousands upon thousands of innocent lives.

They wanted him to lead the program. With the promise of secrecy, protection from lynch mobs, and a fat, fat research grant, Dr. Pollard agreed.

Initially he chose dogs for his research subjects, both for their native intellect and their susceptibility to the rabies virus. With its convenient ability to cross the blood/brain barrier and infect the brain tissue directly, rabies was the ideal delivery vehicle for genetic material meant to enhance mental capacity.

Though the idea was sound, the task was daunting. The exact sequence had to be determined which would have the desired effect on intelligence; once that was accomplished, the "tweaked" DNA would have to be introduced into rabies particles from which all native DNA had been eradicated. If any remained, the test subject would die frothing at the mouth within two weeks. Vaccination was out of the question, as it would defeat the purpose of the experiment by destroying the virus once it entered the body. Even if the new DNA were successfully implanted, there was still the question of whether it would do what it was meant to do.

Dr. Pollard worked many long days sequencing, testing, resequencing, testing again. He worked many longer days scooping out the guts of viral particles and refilling them with his own artificially created strands of DNA. Then there were months of watching and waiting. Secrecy was maintained at all times, and Dr. Pollard referred to his work only by saying he worked with animals that were "tweaked in the head."

The first breakthrough had been a Labrador retriever named Jack who had progressed to college-level trigonometry by the time he was four years old. Sadly, Jack's remarkable life was tragically cut short when he jumped up to lick the face of the visiting President and was shot dead by a nervous Secret Serviceman. Old habits do, indeed, die hard.

The incident dealt a terrific blow to the program, especially after the President, who was not fond of dogs, proclaimed that canines would henceforth be off-limits to further experimentation. Dr. Pollard's vehement protests were ignored; the Executive Branch, thoroughly ignorant of the scientific basis of the project, stood stubbornly by its decree and ordered Pollard to choose another species or risk losing his funding. An influential member of the Joint Chiefs of Staff quickly stepped in and persuaded (rather, bullied) the unhappy scientist into considering birds of prey. The General obviously felt than an enhanced hawk or owl would not only be a more dignified sight than some old slobbery dog, but would also make the perfect spy, sitting unseen in a tree while quietly noting all that was happening in the range of its keen vision. Had he known what this endeavor would bring about, he would have kept his bright ideas to himself, or perhaps even stepped into the latrine and blown his brains out. Either way, it would have been a boon to national security.

Science raced blindly forward, however, and the result was Red.

Red had arrived in a flurry of feathers and lashing claws on a hot summer afternoon a year after the death of Jack. The animal technician who carried him in was unfamiliar with birds of prey and was carrying Red around the middle, leaving the bird's feet free. Pollard tried to give a warning but was too late. In a heartbeat, the hawk lunged forward and freed first one wing, and then the other. He scrambled away from the stupefied technician and made for the nearest window, which was closed, and upon which Red soundly cracked his head. He fell, dazed and panting, and lay on his back with his feet waving comically in the air.

He began to chirp in alarm as Pollard approached. Eyes wide, he raised all of his feathers and brandished his talons, daring the man to even try to touch him. *Back off!* his gaze said. *I know how to use these!*

Pollard crept closer, eyes on the bird's. He knew that he only had to control the feet and the hawk would be defenseless. Getting past those vicious claws was always the trick, though. Carefully, Pollard raised one hand to hold the hawk's attention, and with his other he began to reach for Red's legs. He kept his movements slow and fluid. He watched Red's eyes, dark and defiant, to make sure that the bird's attention stayed on the diversionary hand.

"Here—this might help." Pollard was distracted for just a second by the handle of a net being waved in his face, and in that second, Red struck. Four talons seized Pollard's upraised arm and clamped down hard.

Pollard sucked in his breath and stifled a yell, and through a superhuman effort he managed not to jerk his hand back; to do so, he understood, would only have encouraged the hawk to squeeze harder. Red had stopped his chirping now, his icy glare holding more triumph than terror.

Slowly, Pollard turned his head toward the ashen-faced technician. "Don't say it," he croaked when the man began a feeble apology. "Just give him the injection while he's busy with me."

Nodding nervously, the technician hurried to the bench and returned with a syringe. Red paid no attention to him and gave Pollard's arm an extra squeeze, as if to emphasize the fact that Pollard had made a big mistake in trifling with him. He did not let go, nor did he take his intense gaze off the scientist, even after the technician had given him the first injection of the virus that Pollard had spent the last year engineering.

"There," Pollard said shakily. "That wasn't so bad, was it?" Again he turned toward the technician standing nearby. "Now, if you would be so kind as to help pry his talons out of my arm. . . ?"

Dr. Pollard worked with Red then on a daily basis. He would spend hours talking with the bird, showing him pictures and reading to him. Periodically, Red would have to endure another injection of the virus, an artificial strain of avian pox which Pollard had engineered himself after exhaustive research, and whose core contained the rare mixture of nitrogenous bases that had granted Jack the dog such high marks in mathematics. Every injection meant another wrestling match, during which Red would try his level best to draw blood from Pollard. He often succeeded.

For months Red showed no interest in the pictures. He would preen his feathers during Dr. Pollard's reading and sit motionless during his monologues. "Subject 'Red' continues to show no sign of enhancement," Pollard would mumble into his tape recorder at the end of every day. "No reaction to verbal stimulus, and no discernible interest in the selected imagery." He grew increasingly frustrated, and increasingly worried about how much longer his funding would last at this rate.

One spring morning, Pollard stepped into Red's cage as he had hundreds of times before. "Hello, Red," he mumbled as he sat down on a well-whitewashed stool. "Hello. Hello?"

Red peered levelly at him.

Pollard took a little red ball from the pocket of his lab coat. "This is a ball," he said patiently. "A ball. A . . . ball. I'm holding a ball."

"Oh, shut up."

Pollard gasped. The ball fell from his fingers and bounced away. "My God," he stammered. He thought at first that one of his technicians was playing a far-from-funny joke on him, but a hasty search revealed no one else in the corridor, no hidden speakers, no laughing underlings sweeping into the room and clapping him on the back. "Red," he ventured again. "It's . . . a . . . ball. Say 'ball.' "

Red had tucked one foot up into his body feathers while Pollard was searching the room. Now he lowered it again and gripped the perch. He raised all of his feathers and shook them out thoroughly, ending with a little shake of his red tail, newly molted in just that year. "Shut up," he rasped again. "Go away."

The technicians barely recognized the wild-eyed man that burst, babbling, into their coffee room. One of them dropped a full cup and sent coffee splashing across the floor. Pollard bore down on them like a crazed animal, whooping and yanking at their lab coats. He half-led, half-pulled them down the hall into Red's room. "Ball!" he shouted. "Shut up!" Go away!"

Red peered at him as though he were mad. So did the technicians. "Shut up!" Pollard repeated, exasperation creeping into his voice. "Shut up!"

The technicians glanced at one another uncertainly. One of them raised a hand tentatively. "Dr. Pollard. . . ?"

Pollard whirled toward him. "Shut up!" he shouted hoarsely. "Go away!"

The technicians hurriedly complied, leaving Dr. Pollard alone, red-faced and out of breath. He looked around helplessly, and then suddenly remembered the tape recorder in his pocket. He fumbled for it, dropped it, snatched it up again and jabbed the "rewind" button. He counted ten breathless seconds, and then pushed "play."

"Shut up." The words on the tape were unmistakable. "Go away."

Raising his eyes to the perching hawk, Pollard broke into a tremendous grin. "You did it," he panted. "You feathery bastard, you said it!"

Red fluffed his feathers regally, paused to preen a wing, and then peered straight down into Pollard's eyes. "Bastard," he repeated.

Science had triumphed once again.

The celebration was short-lived, however, as Red took little interest in the items Pollard brought in to show him over the next month, nor did he seem inclined to engage the good doctor in conversation. Indeed, he showed a remarkable inclination for retaining only those words and phrases that Pollard would have preferred Red not to learn. After a peculiar increase in the number of four-letter words that Red was picking up, it was discovered that a playful technician had been sneaking into the lab after hours and teaching the bird the more colorful aspects of the English language. That technician was sent packing over Red's loud protests.

One day, on the notion that Red would most likely be interested in items that would appeal to his predatory instincts, Pollard brought in a cage containing two white laboratory mice. "Now, Red," he began, "These are—"

"Mousies."

Pollard nearly dropped the cage. "That . . . that's right!" he exclaimed, but then he realized that Red was staring not at the cage, but rather out the window into the courtyard.

"Mousies," Red repeated. "Crispy fries, choc-choc-chocolatey shakes."

Confused, Pollard stood on his tiptoes and peered through the window. Only after fetching a pair of binoculars from one of the guards at the front gate did he discover that a television set was visible through the window of the lunchroom on the far side of the courtyard. At that moment another commercial aired for Mousie's Burger Bistro, and on cue, Red raised his wings and loudly proclaimed the virtues of the popular restaurant's choc-choc-chocolatey shakes.

"I'll be damned," was all that Dr. Pollard could say.

A requisition was hastily drawn up for a television to place in Red's cage, but the bird showed only moderate interest in it, preferring to stare at the far-off screen in the lunch room. It made sense, of course—hawks are designed to perceive things at great distances. Pollard thus had the television mounted in a room on the opposite side of the compound and facing a window that Red could easily see, and ordered that it remain tuned to educational and "socially fulfilling" programming.

Red watched his television avidly for many

weeks, and it soon became clear that he preferred its company over that of Dr. Pollard or his technicians. At first, Pollard tried to discourage this behavior, but with Red's vocabulary growing at a pace far beyond every reasonable expectation, Pollard reluctantly allowed him to watch as much as he wanted to. The programming, at least, was wholesome.

Soon, however, Red began to repeat off-color jokes and to utter some decidedly ungentlemanly propositions to the female technicians. Pollard dogged the staff, demanding to know who was teaching the bird such outrageous language. It was then discovered that whereas the scientific crew had been behaving themselves, the janitorial staff had been taking nocturnal advantage of the big television across the courtyard and had even hooked it to a cable feed. The evening programming was far from what Dr. Pollard considered proper, and he proclaimed that the television was to be turned off for good.

Red rebelled. For a full week he refused to speak a word, and the next week he stopped eating. A week later, Pollard ordered that the hawk be force fed. He was concerned, of course, but stubborn in his resolve not to allow his subject to be exposed to the polluting influence of prime time cable TV programming ever again.

At last, one of the senior technicians intervened. "Why don't you just let him watch the television?" she asked.

"No," Pollard growled. "He has to learn."

The tech crossed her arms. "You don't have any children, do you?"

"Me? Why . . . no, I don't. Why?"

"It shows." She suddenly strode past him. "Allow me to demonstrate."

Pollard followed her, sputtering in protest, as she marched into Red's room. The bird turned his back to her and pointedly whitewashed a portion of the floor at her feet. She stood firm. "I've had just about enough of this," she barked sternly. "Do you want your TV back?"

Red turned his head around and peered at her.

"Do you?"

With a flap he turned fully to face her. "Yes," he rasped.

"Then you're going to have to be a good bird and do what Dr. Pollard tells you. You will eat all of your food, and you will answer Dr. Pollard when he talks to you. Otherwise, no more TV. Is that clear?"

Red glowered at her and raised all of his feathers indignantly.

"I said, 'Is that clear?'"

After a tense moment, the feathers slowly came back down, and the fiery defiance in the hawk's eyes cooled. "It's clear," he muttered sulkily.

Red's mental capacity continued to advance, breaking new ground on a daily basis. The military, of course, was ecstatic, proclaiming the project a rousing success and ordered the project expanded, and new targets for the treatment identified. Pollard complied, but remained troubled by Red's persistent defiance. From the very beginning Pollard had worried that the fierce independence inherent in all hawks would be a stumbling block in training them to perform on command, and Red's attitude seemed to be confirming his fears. He tried to convince himself that Red was simply suffering the usual growing pains, and that once he had progressed to a more mature level of intellect he would become more manageable.

Day by day, however, the hawk grew both wiser and more troublesome, and he began to acquire numerous bad habits. One day, he somehow managed to obtain a cigar—Pollard never found out who gave it to him—and from then on insisted being allowed to smoke. Naturally Pollard refused, but the bird retorted, "I saw the General smoking them. Why can't I?"

"Because they're bad for you."

"They aren't bad for the General."

"Yes, they are."

"Then why does he smoke them?"

"Because . . . he's the General, and he's allowed."

"So let me ask him if I can have some."

"No, Red. You can't smoke cigars, and that's final."

Red fluffed his feathers peevishly. "Final, eh? I can't wait to see the General again. I'll say to him, 'Pollard says you're an idiot for smoking cigars. Can you believe that guy? If I were you, General, I'd hire another principal investigator.' After all, near as I can figure, I'm the star of this show, not you."

Pollard was shocked. "You wouldn't . . ."

"In a heartbeat. Now give me the damned cigar."

Pollard gave it to him.

Now, two years and countless cigar-butts later, Pollard stared at Red's back as the hawk stood on the sill and watched the football game on the distant television. His intellect now rivaled that of a college student; so, unfortunately, did his attitude. He was surly, obstinate, self-reliant and self-assured—in short, the quintessential hawk. Still, Red's enhancement had been the crowning achievement of Pollard's career, and Pollard had to admit that he had grown fond of the bird; and despite the apparent hostility, he liked to believe that Red cared for him, too, if even a little.

It made it so hard. Red was such a profound scientific accomplishment, perhaps the greatest ever made. The military were the ones footing the bill, however, and Dr. Pollard's reports could not hide the truth forever. The goods were simply not being delivered. Red's refusal to submit to any human authority did not meet their expectations. They wanted an obedient drone—Pollard had given them a person. Annoyed with what they perceived to be an expensive failure, the military had finally handed down the order. It formed a painful lump in Pollard's throat to think of the one word that he had never had the heart to teach to Red: Euthanasia.

He took a deep, faltering breath. "Red," he began, and then paused, swallowing. He did not want to say good-bye. "Red . . . I just wanted to tell you . . . that I really, really am proud to have been able to work with you these past couple of years."

Red grunted in annoyance. "Yeah, yeah. Me, too. Can it wait until half-time?"

Dr. Pollard closed his eyes tightly. "Red, please listen to me, just once." He sat forward and put his head in his hands for several moments, thinking of how to tell the bird, or even if he should. Maybe he should just let it be done. At least Red would not suffer—Pollard would never permit that.

When he looked up again, Red had turned to face him. The usual fire in the hawk's eyes was subdued, and Pollard realized at that moment that Red already knew. "Save it, Doc," he rasped. "I guess I feel the same way. You're human, but you've got your good points."

Pollard smiled and nodded. "Thank you, Red."

"Don't mention it." Red looked back over his shoulder, through the wire mesh, at the sky. "You know, Doc, I really wish you'd have given me a chance to fly around free, just once."

"I wish I could have let you."

Red flexed his wings and shook himself. "So why didn't you?"

"Because I couldn't. They wouldn't allow it. If I had, I'd have ended up in jail."

The hawk turned and stared fixedly at him. "Like me."

There was a long, awkward silence. Finally Red flexed his wings and sighed. "Yeah, I know. They wouldn't want their precious specimen to fly off and spill his guts to the media."

"Would you have done that?"

"Hell, yes I would have! I'd have sung like a canary. Told'em everything I know about this project, and all the other stuff that goes on here. I'll bet the President wouldn't last two hours in office after I told the world about Jack the Dog."

Pollard managed a melancholy smile. It seemed that Red shared his own feelings about the government. The only difference was that Pollard would never be able to stand up to them the way Red would—the way he *had*. Since that very first day when he had sunk his claws into Pollard's hand, Red had never let his spirit be broken. Pollard could not help but admire him. "So then what would you have done?"

"Hell, I hadn't thought about it." He cocked his head pensively. "I guess I would've gotten a job at a local newspaper. Eye in the Sky—get it? I'd have done just what the boys who sign your paychecks wanted me to do: be a nice handy little spy, except I'd be watching *them*, and letting John Q. Public know exactly where his tax money was being spent. All the secrets, all the crap the military gets away with. They wouldn't be able to take a dump in their billion-dollar latrines without the Eye in the Sky plastering it in the headlines."

His feathers had puffed up proudly; now they sank back down, and Red peered out the window again. After a while he said, "At least let me finish watching the game."

Pollard folded his hands in his lap and stared at them. "I wish there was another way, Red. I can't do anything about it, though."

"No, you can't." Red kept his back turned. "You wouldn't want to lose your precious funding."

"Red, please."

"You're right, Doc. I'm sorry. You've got to do what they tell you, after all. Good little puppet. Damned shame you won't ever be able to publish your findings. They can't have you sharing your secrets with all the other scientists, after all. At least the money keeps rolling in— that's what matters, right? You get to keep your job." He snorted and added in a sour tone, "Too bad you gotta lose your soul to do it."

"That's not fair."

Red chirped in cold amusement. "Right. Tell me about unfair."

Pollard had no reply. He watched the hawk for a long time as it sat unmoving on the windowsill. Red was pretending to watch the game, but Pollard could see that the bird was really staring at the sky instead. At length, he asked, "Would you really have gone to the press?"

"As fast as my wings could carry me," Red said without missing a beat. "You could bet on it."

Pollard hummed softly, pondering for a while, and then made his decision. Reaching to either side of the astonished hawk, he grasped the latches that held the mesh in place and heaved upward. Dry old paint cracked and trickled downward as the mesh came away from the window and clattered out into the courtyard.

Red's wings flapped in alarm and he turned to face the man, who was smiling softly. "Make sure they spell my name right," Pollard whispered.

The hawk hesitated, bewildered, and then his eyes mirrored Pollard's smile. "Deal." He gripped the windowsill tightly with his feet and leaned his head out, peering this way and that. He crouched, wings stretching out wide. "Take it easy, Doc," he rasped. "Give my regards to the General."

With that he gave a mighty beat of his wings and leaped from the window. His flight was somewhat awkward after so many years cooped up indoors, but he quickly gained altitude, soaring over the window where his television set had been kept. The last that Dr. Pollard saw of him was the sunlight shimmering off of the hawk's magnificent red tail feathers, and soon that, too, was lost in the distance.

Dr. Pollard stood at the window for some time, just staring at the sky, and then he turned away and took his lab coat off for the last time. He made no stops on the way home, wanting to be there in plenty of time to catch the six o'clock news.

ONE WING DOWN

by Susan Shwartz

Nominated five times for the Nebula Award and twice plus nominations for the Hugo, the Edgar, and the World Fantasy Awards, Susan Shwartz is a frequent contributor to anthologies. She lives in New York, which is sufficient justification for writing fantasy and horror. Her recent *Star Trek* novel coauthored with Josepha Sherman, *Vulcan's Forge*, made several bestseller lists.

GAWAIN woke dizzy, swaying back and forth.

God, this was worse than when Lancelot's blow had fallen on the old bad wound, and he knew this time it would be the death of him. He'd even written that damned French renegade who'd carried off his uncle's wife and begged him to return to aid Arthur against Mordred. And he'd signed the appeal in his own heart's blood before he surrendered to the sleep he knew would last until Judgment Day.

Apparently, his judgment had been off. Not for the first time.

Now what? First things first. Where was he?

Instinct told him: he was outside. It was night.

He was near a battlefield. Judging by the stink of blood and death, he thought the battle was winding down or had just ended. He extended his senses, trying for the razor-sharp awareness that had made his brothers back in Orkney compare him to the hawk for which he had been named in the Old Language. He reeled again.

Jesus, he was blind.

He tried to raise a hand to his wound and heard the high peal of tiny bells. He had no hands, but felt unaccustomed muscles twitch. Was he a prisoner? Was he maimed as well as blind?

Goddess. Triple Goddess, help. So his mother, his aunt, and those witches who hid beneath a veil of Christian faith had been right, and the priests with their Grails and their talk of heaven and hell had been wrong. Live your life wrong and you had to come back and do it over. Much like an armsmaster drilling boys who might grow up into warriors, assuming they lived that long. And learned from their mistakes.

Warriors like Gawain. He tried to move again. More bells. He tossed his head and smelled leather binding him about. Not bandages, then, wound about his cracked skull, over his eyes, but a leather hood. He was no longer a man, but the raptor for which he had been named.

His Aunt Morgan, who had always been a creature more suited to the hollow hills than to court life, had a fancy name for what he had undergone. *Trans-mi-gra-tion*.

Now that was a tricky word, especially for the lines of Gawain. Quick with a curse, quick with a blow, even quick to forgive until Gareth died and all forgiveness along with him. Gawain had never had time for fancy words. And tricky words were for the likes of Merlin and the sly young men that the Bastard had brought in: Gawain trusted no one who talked too fast or too fancy.

Better make time to understand what's going on, he warned himself. *Assuming you have it, after a battle of this size. Mordred must have called in not just the Saxons but the Danes. He makes Vortigern look like a puppy dog.*

He tried to make himself laugh. If only the sun would rise! Even if he couldn't see it, he would feel it. He always had more strength after dawn, had always counted on it. He tried to laugh again.

Skreeeeee!

The enraged hawk's shriek nearly deafened him. He began to topple backward and was caught.

By jesses.

He would have sold his patrimony, assuming anything was left of the kingdom he had inherited from Lot, if he could Sign himself, but the bells rang again. Trinket bells, bestowed upon a prize hawk.

Gawain, lad, he told himself again, just so

he'd be sure of it, you've been transmigrated. Translated, you could say. Into the body of a hawk. Left here on this . . . what was it, what was it . . . it was an oak tree . . . while his uncle Arthur fought his son for the mastery of Britain.

Skreeeeee!

Oh, God, his head.

He reeled again, to be rescued by his jesses.

Arthur had needed Gawain, needed his support, and he had failed him. Once, he'd failed in charity, turning against his uncle when he knew that Lancelot would have sacrificed anything to save brother Gareth—except the Queen. A second time, Gawain had failed in strength, when he had fallen and died. So he had had to come back and "this time, do it right!" The old armsmaster's command.

What did Whatever—he doubted it was God—think he could do in the body of a hawk?

"Ah, so you are awake now?" a voice whispered in the oak leaves, still tender in their early-May growth. When the sun struck them, they would be almost transparent, like green silk. Assuming he could get this damned hood off.

He knew that voice. He grimaced, and heard the snap of his sharp beak on nothingness. *All that blood and no tidbit for the hawk?* He had taught his young warriors better falconry than that.

Belike, they were all dead now. And he was trussed past his power to fly away and teach the selfish bastards what it meant to stint a hawk.

I seem to be fresh out of mice, the voice rustled again in the leaves, husky and ironic. The tree seemed to shake, as if a man chuckled deep in his chest—and the joke was on Gawain.

Jesus, he always had hated it when Merlin got sarcastic.

You are not the only one named for a raptor, you know. But for the past few years, since Nimue locked me in this tree, I have dined on sun and rainwater and soil—a surprisingly pleasant diet.

Shut up, old wizard, Gawain wished. He hadn't been the only fighting man who'd breathed a sigh of relief when Merlin disappeared. Arthur's mage—who had just had to turn out to be some sort of cousin, too—had been as bad as the old women. Talking, always talking at him about old ways and strangenesses when there were battles to be won, kin to be protected. If this hood were off, he'd peck strips of bark off Merlin's tree, see if he did not.

We have no time to waste on these pleasantries, Merlin told him, as arrogant in his prison within the oak as if he still stood behind Arthur's chair, intimidating his household. *We are family, of a sort,* Merlin continued. *We owe it to our blood to lay any quarrels we had aside.*

Like the battle that's still going on?

Of course, his question came out *skreeeeee!* Not as angry as Gawain's last outcry, but then hawks, like men, had different tones and different voices. In the name of God, Gawain didn't even know who was winning this fight!

We were so close to peace! the wizard's voice lamented. *One moment longer, and Arthur would have made peace with his son on the field at Camlann. Not a good peace, but it would suffice to let us build a better. And then, that idiot had to draw his sword upon an asp, breaking peacebonds. All my hopes, shattered again.*

It must have been hell on Merlin, knowing himself trapped, unable to act. As hard as it was now for Gawain to listen to the final throes of this battle, to know his uncle needed every man, to realize that he had been raised from the dead, but now was no man at all, but a hawk. For the first time in his life—his lives—Gawain felt a pang of fellow-feeling for the wizard.

By now, said Merlin, dispelling Gawain's brief flicker of kinship with him, *even you must realize that your soul has transmigrated. You have what men have always wanted—a second chance. Make amends, reparations for your sins, and then fly free.*

Damn the wizard, he wasn't teaching fledgling mages. Warriors survived by planning as much as by heart and prowess.

Gawain shifted on his oaken perch. Swordplay echoed in the distance, the sound cupped by the valley, magnified by the water. He could smell smoke: the Saxons' ships had been burned. Someone screamed, then gurgled. Another voice, high as the witless song of an old man turned childish, called out three names before falling silent in its turn. All that blood—blood, flesh, waste from gut wounds, but not so much

as a haunch of rabbit or even rat for the likes
of him! Gawain mantled in hunger, rage, and
dismay.

Hush!

Rustles, not leaf-sound, but footsteps, imper-
fectly concealed, and the occasional crack of a
twig drew nearer and nearer. Gawain heard a
whisper of music, breathing along his nerves.
Hawk he might be, but his blood was of the old
line and the Old Way ran in it.

Merlin was working a spell, perhaps one of
the few left to him.

You had better work fast, Gawain told him.
Something is coming.

In the aftermath of a battle, the pillers and
reavers slunk out to plunder the dead or hasten
the living after them. A fine falcon, left on its
perch by a warrior who never returned, could
be easily snatched and sold.

Gawain had had little truck with such human
carrion in his human life. Just let a robber lay
hands upon him . . .

Not so bold, my feathered kinsman, Merlin cautioned. *This is a thief you need.*

Abruptly, Gawain's mind flashed back to a
happy evening when Arthur and his men
lounged around the firepit, Gawain's aunt the
Queen pouring wine for them all—a Saxon custom, though they called it Roman to put her in
heart—and Palomedes told of a creature of his
homeland, caught and imprisoned in a bottle for
years and years on end. A djinni, he called it.

For the first century, the djinni vowed to give his rescuers power and gold. For the second, he promised thanks. But during the third hundred years of his imprisonment, he swore to kill the laggards who had not found him and released him.

The knights had applauded the canny fisherman who'd tricked the djinni back into its bottle, calling the tale a wonder fit for Arthur's hall, and then they wandered off to bed. Even then, Gawain knew better than to speculate who would wind up in bed with whom.

I will kill this thief, Gawain told the imprisoned wizard. *Would not you? I will. I will.*

The rustling grew nearer. The music thrummed again. More of Merlin's work.

Gawain forced immobility upon himself. The thief would have to take him down from his perch before unhooding him. If he mantled, he could startle the man, and then his beak, sharp as any blade, would serve to maim or kill. He'd peck himself free of these damnable jesses.

And then what?

Not strategy, perhaps, worthy of an Alexander or even an Arthur, but it would serve against offal.

Nearer.

Come closer, prey. Gawain shifted on his perch, hoping that the tiny bells adorning him—a falconer's vanity—would lure the thief in closer. Hood and bells might fetch a good price all by themselves. He remembered the sounds of contented falcons in their mews. He made them.

The branch rocked as a hand, tentative at first, then grasping, reached for him, placed him on a padded arm, drew breath in admiration, and then—an idiot as well as a thief—removed his hood.

Moon and starlight struck Gawain's eyes. His sight was changed from human sight, but even so, keen senses told him it was a fine May night, or would have been, if any night so full of treason, pain, and death could be called fine. Now, he would add to it.

He mantled, screaming threat and fury.

And felt himself dropped.

He caught himself, a beat of his wings on the smoky air. In the moonlight, he saw his prey: a bloodsmeared, ragged boy, more wild thing than thief.

Take his eyes, Gawain. Go ahead, do. Take his life, Merlin challenged. *He fears you. He even admires you—such a fine, fierce, valuable hawk. What stops you?*

If I fail now, what becomes of me? Gawain asked the mage.

He spared a glance for his would-be falconer. Terrified, scrawny the young thief might be, but he watched Gawain with admiration.

Here was a boy, Gawain saw it clearly, who wanted more than he had. He wanted to be more than he was: a warrior, perhaps, with helm and shield, bright sword, and hawk. He had helmet and shield: Gawain recognized the heraldry, although his vision was changed from when he had walked as mortal man.

I can't kill a child, Gawain said.

He belled, then settled his wings and stroked his beak against his feathers in a grooming reflex he had not known he possessed.

I knew a cat like that, said Merlin. *Let him stumble in midleap, and he would groom himself as if telling the world, "I meant to do that."*

Quiet, wizard. But Gawain's attention was mostly for his would-be falconer.

Gawain made himself chirp. The boy's eyes widened with astonished joy. He wrapped a cloak too long and too fine—and too sword-rent—to be anything but spoils about his arm and offered the makeshift perch for Gawain's approval.

Do not grasp too hard, the wizard, contrary as ever, exhorted him.

The boy started toward the water, Gawain weighing down his arm.

But what do I do? he called back to Merlin, trapped within his oak tree.

The child, undaunted by the hawk's scream (a point in his favor), attempted to soothe his prize with fingertips, prudently avoiding his beak. His touch was not inexpert, Gawain marveled, but, damn it, he had not returned from the dead to be a falcon manned by a woodwose or peasant brat.

Find the king, Merlin cried, a rustle of leaves in the night wind. *And follow his commands.*

Gawain could feel the boy adjust his balance to take the hawk's weight. Already, he raised his arm in the studied, elegant gesture of the falconer. And turned his back on Merlin's tree.

Fortune attend you! cried the mage. The leaves rustled.

Up ahead, a clash of arms, a death shout, erupted. Gawain decided Merlin could not have pronounced a blessing. It was not his way.

The boy dodged through the trees that surrounded this side of Camlann's battlefield. It would be better to call it butchery than battle.

The stream they passed ran dark with blood. From time to time, they edged past bodies. From time to time, Gawain recognized the slashed devices on shields. He would have Signed them, but he had wings, not hands. Well, John the Beloved Disciple was an eagle: that would have to serve, he thought, not that he had ever been one of the knights noted for holiness.

Wrapped in his own thoughts as completely as if they hooded him, he became only tardily aware that the boy was talking, telling his fears and dreams to the creature he thought of as "his hawk." Or perhaps, he spoke to himself, "Thomas this" and "Tom that." Already, the storyteller's cadence rippled in his speech, not burred like the bardic voices of Gawain's North, but like enough for pleasure.

Like enough for music.

Merlin, what do you know about this child that I do not? Is he your pawn as Arthur was?

No answer from Merlin, but Gawain expected none. The boy was talking enough for an army, all by himself. It was a wonder no one else heard him.

From this Tom's relentless babble as he sought to reassure himself, Gawain learned that the boy, though ragged as one got after a battle, was at least of birth that Gawain in his human incarnation as king's son, queen's son would have deemed at least marginally gentle. But he was a dreamer and poor: such lads took chances.

As Gawain had assumed, Tom's first plan had been to sell him. But now? Dreams of grandeur floated up in clouds of words. Tom now had sword, shield, helm, and hawk. Let him but find a horse . . .

And let any surviving warrior identify any of his takings, and Tom would speedily become not warrior but corpse.

Perhaps one shrewd peck, a bite, a deep scratch, and I can fly free . . . I am a risk he does not need.

Tempting as the thought was, Gawain knew he would not act on it. Raptor though he was, the habit of protecting the weak was still too strong.

Moonlight spilled onto the sodden ground. Blood mixed with the dirt, making clay that would never hold the breath of life. Camlann's field was dark, except for the skulk and rustle of those who crept out to rob the dead.

Tom stopped so quickly Gawain wondered if he had tripped over a root or mistaken one for a serpent like the one that had cost Britain its peace.

"Up ahead," he whispered. "Sweet Jesu, do you see?"

Gawain did not see before he heard. My God, that was Bedwyr's voice, pleading with someone not to fight. "He is unhappy."

Unhappy? On this battlefield, Bedwyr was indulging in understatement. Who was unhappy?

"He wears the Dragon," Tom whispered. "They both do, the old man and the young, though the younger man's is barred. Sweet Jesus, it is the king. Both of them."

Bedwyr's voice rose, imploring king and king's bastard son.

Tom crept closer, trying not to breathe or tremble. And failing.

As they neared, Gawain could hear how the men panted, could smell the blood of the wounds suffered and inflicted. Arthur, when his blood was up, could be as fierce as any Orkneyman. His blood was up tonight, what remained to him. "Tide me life, tide me death," he screamed, then charged his son.

Arthur was king, had Merlin's training, decades of victory in battle. But Arthur was an old man, and swordplay was a young man's game.

Mordred was desperate, wounded, in fear of his life. And alone, where Arthur had Bedwyr.

But Arthur waved his kinsman back. And Mordred was younger.

My uncle! Gawain thought, pride piercing the rage and terror. Aged, heartsick, exhausted, but by God, there was still enough of him left that he would try to wreak justice on a traitor.

Aye, and get himself killed and the kingdom with him, Gawain could practically hear Merlin saying.

He felt himself jolted from side to side, and up and down as the boy Tom all but danced in fear and excitement, his absurd plundered sword drawn. Hawk on one arm, shield slung on his back, waving a sword more than half his length: what could he do?

Get himself killed. Stupidity was a hell of a way to die.

Release me!

Neither Arthur and Mordred turned to see where the hawk cried. Now they danced wearily together, their blades clashing like bells on a hawk. Bedwyr held back, bound as much by fear of striking the wrong warrior as by the king's command. And the boy Tom danced in an agony of doubt.

The sky paled. By dawn, the survivors would be out and about. The boy would be caught, and all the work that had hailed Gawain back from heaven or hell to perform would be left undone.

"What shall I do?" the boy asked himself.

Race in and be struck down? Race away and be
forever condemned as coward by such con-
science as he had?

Release me!

Tom was no Celt, but clearly he had the gift
of tongues. As the hawk's rage shrieked out, the
boy flung up his arm, and Gawain was free.

The sky was lighter now, a white line at the
water's edge, and that was good. He was not a
nightflyer like the great owls or the *gwynhwyfar*
that betrayed them all, for treachery ran in the
women's kinlines as well as the men's.

He flew above the duel, circled three times,
and swooped down. A feint, a parry, followed
by a deadly lunge: he had taught the royal bastard himself and knew his tricks. As Mordred
lunged, Gawain swooped as if upon his prey,
deflecting the sword.

It sliced feathers from his wing and, from the
fire he felt, a slice of flesh. Hawk's blood fell to
the earth. He screamed in outrage and astonishment and began to fall, startling Mordred so that
he stepped forward, evading, his head
down. . . .

And Arthur brought his blade down upon
Mordred's helm. Sparks flew in the darkness before dawn; the helm split. Blood sluiced down,
with paler matter. Brains, not that Gawain
thought the traitor had had that many to spare.

Gawain screamed in triumph. His wounded
wing burned. If he perched now, he would
never have the resolution to fly again, and he

would be a target. Merlin had not intended that. . . .

But what? He glanced down at Mordred.

The Bastard was dead in that moment, he had to be. But just as a bird, its head cut off, jumps about the farmyard for an instant more, the bastard's body jerked, bringing up its blade and piercing the king's side.

He fell. Bedwyr, released from his trance of duty and terror, caught him and eased him to the ground.

"God, is there any aid? Who's there?"

Blood pulsed from Arthur's side, beat in Gawain's temples. He heard a clatter of harness—the boy, throwing down his arms and seeking the nearest priest, perhaps?

He might arrive in time to shrive the king, and then he might not.

The wind blew, bringing with it smells of oak and water, cleansing the stench of war, reminding Gawain of Merlin's spells.

He could not have saved the king. He could not save him now.

What could he do? One need not be a mage to realize he had been brought back to do *something*.

Instinctively, he banked, caught a thermal, and soared. The sensation exhilarated him past consciousness of pain, though he knew he was losing blood and must land soon. But where?

Beneath him, the battlefield grew tiny. He could see Merlin's tree and far beyond it, the

Abbey where St. Joseph's thornbush no doubt wept at a fresh martyrdom.

At the shrine there . . . but the boy had gone to fetch priests, healers, guards—

He sought beyond, his farsight taking in the broken needle that was St. Michael's Tor.

Michael, Prince of Warriors, aid us now!

Music raced across the wind, turning into laughter like tiny wicked bells.

Put not thy trust in princes.

He heard a woman's voice sing in the dawn wind. Not Michael, then.

Gawain turned away from the Tor, the battle, the tree, and out toward the water. Drops of blood fell from his wing, splattering the wrinkled gray surface below.

Guard your strength, he warned himself. He had fought wounded before, he reminded himself. But now, he was hawk, not man. Or, for that matter, not waterfowl; if he fell, he fell from a height and he would sink, one wing down.

Something flew beneath him over the water. It was seized and shaken—once, twice, three times, by light that rose from the water's depth, rippling its surface like wind upon feathers. Light erupted, then died, sinking into the depths. What had that been? A seamonster? He could neither eat it nor fight it. He forced himself to gain altitude. His wing ached, and he knew he could not fly much longer.

A shadow rose between the water and the dawn, fragrant with the scent of appleblossoms, shimmering now in the mists: Avalon drew near. Could he reach it before his strength failed.

He could see a tower there, a broch built in the old way of stones piled on ancient stones upon the headland. He screamed a warning. His hawk's voice sounded strained.

Three ladies emerged.

Mother?

It came out *Skreeeeee*! The lady raised her head.

He had seen her dead, lying at Lamorak's side, their blood and their hair flowing together as Agrivaine sweated and shook and tried to make excuses. Dead, betrayed, corrupt: but if Gawain could return from the dead to redeem unfinished work, why could not his mother? She had studied with Morgan, he knew that.

Three ladies hastened toward the shore and the boat tied to an oak tree by the shore.

His mother and his aunts, all ladies who were enchantresses. The sun rose, glinting off their hair and their rubies, like gouts of blood.

Morgause flung up an arm, calling Gawain down from the sky much as she had called him in from play so long ago in the Northern islands. He wobbled, his strength flowing from him like blood now that he saw an end to the ordeal of flight, but he managed to descend, rather than fall. He looked out for a perch.

Not on her tender arm, Gawain thought, and settled deadly claws upon a low oak branch. He was glad his landing was fairly neat: Morgause had always lacked patience with weakness.

Merlin, are you here, too?

He heard the music, but it was not Merlin's.

The lady stepped forward and gazed into his eyes.

"The hawk came with a warning. Our brother the king. . . ! We are late, my sisters! By now, the king's wounds have caught cold. And the brave hawk is wounded."

The women keened as women of the Celts had always done, but, true to their blood, did not pause an instant to wipe their tears. They tugged the boat down to deep water, unbound a glowing sail, and prepared to cast off.

Their skirts streamed water. Their hair flowed free under their gleaming circlets.

Two boarded. Morgause still held Gawain's eyes.

"I see," she said. "And I know you." She tore a long strip from her sleeve and bound his wing. "Come with me, my son. We will bring him here for the healing of his wounds, against a time of need when he will return.

The king had been her husband's foe, her brother, and Mordred's father. They had been enemies, lovers, and kin. But in the end, it seemed, the call of blood drowned out the call of hatred.

"Blood calls to blood." Morgause inclined her head. She raised a hand to Gawain's wing, the blood dripping there. "We must find you better healing."

And then what? Could he fly free? Would he rest?

"I cannot return you to your old form," she said.

"Sister! We must hurry!" came a cry from the boat, hawk-shrill.

"I offer you only service," his mother said. "Come with us. Wait with us. A time will come when he will need you."

Gawain inclined his head. He flew after Morgause, a little pain-filled flying hop toward the boat.

She climbed into the boat, released its sail, and let fly a battered banner of the Red Dragon. Gawain perched above it like the eagle on a legion's staff as they sailed from Avalon toward the shore of the waking world.

Arthur lay upon the shore as the boat drew up, his head in Bedwyr's lap. His sword was gone. The ladies keened again. This time, Gawain added his cry. He mantled in painful salute.

Wordlessly, Bedwyr bore up the king and carried him to the boat, spreading his cloak over him. It was too tattered for warmth, and Arthur was cold, so cold. He would never survive a journey on the water.

Morgause had been right. Already, Arthur needed him, even in this new body.

Painfully, Gawain dropped from his perch,

spreading his wings—the hale and the wounded—over his uncle. A hawk's blood burned hotter than a man's. Let it warm the king.

Bedwyr set shoulder to the boat, pushing it out from the shore. Beyond him stood robed figures and a smaller one, his eyes avid.

At his *skreeee*, the boy started forward, but a monk restrained him.

Watch, child. Watch and remember, Gawain thought.

He stared into the rising sun, as able as an eagle to bear its light, but not the sight of the wounded man whose body he warmed. After a while, Arthur's hand rested upon his head, ruffling feathers, then smoothing them as a falconer will when day is done. A while longer, and his hand lay still. Gawain thought he slept.

Rest, my uncle. I will keep good watch.

The tiny boat turned back toward Avalon.

OWL LIGHT

by Nancy Asire

Nancy Asire is the author of four novels,
Twilight's Kingdoms, *Tears of Time*, *To Fall
Like Stars*, and *Wizard Spawn*. She has also
written short stories for the series anthologies *Heroes in Hell* and *Merovingen Nights*.
She has lived in Africa and traveled the
world, but now resides in Missouri with
her cats and two vintage Corvairs.

IF the sun's angle was right and she squinted
slightly, Yslinda could make out the Prince's
banners flying from the summit of the governor's palace. Lord-Hill, the local people called
it, for of all the buildings in the region, it alone
rose high above the surrounding countryside—
a man-made hill erected as if to glorify hu-
mankind's triumph and mastery over the earth.

Yslinda's own home was similar to other
dwellings in her country, built to reflect the
world about. Low-lying, generally of a single
story, wide-eaved and open-windowed, they in-

vited contemplation of their surroundings. Only the ruling class, descendants of the conquering Asketi, whose invading legions had swept over the old sleepy kingdom of Delad three generations before, considered themselves beyond the touch of nature. The world was theirs for the taking, to be used, harnessed, and turned toward their will.

This morning was a quiet one, a gentle breeze barely stirring the dense leaves of the trees above Yslinda's head. She left her doorstep and her feet found the well-worn path leading from her house into the forest. Behind, she left the gentle lap of waves on the shore of the lake wherein her island stood. Before her existed only the quiet of the woods, the call of birds, and the hush of hallowed places.

Priestess of Savanya, Yslinda trod the same path toward the shrine her predecessors had taken for hundreds of years. The trees grew closer away from the shore, the light more diffuse. Soon, she moved through a green-drenched world where silence reigned.

Drawing deep slow breaths, Yslinda stilled her heart, her mind, her soul. One did not enter the goddess' presence beset by cluttered thoughts. Automatically, ancient words came to her lips, prayers uttered in praise of life, thanks given to the goddess of wisdom who ruled over the unlimited reaches of the human intellect, who was patroness of Delad.

Suddenly, she stumbled. Some small exposed

root, perhaps, or, more likely, the intrusion of thoughts she had been keeping at bay for days now. She stopped, her hands trembling, closed her eyes, and sought in that darkness to resettle her mind, to regain the calmness necessary to perform her duties as priestess.

The statue rose from the center of the clearing into which Yslinda stepped. No one knew how old it was, this rendering in stone of the goddess of wisdom, nor who had carved it in the deeps of time. But the centuries themselves held small dominion over the statue—the facial features and other details remained so crisp and defined that one could imagine the artist only yesterday had made the last finishing touches to the white stone.

As always, when her eyes met those of her goddess, Yslinda's heart seemed to expand, to grow warm within her. Savanya stood there in quiet majesty, clad simply in a flowing robe, with her great owl riding her shoulder. Yslinda bowed low before the statue, then sank to her knees.

"O Savanya, Mother of Wisdom, still my mind," she prayed, lifting crossed hands and covering her eyes. "Tell me, Mother, what should I do? Guide me, Giver of Wisdom. Let my choice be as wise as your name and the winged symbol of your thought."

She had always dreamed of owls, one of the early signs that had set her on the path to become Savanya's mouthpiece. In addition to her inborn healing powers, from an early age she had been so in tune with the purposes of the goddess that people had sought her wisdom when she was still very young. Yslinda's formal training had commenced when she reached the age of nine, a source of wonder and pride for her parents. But always, aside from skills quickly developed under the kind tutelage of the old priestess, Yslinda had been attracted to and had dreamed of owls.

For seven nights now, her dreams had been full of wings.

Prince Gonten leaned back in his cushioned chair, swatted absently at a passing insect, and watched his companion prowl the room. Though painfully aware of the importance Hvandi wielded in the Asketian Empire, he both loathed and feared the High Priest of Keti. Few had ever given Gonten pause, but this one did, as evidenced by the Prince's presence in this godforsaken corner of the Empire, bored nearly to tears by the lack of entertainment and creature comforts.

"I *must* have her," Hvandi said at last, planting himself before Gonten, his dark eyes smoldering. "Her goddess *must* be brought to heel at the Bright Lord's command."

Gonten reached for a goblet of too-warm wine. "So you've said, more than once since dawn. And I believe I understand what—"

"You don't," snapped Hvandi, perhaps the

only man save the Emperor himself who could use that tone of voice to the Prince, Heir Apparent to the throne. "It is something those untutored in the mystic arts can only glimpse. But I will try to explain. Again."

The Prince nodded, despising his fear of the priest. Though he had never spoken of it, Gonten had always sensed something dark, something at odds with Hvandi's position as Priest of the Bright Lord whose power sustained the Asketian Empire. But he had also witnessed evidence of Hvandi's vast power and was not foolish enough to challenge it. Not yet, at least. Let the priest talk on; it was only slightly more boring than listening to the governor complain.

"My powers come from the god," Hvandi said, his voice falling into a lecturing tone, as if he spoke to a young child. "Every kingdom we conquer has its own gods, its own beliefs. All must be subjugated before Bright Keti. This Savanya—this purported goddess of wisdom—must bow before the Lord of Heaven or we are diminished. I can accomplish this task only by wedding the priestess."

"As you've wed other priestesses before," Gonten said, refilling his goblet. Gods, how the priest could go on. "But this one—she's refused you."

Hvandi's eyes flashed. "So did the others, but eventually they yielded."

"This priestess seems different," the Prince observed, keeping his voice level. "Just like the people of this damnable kingdom! They didn't even raise an army to defend their country when my grandfather conquered them. Oh, to be sure, isolated groups of men took up old and rusty arms to protect their villages and towns, but they never mounted any serious resistance. It was as if they had forgotten war and how to make it."

He stood and walked to the window that opened onto the sleepy countryside. "This place is like living in some drug-dream. It's enough to drive any sane man mad. Nothing ever happens here—the people go about their simple, ordinary lives, and raise their grain and fruits and livestock. Aside from the pursuit of learning and the arts—" Gonten snorted derisively. "They do as we demand, they pay their taxes, they give way to us in all things. Sometimes I wonder why my grandfather bothered conquering Delad. It has no real wealth save its learning, and that alone shouldn't have been enough to tempt our legions. We have learning and arts aplenty in the Empire. The defeat of peasants wielding ancient weapons is no source for pride." He fixed the priest with what he hoped was an innocent look. "How can a goddess of such a gentle people compromise the power of the Bright Lord, whose strength and power and majesty are beyond comprehension?"

Hvandi threw both hands over his head and muttered something the Prince was earnestly glad he did not hear. "Ignorance can be dangerous, Prince," he said. "This may seem to you a backwater kingdom with nothing of great value to be found within its borders. But there is much power to be won from this goddess. If I am to have it at all, it must be achieved through the marriage act."

Gonten closed his eyes and rubbed them wearily. He and Hvandi had gone over and over this point, and, try as he might, he still could make no connection between marriage and the assimilation of power.

"Why not just rape her and be done with it?"

"Your father, Prince," Hvandi replied in an icy tone, "has instructed me to treat this priestess well. Her people are meek, yes, but we don't know how far we can push them before they break. She is a national treasure, the mouthpiece of the goddess who rules this kingdom." His eyes hardened. "Your father is facing rebellion to the north and west; even *you* should be able to see that he hardly needs another uprising on his hands."

Gonten tensed at the implied insult but kept his face expressionless, yielding the point to Hvandi. "Well, then, if she refuses to wed you, we must convince her otherwise."

"And how might we do that?" the priest asked. "No one has any dominion over her, not even the King."

So you don't have all the answers, do you? Gonten thought. He smiled slowly, hoping he appeared more sure of his reply than he felt.

''There are ways, priest. Believe me . . . there are ways.''

Fatigued from the labors of the day, Yslinda blew out the last lamp and stood for a moment in the warm darkness. More folk than usual had taken the boat ride to her island asking for her help. She had given freely of her wisdom and her healing touch as always, but tonight she felt especially drained.

As she stretched out on her simple pallet, she shivered and drew the thin covering up to her chin. *O Savanya*, she prayed silently, *tell me what to do. Guide me. I cannot wed that foreign priest— I can't! He'll use me, drain me of my power, and leave our people without your guiding light! Give me a sign, O Wise One! A sign!*

But the darkness of night remained simple darkness, and the soft wind was only a wind. Yslinda closed her eyes and slept.

Wings beat across the heavens. Wings star-bright, vaster than worlds, more powerful than time. Eyes, huge and golden against the blackness of space, glinting in a light more than light, seemed to see through Yslinda into the core of her very being.

Owl Light, Owl Bright, speak to me, give me sight!

The huge bird sat silent on the lower crook of the moon, then spread its wings until they hid the wheeling stars. Its head turned, its feathers ruffled in a wind that blew through Yslinda's mind. Softly, surely, the Owl descended from its perch and wrapped those wings around her, the touch of down-soft comfort keeping the gibbering shadows at bay.

By torchlight, the young King's face appeared paler than usual. Clad, as always, in a simple white tunic over white breeches, save for the slender golden circlet on his dark head, he might have been any of the young men who had journeyed to the capital to further their education. His gold eyes caught the light, and for a moment Prince Gonten seemed snared by his gaze. But he had stared down opponents far more mighty than this fourteen-year-old boy who stood before him, and he shook off the strangeness, refusing to be cowed.

"So you see the problem here," Gonten concluded conversationally. "We ask very little of you, King. We will not take your priestess from you. We honor you that much, to be sure. Tradition, however, must be upheld, and tradition demands that Lord Hvandi wed this woman, a symbolic union between our gods and yours."

"I have no power over her," the young King murmured, repeating himself for the third time. "I can't command her."

"Ah, but you *can* recommend, most strongly, that for the good of her kingdom—for the greater good of the entire Empire—she do this thing."

The boy lowered his eyes momentarily, then raised them again. "I can," he admitted, "but whether she listens or not is entirely up to the goddess."

Gonten smiled slightly. "Perhaps. And perhaps I can do more than you think to persuade the goddess to give strength to your words."

Yslinda waited by the dock as the royal barge came to rest. The King was first to alight, followed by his guard and Prince Gonten's men. The Asketians, she noted uneasily, far outnumbered her countrymen.

"Goddess bless, King" she said as he reached her. She bowed her head, in deference both to him and to the unbroken line of kings that stretched back longer than memory.

"Goddess bless, Priestess," he replied. His face was shadowed, as if he had not slept well. "We will talk in private."

She bowed again and led the way from the shore to the front steps of her house. Neither the King's guard nor Prince Gonten's men followed.

"I'm afraid I know why you're here, King," Yslinda said, once they had stepped inside. "And I can't pretend I'm pleased to see you play the role of messenger."

The young man blushed slightly. "You must listen to me, Yslinda," he said "For the sake of our kingdom, you must listen. Do you think I enjoy coming to you like this . . . like some paid lackey of the Asketi? But I must. I don't see that I have a choice. Prince Gonten would have you wed this priest Hvandi—" He lifted a hand to forestall her reply. "—and there is little I can do to prevent his."

"But the goddess *can*," Yslinda said, her voice trembling. She struggled for composure. Surely she could not be hearing the words coming from the King's mouth. He had always supported her in all that she had done. *But not in this,* an inner voice spoke. *What are his choices? Say no to someone who could crush this kingdom like an eggshell beneath his legions' feet?*

"Of the goddess' power I have no doubt. But at what expense can this demand be turned aside?" he asked, echoing her thoughts, as if he, too, had the ability sometimes to see into another's mind. He looked directly into her eyes, his own very steady. "The Asketian was very blunt. I have no heir; I am an only child. No issue of my family survives save me. If you do not agree to this thing, an—accident will be arranged. The line of kings will end with me, and our kingdom will go down in darkness, our link to our ancestors gone."

A cold wash of fear ran through Yslinda's veins. "He wouldn't!" she exclaimed, shying away from the very notion of an ending to the House of Kings. "How could he even *dare* to—"

"He can," the King said, his voice full of a weariness that went far beyond his age. "And he will. Unless the goddess herself intervenes in ways I cannot imagine."

Owl Light, Owl Bright—

"O Savanya," Yslinda murmured. "O goddess! Let it not be so!"

"Prince Gonten also said the priest will arrive at sunset three days from now to take you to Lord-Hill. He gives you that time to prepare yourself and for him to make the palace ready for the ceremony. You will be married at sunrise of the fourth day, for that is the time when his god ascends over the world."

Owl Light, Owl Bright—

A fragmented mosaic of alternatives to her forced marriage scattered across Yslinda's mind, choices she could make and the repercussions flowing from them. At the end of each pathway into the futures lay a curtain of darkness, beyond which even she could not see.

"Have I no choice in this?" she whispered. "No choice at all?"

The King's face grew more shadowed yet. "That, Yslinda, lies with Savanya. Pray as you have never prayed before. Our lives and the survival of our kingdom lie in the goddess' hands."

The King had disembarked and had been escorted to his home by his guard without so much as exchanging a word with the Prince. He had favored Gonten with only a brief nod, a wordless acknowledgment that he had kept his word and had spoken to the priestess.

Gonten inwardly admitted to admiration of the boy-king. In the past few days, he had wondered many times if he could have handled himself with such aplomb had their roles been reversed.

"So," drawled Hvandi who stood at the Prince's shoulder. "You've arranged it, then."

"I've arranged nothing," Gonten corrected the priest. "I've only passed on a promise of the King's demise if the priestess refuses to return with you. These people revere their kings, seeing them as an unbroken link to their ancestral past. The life of their kingdom is the life of their king. If this priestess *does* refuse, then we'll deal with the King at our leisure. An accident, this close to the water, should not be hard to arrange."

"But what of the people? Don't you think they'll recognize our hand in this?" Hvandi asked. "Be very careful here, Prince. Remember your father's predicament."

Remind me again, old dog, Gonten thought, *and by the Bright Lord, priest of his or not, you'll suffer for your impudence!* He allowed the slightest of cold smiles to touch his lips. "If enough of our people die with the King, how could anyone suspect us?"

For the first time in years, Gonten saw the priest blink slightly. *Good, you old tyrant,* he thought. *Learn now that I, too, have teeth!*

The two days that followed the King's visit to Yslinda's island had passed in what seemed to her a blur of confusion. She held to her duties, offering up her prayers to the goddess and meeting all those who came from across the lake for comfort, healing and hope. But for her, hope was slowly dying. Even the goddess kept silent, though her owl continued to visit Yslinda's dreams at night. But the owl, like the goddess, offered no words of comfort, no hope that the marriage could be halted. Despair took root in Yslinda's heart, though she refused to allow its darkness to show on her face as she ministered to the people.

Only one constant remained in the world for her now: her faith and a certainty that, when the time was ripe, Savanya would speak at last.

On the second day after the King's visit, some of Yslinda's visitors recounted the arrival of Asketians in their chariots to the capital city. Important arrivals, these local lords, if importance could be assumed by the number of their servants. Yslinda held her tongue as she listened to these tales, not wanting to vocalize her fears. First and foremost, she was Priestess of Savanya and her duties were those of a priestess, not a young woman who trembled before a dreaded event.

But the people who visited her island could not understand the danger she faced, the peril behind this supposedly ceremonial marriage of Asketian High Priest and Deladian High Priestess. They could not guess how the very powers that made her priestess would be jeopardized by marriage to the Lord Hvandi. How he could, in the moment he consummated their marriage, bind an invisible chain to her and her mystic powers, lessening the ease with which the goddess could manifest in the physical world. They had no idea of the threat she faced. They thought the event merely symbolic and, consequently, remained undisturbed by the upcoming ceremony.

Only the King, she perceived in some vague manner, was capable of understanding just how terrible this event would be. And, like Yslinda, he appeared powerless to prevent it.

Her duties done for the day, Yslinda took a slice of cheese and some greens one farmer had brought as payment for healing his youngest son, and settled down on the front steps of her house. Nibbling at the cheese, she gazed over the waters of the lake, at the glowing colors the setting sun painted on the water. Never, in all her years on this island had loneliness plagued her. Now that emotion overwhelmed, rocking her self-assurance to the core.

Tears misted her vision as she looked across the darkening lake toward Lord-Hill. Only one day left. One day.

Suddenly, in ghostly quietness, a great white owl dipped down from the trees at her back and snatched up a mouse nearly at Yslinda's feet. The surprise she felt at seeing the bird claim its prey so close was only slightly less than that elicited by its presence. As a night hunter, sunset was not its preferred choice of times to hunt. Did a message lie here that she could not read?

The owl stood for a moment, one foot on the dispatched mouse, and its eyes met Yslinda's. She held her breath, waiting for the owl to speak, but this one did not. It merely spread its wings and lifted effortlessly into its worlds of trees and coming nighttime.

There was no message. There were no words. It was only an owl, not the Owl of her dreams.

Irdun, King of Delad, last link to all the kings that had gone before him, awoke from a night of dark dreams and clamoring voices. All he could remember of those nightmares was a sense of despair and a feeling of impotence greater than he had ever known before. It was not the same emotion he experienced when dealing with the Asketians, for he had grown from infancy to young manhood knowing he was King in title only, that the real power in the land was the Emperor's, exercised by the governor who ruled from the shadows behind Irdun's throne.

No, this was a knowledge that he should be doing something—something he instinctively shied from, something that no one had attempted since the Asketians had overrun Delad. The rising tide of terror that gripped him was nearly enough to ruin his morning meal.

The governor's palace hummed with activity this morning; courtiers hurried back and forth on what to his eyes seemed meaningless errands. The Asketian guests stood on the broad terrace overlooking the lake, bowing and murmuring unctuous words to Prince Gonten and the priest Hvandi. Irdun gazed at the lake as well, toward the goddess' island, and wondering how Yslinda had passed her last night of freedom.

He shook his head, as if he had taken a fall and was not clear-minded after. The memories of his nightmares returned. He tried to grasp at them, to bring them into focus. What was it he must do? What? And how?

He looked away from his view of the lake and returned to his house that stood in the shadow of Lord-Hill. Silent servants bowed as he passed, touching their foreheads in homage. Irdun drew a deep breath. His hands trembled slightly, and his stomach threatened to reject what he had eaten earlier. He rubbed his eyes, his mind still clouded, and entered the small chapel of the goddess next to his rooms.

Bowing before the statue of Savanya that sat on a small altar, he knelt and some of his fear and confusion subsided. He murmured prayers he had said since he could speak, but this time felt an urgency to utter those words with all the strength he possessed. He closed his eyes and sought in the silence of the room to achieve some measure of calm.

An owl appeared before him with a suddenness that made him gasp. He knew this to be no ordinary bird, though he had contemplated owls in his prayers before. Here was an Owl of owls, huge—impossibly huge—and glowing from within with a pure radiance that outshone anything he had seen before. And in one of the Owl's feet there was a dagger.

Irdun flinched backward, his eyes snapping open. But instead of seeing the small familiar statue of Savanya, he knelt face to face with a huge Owl, white as the light of stars . . . an Owl that sat where the statue usually rested. Irdun's heart pounded in his chest as he stared at the bird and at what the bird carried.

Follow your heart, a voice whispered in his mind. *Trust in me. I will not fail you.*

As if he were someone else, Irdun watched his hand reach out and take the dagger from the Owl's talons.

The sun was sinking low in the sky, and the feast had entered a new phase of excited merriment. Prince Gonten sat at the head of the table, his eyes never still, weighing and assessing the words and actions of the nobles who had gathered to honor the upcoming marriage of the High Priest of Keti and the High Priestess of Savanya. He had been accused of many things in his life, but no one had ever so much as hinted he was stupid. He had learned well at his father's knee, how to listen without seeming to listen, how to make small conversation without those he spoke to knowing he was keeping track of every word they uttered.

Now was no different. He was well aware, even without Hvandi's prompting, of the situation facing the legions of Asketi to the north and the west. And, sensing a hidden current of discontent swirling through the room, he listened to the hum of conversation with more than what to others might appear bored ears.

The two nobles who sat several places away had lately come from those regions of unrest and he heard, in their seemingly innocent conversation, hints of uncertainty as to the strength of his father's hand in leading the legions. *Click.* He made a mental note of that, prepared to repeat nearly word for word all they said to his father. Another noble spoke casually of the recent acquisition by one of his friends of lands to the far west, an odd move for someone who had gained fame for being wildly in love with the comforts of the Empire's capital city. *Click.* Another mental note taken and stored.

"Ah, Prince Gonten," said a slightly nasal voice in his ear. He cringed inwardly, but assumed his most gracious smile as he gestured the man to a seat at his side. The governor's timing could not have been worse, having ended for all practical purposes Gonten's eavesdropping. "Do you think Lord Hvandi can stand another hour of waiting? Look at him. He's nearly beside himself with anticipation."

Gonten looked. The governor was accurate in his observation. The Prince could not remember having seen the priest in such a state before. Something nudged at the back of his mind. Maybe there *was* more to this priestess than he knew. Maybe Hvandi *was* correct in thinking much power could be won from this woman and her goddess. Maybe.

"She's an extraordinarily beautiful woman," the governor continued, "and I'm sure that fact alone would kindle anyone."

"Oh?" Gonten kept his voice pitched to polite boredom. "I was unaware that Lord Hvandi had ever met the priestess."

The governor waved a languid hand. "He hasn't, Prince, but he has ears. I've met her many times myself, when I've been obliged by my position to visit her island. She *is* beautiful, in a very un-Asketian way. Those gold eyes of hers, though, are unsettling. There are times when I swear she's looking straight into my heart."

For an instant, the Prince remembered the young King's eyes, golden as were those of his countrymen. Beast eyes, bird eyes. Eyes hardly human. His grandfather's legions had brought home tale after tale of the silent, gentle people they had conquered—a people with eyes of gold.

Servants lit torches in the feast hall, as well as hanging lamps, and the shadows that had begun to creep into the room were pushed back by the warm light. The Prince looked around casually, but did not see the King. That in itself was not odd. The boy was known to come late and leave early from the feasts held in the governor's palace. At any other time, Gonten would have dismissed the lateness of the King's arrival, but on this night in particular . . .

Lord Hvandi approached the Prince's place and bowed slightly. Gonten returned the nod, glanced out the windows and noted it was nearly the hour of sunset, the time the priest had chosen for his trip to the island to claim his prize.

"Walk with me to the barge," Lord Hvandi said. "I'll be leaving momentarily."

Though Gonten sensed the order behind the invitation, he nodded and shoved back his chair. At that moment, there was a stir at the wide doorway to the feast hall, and the young King entered. Dressed simply as usual, he still seemed more subdued than the norm. He walked slowly toward the Prince as if in some dream, his cloak drawn close though the air was warm.

The Prince heard his guards shift positions behind his chair. He sensed something strange here—something he could not put a finger on. His guards had noted it also, though no one else in the room, including the priest, appeared aware of anything odd.

"Prince," the young King said, nodding politely. "A fair banquet you have tonight."

"It is," Gonten allowed. His gut tightened slightly and he glanced sidelong at the priest, but Hvandi's attention was focused out the window toward the island in the middle of the darkening lake.

"And for such an occasion," the King said in a curiously uninflected tone, stepping closer, "I have brought you a gift."

What happened next took place nearly too quickly for the eye to follow. Before the Prince could set himself, the boy-king drew a dagger from beneath his cloak and sprang at Gonten, his youthful face untouched by any emotion at all.

The hall erupted into chaos. Tripping over his chair, the Prince fell backward, and felt cold fire burn along his arm as the dagger barely missed his chest. Lord Hvandi cursed, lifted a hand, and a streak of red fire lanced toward the King. From his vantage point on the floor, his guards standing above him with drawn swords, the Prince watched the young King falter, drop the dagger, and slump slowly to the ground without uttering so much as a groan.

Silence fell like a leaden weight on the room, then exploded into a hubbub of voices. Prince Gonten, helped to his feet by his guards, stared down at the boy-king, still too startled by what had happened to think. As the shock wore off, he snatched up a napkin from the table and dabbed at the wound in his arm.

"You're not injured badly?" the governor asked, his voice trembling. "O gods! To think of it! To *think* of it! What possessed the King to—"

"Whatever it was, it's gone," Gonten said, only now feeling the pain that followed his wounding. "Thanks to Lord Hvandi, I live."

The priest stood by the slumped body of the young King, his face bewildered. "I aimed to kill, Prince," he said to Gonten, "yet the boy's alive."

Gonten brushed aside the priest's puzzlement. "All the better to make an example of him later," he growled, holding out a hand. One of the servants extended a goblet of wine which he snatched and downed in only a few gulps. He tossed the goblet aside and it rang in the silence as it bounced on the floor. He felt his face harden into a mask. "Guards, take this young man to his chambers so we can—" He glanced up at the priest, and smiled coldly. "No, a better idea yet. Lord Hvandi, I will accompany you to the island for your bride. And, to make the trip more entertaining, the boy will come with us."

Yslinda grew aware of the sun setting without the need to look. She knelt before the statue of Savanya, her pulse beating at her throat in an uneven rhythm. Now. It must be now. She must make her choice. Should she rise and go to the dock, to wait like some sacrifice for the Lord Hvandi to take, or should she refuse to bow to his demands? What would be the outcome of either choice?

Her mind raced wildly ahead, filled with the ramifications of both choices. If this, then that. She felt overwhelmed by the mere fact that she could choose at all.

She lifted her eyes to the statue, a dim white

now in the fading light. Still the goddess kept her silence. Still she refused to give a sign, or to answer the repeated prayers her priestess had offered. Or, Yslinda wondered, had the goddess answered in some language that she was ill-equipped to hear even after all her years of service?

A pang of fear swept through her heart, and she doubled over in her kneeling position, her head touching the ground. *O Lady of Wisdom, Mother of Delad, what must I do? What answer can I give this priest when he comes to our island? I'm afraid, Mother, but not so much for myself as for what will happen to the kingdom. I have no priestess-in-training. I am the only link you have with this world. And I know what the priest can do to that link, to my powers. Please, Lady, please! Fount of Wisdom, grant me the knowledge to know what to do!*

Of a sudden, the hair on the back of her neck stiffened, and she felt the closure of another place and time on that in which she and her world existed. She raised her head and looked up at the statue. Far from growing dimmer in the gathering dusk, the statue began to glow with a steady, strengthening light. A faint buzz and the distant sound of tiny bells filled Yslinda's ears, and the air seemed charged much as it does before lightning strikes from a storm.

Child, a voice said, and she trembled with joy at the words, knowing it was the goddess her-

self who spoke. *Have you so little faith in me that
you think I cannot shield those I love?*

"No, Lady. I am only mortal, and I fear."

Then fear no more, child, the voice continued.
*Rise and take your place between the two trees
closest.*

Yslinda did as she was instructed, feeling de-
tached from her body as if she watched another
perform the motions. Once between the two
trees, she stood silent, waiting.

The priest comes, the goddess said, *along with
the Prince and your King.*

"Lady? The King? What is he—"

*Later, child. For the moment, all you need to know
is that he has played his part in this thing. Now,
trust in me and do not be afraid of what follows next.*

Yslinda stood motionless, her eyes fixed fast
on the gleaming statue. A strange feeling rose
from her feet, one of rootedness, of connection
with the earth. Higher and higher the sensation
spread, and, suddenly, a cocoon of safety
wrapped all around, and she existed in a place
where she could see but could not be seen.

And now, the goddess whispered in a voice
like the rushing of wings, *let us show these for-
eigners that there are other powers in the world than
those they own.*

Prince Gonten was the first to step from the
royal barge. He heard Lord Hvandi disembark
next, then the scuffling sounds of his warriors
as they set the unresponsive King on the

wooden dock. The Prince gestured, and ten guardsmen, swords drawn and shields at the ready, preceded him from the shore toward the priestess' home. The remaining nine and their captain, followed at Gonten's back.

His arm still burned from the knife wound he had taken, but, bound now and swathed with healing herbs, his injury was more of a nuisance than a hindrance. He glanced sidelong at the pliant King who still walked as if in some dream. *Something isn't right here*, he thought. *Hvandi never misses what he aims at, and he swore he struck to kill. What is it that protected this boy from Hvandi's power?*

There was a subtle stirring in the air, as if a wind had sprung up from across the water, but when he looked, he saw the lake lying glassy and calm, some vast mirror that would soon reflect the light of the stars. Set on edge by the oddness of the evening, Gonten reached out to touch Hvandi's shoulder.

"You walk into this goddess' realm now, Priest," he said quietly, "and Keti has dropped below the horizon. Is your power sufficient to withstand the marshaling of Savanya's power?"

Lord Hvandi turned his head and it was all that Gonten could do to keep from gasping. The priest's dark eyes were full of fire now, a fire that was presently banked but could and would spring to blinding flames if called upon. The Prince lowered his gaze, knowing his silence spoke more than words.

Hvandi's thin smile acknowledged Gonten's unease. "You," he said, shaking the young King's shoulder. "Do you know where your priestess might be at this hour?"

The King remained silent. Only his golden eyes registered any evidence he had heard something other than his inner voices.

The guard captain, followed by half his men, emerged from the house and shook his head.

"The priestess isn't here," Gonten said, stating the obvious and hating himself for having done so.

"So it seems," returned Hvandi, openly enjoying the Prince's discomfort. "Send your warriors out to search for her. She can't have gone far."

Gonten nodded and called forward the captain of his guard. "You and nine of your men split into pairs and scour the island from its farthest side to this shore. It's not large, so it shouldn't take you long. We'll wait here for your return."

"And," Hvandi said, "do not, I repeat, *do not* enter the grove of the goddess. To do so now might imperil your lives."

The guard captain saluted, gave his orders, and disappeared into the gathering darkness with his men. Once more, the Prince sensed a wind that was not a wind blow across the water, and he shivered through the night was far from chill.

Time seemed to crawl by as Gonten, Hvandi,

and the young King waited by the doorway to the priestess' house. The remaining guards sensed the Prince's unease; their hands never strayed far from their sword hilts, and he caught one of them licking his lips nervously. He wished he could give in to his own nerves, but a leader of men never let his subordinates see anything but confidence.

The evening had deepened to darkness by the time the captain and his men reappeared. Gonten had ordered torches lit and, from the expression the guard captain wore as he stepped into the flickering light, the Prince knew he and his men had found nothing.

"So," Hvandi said, his voice so cold that it caused an involuntary shiver to skitter down Gonten's spine. "The battle lines are drawn." He reached out and lifted the King's chin in his hands and stared for a long time into the withdrawn, golden eyes. "You will lead us, then, my lord," he said in a mocking voice. "Surely you, better than any of us, know the way to the goddess' grove."

For the first time since he had attacked Prince Gonten, the young man nodded and, steady once more on his feet and without any help from those around him, he set out at a slow walk into the forest. Lord Hvandi lifted an eyebrow, gestured to Gonten and his men, and followed.

*   *   *

Irdun felt the closeness of the grove now, but was still unable to experience any emotion other than patient waiting. Another guided his footsteps; another held his mind. Before him, unseen by the priest, the Prince, or any of the accompanying warriors, flew a ghostly shape, wings silent in the clinging darkness.

Owl Light, Owl Bright—

The old prayer sprang up from some deep well in Irdun's being as he led the way beneath the clustering trees. A warmth filled his heart as he walked. He was not forgotten. He had played his part, done his deed, though another had moved his hand. A small smile touched his face, unseen by those who accompanied him.

His mind was filled with wings.

The statue of the goddess was the only thing that stood in the center of the grove, but Prince Gonten looked about uneasily, as if he expected to see armed men dash out from under the cover of the trees. His eyes snapped back to Hvandi. The priest had come to a halt several paces from the statue. The young King seemed animated at last, but gave no indication that he would move from his place alongside Gonten.

"Savanya!"

Hvandi's voice split the silence of the grove, causing Gonten and several of his men to start. The Prince saw the glowing fire brighten in the priest's eyes, and looked away.

"We have a score to settle, goddess, you and I, and so let us begin!"

The priest lifted his hands and a fiery ball appeared between them. His body rigid with the effort it took to control the power he had unleashed, Hvandi drew back his hands and flung the blazing sphere toward the statue.

And that was the last thing Prince Gonten remembered seeing with his physical eyes.

Irdun recognized Yslinda, standing between two trees at the very edge of the grove, but knew the other men saw her only as one more tree. His heart sang at this simple manifestation of the goddess' power. And when the priest flung his fiery weapon toward the statue of Savanya, Irdun wanted to laugh at the futility of the effort.

But suddenly, there was nothing left to see but the golden eyes of the Owl.

Light met light—fiery light opposing that seemingly fashioned from the stars. Winds tore through the grove: a rush of winds bent the trees about, sent leaves scattering before its coming. From out of the heavens, on wings too vast to be viewed in this world, the Owl descended in thundering silence.

Waiting for the Owl was no longer the priest, but a giant serpent, raised up on its coils, swaying back and forth, its gaping jaws opened to reveal fangs that ran with fire. The two mystic

beasts grappled, the Serpent trying to snatch the
Owl in its coils, and the Owl attempting to
clutch the Serpent with its talons.

Encased in her enchanted armor, Yslinda
watched the conflict, unable to do anything save
pray. The Owl and the Serpent closed again,
both existing in some other world, yet visible to
those who had eyes to see.

The winds howled.

The Serpent's coils entrapped the Owl, and
Yslinda heard a shout of triumph from the
Asketian priest.

But the Owl became Light—a light that consumed, that strove to tear the Serpent from its
human base.

A scream filled the night. Ripped from
Hvandi's throat, it echoed down the worlds. Yslinda barely noticed the Prince and his men,
fallen to the grass. Only the King stood stead-
fast, his face shining in the Owl Light.

Shapes bent in upon other shapes, vistas of
worlds she did not understand warped each
other into worlds even more indefinable. The
winds howled, the winds sang, the winds blew
the unclean light away, spinning down the spi-
rals of conjoined universes into a nothingness
that could not be seen, only sensed.

And suddenly, silence.

The grove stood as if nothing had happened,
as if some titanic battle had not just been waged.
Yslinda's eyes filled with tears as she watched
the Owl settle silently on the edge of existence,

the glitter of starlight in its eyes. It slowly folded its wings, tilted its head, and faded as a dream upon waking.

And its light faded with it, to find a new home in Yslinda's heart.

Freed from her enchantment, she joined the King, whose eyes were still filled with the wonder of what he had witnessed. The expression on his face let her know none would ever see this King as a boy again. Tonight, consumed by wonder, he had been made a man.

Prince Gonten stirred, lifted his head and looked confusedly around. His men had vanished, leaving behind only their swords and shields. The Prince's face was haggard in the moonlight, as if he had seen more than he had ever wanted to. The King extended a hand and, shaking uncontrollably, the Prince took it and stood.

"A lesson, Prince," the King said, his voice seeming to have deepened since sunset. "A lesson for all to learn. Never place your faith in someone who wields heaven's powers for his own end."

"The goddess has no quarrel with the sun lord," Yslinda added, standing at the King's right hand. "She has no dispute with any save those who walk in Darkness. And your priest, though he held himself out as mouthpiece of the sun god, was in league with those shadows." A small smile touched her lips. "By now your people will know what has happened on this island. Remember it. Leave us to our own mysteries, and we will leave you to yours. Now, go. Praise the goddess who has let you live.''

Prince Gonten stood unsteadily before the statue of Savanya. His gaze dropped and he uttered a groan of fear. With a muttered prayer to whatever god of his was listening, he fled the grove toward the lake, running as if the fiends of his nine hells were at his heels.

Yslinda looked down at the base of the statue by the goddess' right foot. There, absent from its usual perch on Savanya's shoulders, stood her Owl, its talons clutching a serpent, the face of which was that of the priest Hvandi.

EAGLE'S EYE

by Jody Lynn Nye

Jody Lynn Nye lists her main career activity as "spoiling cats." She lives near Chicago with two of the above and her husband, SF author and editor Bill Fawcett. Among Jody's novels are the *Mythology 101* series, *Taylor's Ark, Medicine Show,* and four collaborations with Anne McCaffrey: *Crisis on Doona, The Death of Sleep, The Ship Who Won,* and *Treaty at Doona.* Recent works include *Walking in Dreamland, School of Light,* and an anthology, *Don't Forget Your Spacesuit, Dear!*

IMOH crept along the blind edge of the crag, trying to ignore the stones rubbing at his elbows, knees, and bare belly. Though he was slim, there was little room for him to maneuver. His tanned skin and soft leather pants and shoes were already gray with dust, and his freshly washed and oiled black hair that he had braided so neatly had been wrenched and twisted into a mess by the sharp evergreen twigs he'd crawled under. He had never once cried out, although he guessed strands of his long hair hung from bushes from here all the way down the cliff. Nor had he made a sound when that last sapling whiplashed him in the forehead, sending a trickle of blood down into his dark brown eyes. He must be silent as air. From the shrieks and peeps ahead, the great eagle was on her nest, feeding her young. If he thought too much about what he was about to do, his insides quivered. Several times already he had almost turned around to go back to the village, but that would have been too much of a disgrace for himself and his clan.

He was glad that he had to face his adulthood test by himself. It was undignified for one of the Eagle clan to crawl on his face with his rump in the air like a kitten stalking a feather. Worse yet, he would have hated to have anyone know the fear in his heart. The flat truth was that he was terrified of eagles. He'd seen them tear rabbits in half, and haul fish out of the river that were almost too large for him to carry. Imoh would far rather make friends with a wolf or a wildcat, but his family's totem was the great bird of prey.

Every great clan had as its guardian one of the ancient animals of the forest. The Wolves were the leaders. The Wildcats served bravely as the warrior class. Even the loathsome Toad stood for the keepers of the Tribe's wealth, based upon the legend of the jewel in the head of their name animal. Surprisingly, the Toads were very wise people, as wise as the healers of the Turtle Clan, who were hermits by the nature of their specialty. The Eagles were the seers. Their totem saw all, flew over all, and knew things before they came to pass. In order for Imoh to gain the sight that was his family's gift, he must look into the eye of the eagle who would be his guardian for the rest of his life. And to do that, he must brave them in their own habitat.

Not that they were difficult to find. The greatest of the eagles, called Hands-and-face because of their white heads and primary feathers so like outspread fingers, sat in the very tops of trees, surveying their realm with those keen, pitiless eyes. The dead trees were their favorites. The eldest wise man of the Turtles had said it was because the other branches were too pliable to support them. "The eagle stands most securely upon firm supports, much as the tribe stands upon the proven strength of its members," Old Heldeh had said with his eyes raised to the ceiling, speaking as much to the unseen spirits as to him. "Imoh must find the eagle who shares his vision, climb up to him, and meet his eye."

Imoh himself was like a young tree too green to hold the weight of a Hands-and-face. His young body, not yet a full man's height, was still more pliable than mighty. He was growing shoulders on his narrow frame and calves to his legs. His strength increased daily, and he pushed himself to the extent to which his muscles were capable. Some of his capers were risky, like jumping from rooftop to rooftop all around the village circle, but he trusted his body. He knew he could handle whatever part of his ordeal did not have to do with eagles. Mother worried greatly about him, but she was a worrier by nature. Imoh was her fourth child. After three daughters, she hardly knew how to treat a daredevil son.

"He needs to acquire steadiness," she complained to Imoh's father, who shook his head.

"Eagles are wild," he said simply. Imoh's mother sighed.

Whether he liked it or not, Imoh was learning steadiness. The attempt to lock eyes with the mother eagle was by no means his first attempt, nor his first eagle.

The great birds were absolutely territorial, and their territory stretched wide. Within a day's walk from his tribe's winter village, he could touch land belonging to no more than three. The first bird he disturbed so much making his rackety way up the tree where he'd spotted it sitting calmly that it had taken off on huge wings and had not been seen since. Imoh's middle sister made a single reference to cutting the tribe's luck, and was punished by both her parents for trying to cause trouble. It wasn't true, Imoh told himself, remembering it all as he crawled in the dust. His face burned with remembered shame. The eagle would return. It must. If only he could complete his trial quickly and return, the village would forget about his past mistake. He had asked others for help, but no one had easy answers. No other clan member would answer his questions, or indeed, could answer them. Each clan had its own coming-of-age ritual, its own means of gaining acceptance by its guardian and the bestowal of power. He was the only boy of the Eagle clan in their village, and his elder sisters were too canny to talk about how they had managed their ordeals. They would say only he must solve his problems by observation.

Such a notion was indeed against his nature, but that was exactly what he had to do if he wanted to be a man and a full member of the Tribe. He made himself learn to observe.

For his second attempt, he picked the younger of the two remaining eagles, a male just out of adolescence. In his opinion it had claimed the nicest range for its hunting ground. He sat watching it for many days, making friends with it in his mind. *We will speak to one another*, he promised it, keeping watch as the great bird opened its wings and floated down to pick another fish out of the river, or dove like a falling rock on a small animal in a field.

Imoh pursued that bird for almost the full turn of the moon, trying to figure out where it would hunt, when it would stoop for prey. He was disappointed when it refused to alight anywhere he could reach while remaining in safe cover. It was only when he noticed that the male chose the same snaggy tree for its perch almost all the time that he felt hope.

Laboriously, he had climbed the tree nearest the dead one, waiting in the branches until the Hands-and-face lit and closed its huge talons around the uppermost branch. The limb creaked slightly under the bird's weight. Slowly, tremblingly, Imoh had come out of his hiding place and shinned up the rest of the way until he was level with the great bird's perch. Forcing himself to be brave, he stared at the eagle, who watched him impassively. Suddenly, it turned its head, and the two of them were eye-to-eye. Imoh gasped. The brown-red disk with the tiny speck of black was fully on him.

Just as abruptly, the great bird turned away, sweeping its keen gaze over the river far below them. A splash of silver winked on the water's surface. The Hands-and-face opened its wings and lifted off the branch, leaving Imoh clinging to his branch, shaking with reaction and disappointment.

There had been no communion. The young male was not his guide. Its mind was closed to him. Imoh had made his way down from the swaying tree, feeling heavy of heart.

The third eagle, an older female, had alit almost beside him on the bank of the river when he went to wash off the sweat of his effort. Almost offhand, she had offered him a casual, fearless glance. Imoh got a very good look at her, admired her soft gray breast feathers and the snowy brilliance of her cap of feathers, as white as his own hair was black. There was nothing personal in her regard. Although she seemed to offer him the courtesy of one kinsman to another, she was not his companion either. Imoh had gone home to the village, staring at the ground before his feet all the way, never looking up at the empty sky. He was out of eagles. He had failed the ordeal. He would never be an adult.

His grandfather had been sympathetic.

"Don't be upset, young one," he said, bringing the boy to sit with him close to the evening fire. "You will find your guardian. The High Ones promised at the beginning of the world that there was a totem, a guide, a mentor for every human being that walked the earth, and promised it will not take them a lifetime to find it. By that the Tribe believes that it is within a close distance to where one is born."

His mother had leaned over to remind him as she handed them bowls of the supper stew, "Imoh was not born here, Father." Then she stopped in surprise. Imoh had started, too. He knew the story. He'd asked for it time and again at bedtime since he could talk. It was one of his favorite tales. His mother had come on her time while the Tribe was on its semiannual migration, and had to stop to give birth in the honeycomb caverns along the narrowest part of the

passage leading from the Tribe's cold-weather
home to its warm-weather one. She and the infant Imoh had had to complete their journey
alone as soon as she was strong enough to
travel. It had been his first adventure, full of
danger and portents, even though he'd been too
young at the time to appreciate it. Why had he
not remembered that fact before?

Imoh had been excited and danced around the
family campfire. The failure to find his eagle
near the village was not his doing. He knew his
birthplace well. His birth marker was alone in a
small cave along the great river that marked the
Tribe's way two days' walk to the south. He
would go there to find his guardian.

Only two eagles made their nests within the
accepted range of the honeycomb caverns. He
hoped one of the two great birds would be his
soul's guide. Both birds lived on cliff ledges at
opposite ends of a turn of the river cut. The
farther-ranging bird was an old male with a
longer wingspan than any Imoh had ever seen.
Imoh found it hard to believe that a bird of that
age had not found his human counterpart. But,
he thought, holding on to hope, few people had
ever been born near here. Maybe it was yet un-
chosen. The closer of the two eagles was a mature female, whom Imoh spotted standing on
the edge of her huge nest, bending over again
and again. So, she had chicks to feed. That
would mean she had to return to that place fre-

quently. No more chasing about. Imoh had
learned his lesson on that. He would approach
her first.

The edge of the nest showed on a shelf of
rock a third of the way from the top of the bank,
making it inaccessible from above. To reach it
would not be an easy task, but Imoh's muscles
had been growing harder over the course of
time. The land itself was relatively easy. The
river had cut a deep V-shaped channel in the
earth's heart, but in gradual stages. Natural ter-
races rose in layers on either side of the rushing
water. If the banks had been empty, it would
have taken a matter of an hour to walk up. Instead, thick overgrowth had sprouted from the
clay and rock, providing both shelter and obsta-
cle. Imoh sighed at the length of time it would
take him to climb, but the bushes would also
keep the great female from seeing him. He must
not make her think he was a threat to her chicks.
Flat on his belly, Imoh looked down over the
lip of his path at the rush of rapids over sub-
merged rocks over six man-heights below him.
It didn't matter if the mother eagle tore out his
heart herself or knocked him off the bank into
the river; either would kill him. *High Ones, take
me into your care*, he prayed.

A twig reached out and tangled itself in his
hair again. Imoh was forced to creep a pace
backward and reach above himself blindly to
untie himself from its grasp. There, he thought
irritably.

He heard a booming sound as he crept around the last fold in the river bank, and crawled around the corner to look triumphantly at his future guardian. The nest's edge was empty! While he'd been distracted, the mother eagle had gone away again. The booming had been the beating of her wings on the air. He heard the contented peeping of the hatchlings in their nest. Imoh groaned. She might not be back again for hours.

Imoh tried to make himself comfortable, and settled down with his head on his crossed forearms to wait. The sun drew its golden light upward from the river valley, leaving it graystone dark. Imoh realized that the eaglets were the only ones who had been fed. If he stayed here, he would pass a hungry night.

When the sun was only just below the lip of his hiding place, Imoh decided to go. The mother could return in the next heartbeat, or not until dark, when he wouldn't be able to see her eyes anyhow. If he hurried, there was still time to catch a fish for his dinner. Carefully, as silently as he could, he eased to his elbows and knees, and began to move backward. As soon as he was able, he turned around to head down the slope.

Imoh's maternal grandmother was a great fisherwoman. She had taught him to make a spring-pole, a devise that plucked a hooked fish neatly out of the water using its own weight. He cut a couple of willow saplings, one half as long as the other and with a fork at the end, and bent them into a bow at the river's edge. With the string from his hair as a line, he tied on the flint hook he had in his pouch with his tinderstone and a dropped feather for a lure. Fish would do, although he would have preferred a nice rabbit. The cliffs were riddled with warrens, but with the eagle on the wing somewhere above, the rabbits were hiding out of sight.

He sat on the bank with his knees pulled up underneath his chin, almost dozing as he waited for a catch. The sun was scarcely touching more than the clifftops, and the sky was still. Suddenly, the spring-pole quivered and exploded erect with a loud *twang*! Imoh scrambled to his feet. Hanging over his head from the upper sapling was a fine young salmon. Its silver skin twinkled in the dying light as it wriggled on the line. Imoh was delighted. He'd have a feast tonight.

Imoh had no sooner taken out his knife and stared to bend the twig toward him when he heard an unearthly scream. He looked up to see the mother eagle stooping out of the sky toward him. Imoh flung himself down into the bushes against the bank, his heart pounding. The eagle never landed, but swooped low, grabbed his catch—his catch!—and was gone with it before he could draw breath. How dare she? Imoh gasped with frustration. And she'd taken his hook with it.

He had no choice but to go to sleep on an empty belly. He could make a spear out of his knife and another sapling, but it was now too dark to see the fish. He slept uneasily, seeing those outstretched talons reaching for him. In his troubled dreams she was coming to tear out his heart and feed it to her chicks. Imoh woke as tired as he'd gone to sleep. Stiff and irritable, he rose with the sun to fish for breakfast.

The High Ones must have favored him. As he stood astride a pair of rocks in the river, he was sent a whole school of young salmon to choose from. Their bright scales glinted under the brown water like bits of mica. Imoh stood very still, careful not to let his shadow quiver on the water's surface as he waited for just the right fish. He hoped the mother eagle wouldn't steal this one, too! Could she not at least have shared with him? She was surely meant to be his guardian. Maybe if she would teach him the Sight, he could teach her right from wrong.

He didn't want to have to keep chasing the great beast of the air up and down the mountain time and again, he thought. Imoh stiffened as a very fat fish paused for a moment near the rock under his right foot. That one! He plunged the spear down, impaling the fish with a stroke. Could the mother eagle not stay in one place for just one moment? He pulled in his catch.

The school of salmon scattered, but came back to the cool shadows as soon as their brother's blood had washed away downstream. Watching

them, Imoh had an idea. He could bring the
mother eagle a gift to show his respect. He'd
bring it to her nest. She'd go there, if nowhere
else, because she must continually return to her
young. If he came with food, she must see that
he meant her and her family no harm. Full of
plans, he went to cook his breakfast.

The second climb up the riverbank toward the
nest was much easier, because he'd already
blazed his own path. This time he had to con-
tend with a slippery, smelly burden in a net
made of woven willow branches on his back.
He'd caught several fine fish, a fitting gift for a
holy guardian. But the gift attracted other animals, who followed him avidly. It was easy to
chase off the small predators, but a young wildcat stalked him, threatening to ruin his plan.

He remonstrated with the wildcat, telling it he
was not of its kind. The cat just stared at him
with its squared pupils, moving closer as Imoh
edged away. In the end, he had to drop a fish
on the ground. He left the cat to its prize, and
hurried away on hands and knees.

As morning passed, the dead fish got warmer.
Imoh could no longer smell the ground or the
greenery. There was something horrible in the
way they felt, slithering against his skin through
the openings in the willow creel, He reached the
top for the second time, reeking of fish.

He felt this time he must make a bolder gesture. Though his heart pounded in his chest,

nearly choking him, he got to his feet and shouldered his gift. With all the strength of will and the knowledge that everyone at home would soon find out if he failed, he stepped around the last outcropping to behold the huge nest.

As soon as he came into view, the dark-headed chicks began to clamor, partly out of fear and partly out of curiosity. Here was a stranger—not mother—but he smelled of good things to eat! Imoh studied them as they churned about in the nest craning their skinny necks toward his creel. They were almost fledged. It couldn't be long at all before they were ready to fly. Imoh stood tall, just far enough away from the nest that wouldn't be construed a direct threat. Holding up one fish as a lure, he scanned the trees that lined the river valley. Here and there bare snags poked up gray fingers. Imoh's eyes were dazzled with sun. He knew the mother could see him at distances so great she could be invisible to him. No, *there* against the black-green was the white dot, the head of a Hands-and-face. Imoh waved his burden high in the air.

The distant dot lifted straight up from its perch. When it was clear of the treetops, Imoh could see the great white-tipped wings. It was coming at him, faster than it had stolen his dinner last night. He quailed, but stood his ground until the last moment, when she was hovering just overhead. Her huge talons grabbed for the fish, but he dropped to the ground and rolled toward the nest, trying to make her land there so she would be at eye level to him. She grabbed the fish out of his hands and settled on the edge of the mass of twigs and sticks to glare.

Bravely, Imoh drew himself up and met her eyes. And felt *nothing*. His heart went hollow in his chest. She was not the one! He could have cried with frustration. The eagle dropped her fish, opened her mouth and screamed. Imoh backed off, preparing to run for his life.

He felt a tug on the creel in his other hand, and looked down. The four little eaglets had clambered out of the next and bustled toward him with their waddling gait, their hooked yellow beaks open, crying for the fish. His eye still on the mother, he dropped the dusty mess and let them have it. They fell upon it, peeping busily. He backed away another pace as the mother shrilled her piercing war cry. As lightly as a cloth whisked from one spot to another, she rose on her great brown wings and dipped down onto the ledge between him and her children. She shrilled again, stopping Imoh's heart in his chest.

Go away, the call said. *Now!*

Imoh felt behind him for the outcrop of rock, keeping his eye on the mother. Another failure! Now he would have to go south, to the other great bird, and hope the High Ones weren't playing tricks on him, that there was not a third place he must hunt for his guardian. Must he follow the Tribe's trail clear south to their summer home, trying to guess where he'd been conceived?

He backed away. Just then, one of the eaglets peered underneath its mother's feathered skirts and peeped. It blinked at him, its nut-brown eyes bright and unafraid. Imoh stared at it, and suddenly understood it. He knew its fierceness, its feeling of safety being with its mother, and its satisfaction at having a full belly. It was a male, second of the four chicks to hatch. Imoh gasped, almost feeling tears come to his eyes. His guardian, his teacher, his totem creature was an infant Hands-and-face! They bonded in an instant so brief there was no time for Imoh to draw a single breath. He had only one chance to blink at his sacred guide before the mother eagle, out of patience, launched herself off the ledge at him.

Imoh dodged and rolled, trying to avoid the outstretched talons. He plunged toward the narrow neck of the path, worried about falling off the cliff. He caught himself with one hand at the very edge of the rock, and wiggled hard to get back under the bushes out of reach. The mother eagle's talons tore through the thin twigs. Imoh felt a hard claw catch in his skin and rake up along his shoulder blade as he shinnied backward toward the slope. The white-hot pain was masked by the assault of thousands of pine needles and broken branches ripping his skin from above and below until he could get down to the shelf in against the riverbank. His hair was hopeless now. It'd be years before he'd have the shining tails of hair again that he'd been so proud of, but he had his guardian!

In a short while, the mother eagle realized she couldn't reach him and gave up the chase. After all, there were the remains of five fine fish in her nest. Panting, Imoh scrambled downhill, keeping himself invisible from above. Avoid the path, he told himself, staying under the cover of the trees along the path. The mother could come back, and if he was in open sky, she'd have no trouble seeing him from many miles away. He was marked now, and not only on his back. He turned his face toward home.

Inside himself he felt the presence of the little bird, and if he concentrated he could see what it was doing. At the moment it was enjoying fish, snatching tidbits from its siblings and fussing for the best parts. He gave it a name, Sky Claw, and knew that he would never tame it. He might also never see it again, but they were bond brothers now until the end. They would gain strength from one another's successes. The presence of his guardian would keep him from harm. Thanks to Sky Claw, he was less afraid of eagles, but he had more respect for them, as was fitting for one of his clan. And he would have the gift of Sight. Did he? Imoh wondered.

He thought of his mother, and suddenly, he could see her in the village, as if through the eyes of someone near her. Imoh had to stop walking, lest he fall over roots on a path he

could no longer see. His mother was on her
knees pounding corn in a mortar for bread, and
tossing in green herbs as she went. Imoh
grinned. That was his favorite food. She was
making it for him, already knowing that he had
succeeded at his quest. A true child of the Eagle,
she had the Sight, too.

Through his new gift, Imoh witnessed the
fledgling flight of Sky Claw an hour before sunset on the day he reached the outposts of his
village. *A good omen for us both,* he thought, waving to the Wildcat clan warriors guarding the
southern approaches. He grinned at them, and
knew how they saw him: dirty, bloodstained,
with torn shoes, pants and hair, but a man
today. *Today we both learned to fly.*

WIDE WINGS

by Mercedes Lackey

Mercedes Lackey was born in Chicago, and worked as a lab assistant, security guard, and computer programmer before turning to fiction writing. Her first book, *Arrows of the Queen*, the first in the Valdemar series, was published in 1985. She won the Lambda award for *Magic's Price* and Science Fiction Book Club Book of the Year for the *The Elvenbane*, co-authored with Andre Norton. Along with her husband, Larry Dixon, she is a federally licensed bird rehabilitator, specializing in wild birds. She shares her home with a menagerie of parrots, cats, and a Schutzhund trained German shepherd. Recent novels include *Werehunter* and *Black Swan*.

INTRODUCTION

Every so often, a character takes over and demands that more attention be paid to him (or her). This was my dilemma when writing *The Black Swan;* one of the characters, a relatively minor spear-carrier, stood up and insisted that I go into more detail about *her.* Now, the story was supposed to be about the characters of *Swan Lake*—there was no room there for a digression about one of the Prince's bridal candidates.

Honoria didn't care. She wanted *her* story told, and to Tophet with what I wanted. Fortunately, since Honoria is a falconer, I had a place to tell it. So here it is, and I hope you like it.

THE shadowed interior of the mews, redolent with the musky aroma of hawk-mutes and full of the restless energy of birds ready to be hunting, was an odd place to find a princess, but Honoria never tired of introducing the intricacies of falconry to devotees; she was always happy to create new worshipers at the shrine of the mews. It troubled her not at all that most of the congregation were male; she had encountered enough trouble in her own quest to become a falconer that she would not care to visit such difficulty on any other female unless she had the same degree of need for the birds that Honoria herself had. Falconry—*true* falconry, and not merely accepting a bird from your falconer and tossing it into the air without pausing for a moment in conversation—was already difficult enough without that added hardship.

Young Bern, blue-eyed, blond-haired squire to

her brother, Sir Hakkon, watched Honoria as closely as ever he watched his master. She had her favorite peregrine, Valeria, sitting calmly un-hooded on her gloved hand, and the jesses from each of Valeria's feet held ready to attach to the leash that would allow the bird to make a short flight, called a bate, if she was startled, but not to escape. "And see, this is how you make the knot at the end of the jess," she said, deftly tying jesses and leash together in the falconer's knot, doing so one-handed and with the aid of her teeth, much to the amazement of the young squire. The leash was already tied off to the ring in her glove. "Now that you have the falcon on your fist and secured, you can hood her."

She slipped the beautifully crafted hood, orna-mented with a Turk's Knot on top, out of a side-pocket on her game bag. Fixing her gaze on her peregrine's eyes, and making a little "pishing" sound to quiet her, she brought the hood up to the falcon's breast, then popped it on her head in a single, swift motion. Using hands and teeth, she tightened the braces at the back of the hood before Valeria could shake her head to get it off. That was Valeria's latest trick, and she was perfectly capable of playing it for an hour until she consented to wear the hood.

"There!" she said, holding up the hooded fal-con on her leather-gauntleted fist, game bag slung on her hip, leash properly fastened to the jesses and to the ring on her glove. If ever any-one painted a portrait of her, this is how she would choose to be memorialized: in her best brown riding habit—not a fancy court gown with tight sleeves, trailing dagged hem, and fur-lined houpellande—and with her hair tucked neatly under a tight cȯif, and not a single jȯwel. "Now we're ready for the field."

She cast a side glance at young Bern, who gazed at her with awe, and smiled. He wouldn't be in such awe if Valeria had been in one of her moods—for it would have been a struggle to take her up; she'd have bated off the fist at least a dozen times before she calmed, and then she'd have snaked her head around like a serpent to avoid the hood. "Time for your catechism," she continued merrily. "What bird is this?"

"A peregrine falcon," Bern said promptly.

"And why is she called a *falcon*?" she asked, wondering how detailed his answer would be.

"Two reasons; first of all, she has long, pointed wings and she waits on up in the air. A hawk has broad, wide wings and hunts from trees or from the fist." He screwed up his face for a moment. "Of course, you can hunt a falcon from the fist too, but she has a better chance at the prey if you put her up so that she can stoop. It's her shape—that and the way she likes to hunt—that makes her a falcon. That's the first reason." He watched her alertly, to see how satisfied she was thus far.

She was quite pleased, actually. "Good, and the second reason?"

"She's a falcon, because she's a girl. The boys

are tiercels." Bern looked pleased with himself at answering the question with *both* correct answers.

"Excellent," Honoria rewarded him, as she gestured to him to follow, and led the way out of the mews. The birds watched with alert interest through the slats of their stalls, and she wondered what was going through their heads. "Now, why am I hunting with a falcon and not a tiercel?"

"Because tiercels are smaller?" Bern hazarded, as Honoria used her free hand to pick up her skirts as they entered the stable-yard. With spring gradually coming on, the stable-yard was a mess of half-frozen mud, and the current fashion of riding habits still had skirts long enough to mire the hem if one wasn't careful.

As if we women hadn't enough to hobble us already, she thought, as she made to answer Bern's reply. "Most falconers do prefer to hunt with the larger falcons, yes," she told him, continuing his education as an austringer, one of the many skills he would need to qualify for knighthood. "Most falconers will also tell you that females are more serious about hunting, as well. They feel that falcons are more determined in a tail-chase, less inclined to let the prey slip."

Bern scratched his shaggy head, looking earnest. "Maybe that's because they have to feed the babies and can't let anything get away?"

Honoria laughed delightedly. "That might be—but it is also possible that most falconers let greed get the better of their judgment, and let slip at game that is too big, too fast, or too difficult for a tiercel. I seldom take a peregrine tiercel at anything larger than teal, and I have seen no difference in attitude between Valeria and Victor. In fact, since Victor is small and more agile, he's better at partridge and wood-dove than Valeria. But today, we hunt duck, and for duck, we need Valeria's weight and strength.''

There were ducks returning form the south in one of the wheat fields below the castle bailey; they were at a disadvantage there, away from water, though there was a cow pond not far away. Honoria was going to take Bern out for his first lesson in hunting where someone would actually *explain* what was going on, and why. The young squire had been on many hunts before this, and had absorbed quite a bit simply by observation, but no one had ever explained what was happening, step by step.

Bern had a spaniel trained to flush on a lead; he would handle the dog today, and Honoria the bird. Tomorrow, or the next day, if ducks were still there, the positions would be reversed.

He would not be flying Valeria, however. He already had success this winter with his own kestrel, or "tower-falcon," a bird he had not trained, but had assisted with training—Honoria would lend him the use of an older, steadier falcon called Melisande, who had none of Valeria's temper. Melisande had once been as highstrung as Valeria, but that had been in her prime

ten years ago, and with age came steadiness and
wisdom the younger falcon lacked. This bird
was unlikely to fly off if her falconer made a
mistake; birds of prey were consummate oppor-
tunists, and an old bird, conditioned by ten easy
years in the mews, would allow herself to be
called in to the lure and a ready meal rather
than seek freedom and uncertain hunting. Melisande had been Honoria's first young peregrine,
taken as a brancher, as Valeria had been last
year.

She and Bern walked obliquely toward the
field; the ducks weren't visible in the snow and
stubble, but if you listened, you could hear the
quacking. She listened carefully, and paused
whenever the quacking sounded a little nervous.
Finally, she signaled to Bern to let the spaniel
loose.

The dog knew the ducks were there; he could
smell them, and had been so eager to hunt he
trembled. Now he went to his belly and crept
toward the field like a slinking cat, getting down-
wind, in position for a good flush.

Honoria slipped off Valeria's hood; the falcon
blinked in the dazzling sunlight, and Honoria
felt her talons tighten on the glove. She untied
the leash from the jesses, and whispered to Bern.

"Now, while the ducks think we can't see
them, we put the falcon up. While she gets
height, the dog creeps in and holds for the
flush."

She loosened her hold on the jesses and gave

her fist an upward shove that signaled to the
falcon she should take to the air. This was a
tense moment; if the ducks saw her and were
spooked, they'd flush early, before she got
proper height for a stoop. If she got anything at
all, she'd have to take it in a tail-chase—always
a dubious proposition with less than even odds
for the falcon.

But the birds didn't flush, and soon Valeria
was just a spot high in the sky, circling
overhead.

Honoria pointed. "There she is—that's called
'waiting-on.' She's waiting for a signal from us,
or for the ducks to flush. We'll try to give her
both at about the same time."

By now the spaniel was in place, on point,
every hair quivering with repressed excitement.
Honoria gave a shrill whistle and waved her
arm.

The spaniel raced through the stubble into the
midst of the feeding ducks, flushing them perfectly; they flew up in all directions, quacking
wildly with confusion and leaving behind a
cloud of feathers and down that floated away
on the breeze.

But Bern's eyes were on the falcon, who fell
from the sky like a thunderbolt, in a perfect
stoop; her wings tucked in close to her body,
her talons pulled in and fisted, her eyes on one
of the ducks among the twenty or so flapping
heavily to gain speed and distance. Some of
them already knew she was coming, and there

was panic in their voices as they rowed the air, trying to find some means of escape.

But for one fat hen, it was already too late.

Valeria closed with the duck with a audible *crack*, like a thrown stone striking a plank. And striking her was just what the falcon had done.

"There!" Honoria cried with satisfaction, as the duck fell, an inert, motionless weight. "The falcon balled up her talons in a fist, and struck the back of the duck's head! That's the best attack with a bird this size. Look, see how she used the attack to bounce up and get more height, in case the duck wasn't stunned or killed and she had to try again?"

Valeria didn't need a second attack this time; at the top of her bounce, she went into a second stoop and followed the duck down to the ground. Honoria and Bern ran toward the place where both had fallen.

As soon as they got her in view, however, Honoria stopped running and motioned to Bern to stop as well. "All right, this is where inexperienced or overexcited falconers lose their birds," she cautioned. Valeria perched atop the duck, her wings spread over her prey, glaring at them. "See how she's mantling? She's protecting her prey from us. It's our job to convince her that we have something for her that's better than what she just killed. We have to reward her both for making the kill and for giving it up to us. Everything we do has to bring a reward for her, or she'll leave us without looking back."

Honoria reached into her game bag and brought out a pigeon breast, fresh and still warm, with feathers and a little blood on the feathers. She slipped it into her gloved fist and held it up, chirruping to her bird; the feathers ruffled in the breeze, catching the falcon's gaze.

Today, all the gods of hunting must have been smiling on her; Valeria loved pigeon, and she hadn't yet tasted or even seen the hot blood of the duck. Without hesitation, she shoved off the duck and made straight for the glove, settling down on it like the lady she was, and contentedly started to tear at the pigeon meat beneath her talons. She spread her wings again and mantled over her meal, protecting it jealously from any potential rivals. As she ate, Honoria tied her jesses to the leash and secured the jesses in her gloved fingers. Only when she was done did Bern run to fetch the duck.

"Lady Honoria!" the squire said, as he walked back with the duck tucked under his arm, his blue eyes round with amazement. "The falcon broke the duck's neck!"

Honoria nodded, flushed with gratification at her bird's success. "That's the best and cleanest sort of kill," she replied with a touch of pardonable pride. "The next best is when they bind to the duck, either on the way down or on the ground and pierce the heart with their talons. That's why the falcon is called 'the bird of the foot,' because they kill with their talons and not their beaks. What would we have done if Valeria hadn't come to me?" Valeria plucked the bit of pigeon daintily, and bits of fluff and feathers flew away in the breeze.

"Uh—make in to her slowly," Bern said, after a moment of hesitation. "If she looked nervous, or like she was about to fly off, we'd go in on hands and knees."

"Or crawl on our bellies if we had to," Honoria reminded him. "Then what?"

"Bring the glove with the pigeon in from behind and coax her up on it, bring it up under her little by little," Bern continued, more sure of himself now. "You'd want to hide the duck while you were offering the pigeon. Only when she was eating the pigeon would you take her up and secure the jesses."

"Because?"

"Because we *never* want to make her think we're taking her dinner away from her. We always want her to remember that we *give* her dinner." Bern was quite sure of himself now, and Honoria was gratified that her lessons were being recited with real feeling, not just by rote.

"Because?" she prompted again, wanting him to be sure of the reasons behind everything she taught him.

"No falcon or hawk is faithful to anything but its best interest," Bern recited confidently. "She can fly away at any time, and will, if she thinks we aren't serving her. The falconer serves the bird, the bird never serves the falconer."

Honoria laughed. "Good—but do you know

what that means?" She motioned to Bern to walk beside her as they made their way back to the castle; she wouldn't hood Valeria until the bird had eaten her fill.

"I do now," the boy replied. "I used to think you could make a friend out of a falcon, like you can a dog, but all they ever really do is tolerate you. Except once in a long while you might get a bird like Freya."

"Once in a lifetime," Honoria corrected. "And then, only if you are very, very lucky. Stick to what is the rule for the whole mews, and continue." *Hope and even pray for a gos like Freya, and dream of one at night. Maybe you'll get one, little fellow.*

"Well, the best you can get is tolerance—a kind of partner, but a partner that is always waiting to see if you're going to do something she doesn't like. If you do, she's going to leave you." Bern sighed, but with a note of exasperation that tickled Honoria. "Just like Sir Gregof's bird did yesterday."

"And what did Sir Gregof do that was wrong?" Honoria knew very well what the knight had done, but she wanted to know if Bern had seen it.

Bern grinned impudently. He could; Gregof wasn't *his* knight. "What *didn't* he do wrong? He didn't wait for the bird to get enough height, he flushed the partridge himself so the poor falcon had a tail-chase, and when the falcon actually caught a partridge, he ran up to it! And since it was a partridge, and small enough to carry, that's what the falcon did; she carried it off, and the last he saw of her was disappearing over the hill with the partridge in her talons."

Oh, excellent; no doubt, he has the eye and the brain to match. "Very good; you caught all of that. Now, what do you think my father's falconer did last night, while Gregof went off in a temper, cursing the bird and the trainer together?" This part Bern hadn't seen, but she wanted to see if he'd intuit it.

"I don't know what Heinrich did, but I know what I'd do," Bern ventured slowly, as they neared the gates of the palace. "I'd follow the falcon, slowly and quietly, until she stopped to eat the partridge. I wouldn't go after her then, because she'd already been offended. I'd let her eat, then I'd mark where she went to roost for the night; she'd want to sleep right away with a full crop, but she'd do it somewhere she felt secure, and she might be nervous without the mews walls around her. In the morning that meal would have worn off, she'd be in a strange place, and I'd come back before dawn with a live pigeon and a trap, but a different trap than the way she was caught before, if she was trapped and not taken from the nest as an eyas."

"Excellent!" Honoria applauded, and clapped the youngster on the back with her free hand, while he grinned up at her, a lock of hair falling impudently over one eye. "Although with a bird as well-trained as one of Heinrich's, a lure and a pigeon wing would probably be enough to get her. In fact, it was; he brought her into the mews just before you arrived this morning."

"And I bet he never lets Sir Gregof fly another royal bird!" Bern grinned.

"Sir Gregof will be fortunate if he is allowed to fly anyone else's mar-hawks," Honoria told him severely. "Unless he comes to Heinrich and agrees to mend his ways, and begs to be taught the proper way to serve a bird."

Bern trudged alongside her for a few more yards, then asked, "But what if he just goes into the mews and takes one?"

Honoria frowned. "He'd better not try," she said with a touch of anger. "I'll horsewhip him out of the mews myself."

The look on Bern's face said that the boy fully believed her—which was just as well, because she *would* do just that, taking full unfair advantage of her sex and position, knowing that as a knight and her inferior, Sir Gregof would not dare to protest, much less strike back. The birds were worth any amount of her own unchivalrous behavior in their defense.

As they gained the hard-packed, icy road, and walked up the aisle of trees toward the palace, Valeria finished the last bit of pigeon, stropping her beak on the glove to clean it. As she settled down and her talons relaxed, Honoria paused a moment to slip the hood over her head. It was a common thing for young knights to gallop their horses wildly up this road, and she didn't want

Valeria to bate in startled surprise if one did come pounding up unexpectedly. The usual guards stood sentry on the outer walls; they were used to seeing Honoria and her "apprentice" coming and going with hawks, and grinned and waved congratulations to her when they saw the day's catch.

Bern handed the duck to the first servant they encountered once past the gate and inside the outer walls; the servant would take it to the kitchen to add to whatever fowl were on the menu for the next meal. Hunting wasn't just for pleasure and sport; hunting put extra provender on the table, especially in winter, when the promise of hospitality brought more mouths to the table. The Crown Prince, Honoria's father, never turned guests away, but also relied somewhat on those guests to repay that hospitality with the results of hunting parties that were as much necessity as recreation.

"All right, Bern, your lesson is over for today; go back to wait on Father while I put Valeria up," Honoria said cheerfully, as they passed the inner walls and into the stable yard. "If tomorrow is as good as today, and the ducks are still there, it will be your turn to take Melisande out to hunt."

"Provided she's in condition and fit," Bern added, quite properly, though it was obvious how excited he was, and how disappointed he'd be if the falcon wasn't fit to fly. "Please, my lady, don't risk Melisande just to keep from disappointing me.''

"If she's not, we'll contrive a substitute," Honoria promised on impulse. "You're ready for your first hunt with a real bird, and you're going to have it while hunting weather still holds. You know, Freya is so steady as long as I'm around, we might even have you hunt with her.''

Bern's eyes lit up at the suggestion of hunting with the famous Freya, but he very properly bowed as he thanked her, rather than hugging her like the child he had been when he first arrived to serve her father. He was growing up; all too soon he'd be made a knight himself, and he'd probably become one of the horde of young men who either disapproved of her "unmaidenly" ways, or tried to court her, or worse, "tame" her. In any case, if that happened, she'd lose a pleasant hunting companion.

Well, at least he'll be a proper falconer; that's something, she consoled herself, as he ran off to find his master. She continued on through the stable yard to the mews, where she opened the door to Valeria's stall, took off and hung up the leash, unhooded her, and left her loose on her perch. If Heinrich, the falconry master, chose to weather her today, he'd come take her up later and fasten her to one of the outdoor perches. She checked to see that Valeria had fresh water in her pan, and left, latching the door behind her.

"What fortune, my lady?" Heinrich asked, as she passed him, hard at work mending a leash in the tiny equipment room at the end of the mews. The room smelled pleasantly—at least to Honoria's nose—of hawk-musk, leather, and neats'-foot oil.

"Valeria took a hen-duck on the first stoop," Honoria replied with another flush of pleasure. "Bern's to take Melisande tomorrow, if the ducks are still there."

"If not—" Heinrich considered for a moment. "I'll salt the field with young doves. They'll give old Melisande a good stoop, and Bern a success for his first hunt."

"Thank you, Heinrich, that is very good of you," Honoria replied warmly. Heinrich didn't often volunteer to sacrifice his doves, for they were too valuable in training, in catching wild birds, and in luring in lost ones. They were special birds, guaranteed to come home to their cote if not caught, swift fliers, and clever for their kind.

"Yon Bern's going to be a good one; worth going to a bit of extra for. Besides, I need to do some weeding out of the last hatch, for some of them aren't up to standard," the old, grizzled master replied gruffly, and Honoria kept her smile to herself. Bern had endeared himself to Heinrich by helping out with some of the less-pleasant tasks of the mews, on the strength of Honoria's assertion that a *real* falconer knew everything there was to know about the care and condition of his birds. When Bern acquired his kestrel, he even took over all of the duties of caring for it, including cleaning its stall. His rank would have excused him from that, but he never once shirked it, and only stopped when Heinrich told him that the youngster had more than proved he knew what he was about, and his master needed his services more than his bird did.

"Do *you* think I should take him straight up to a real game-hawk, and skip the merlins altogether?" she asked the master.

"You know, lady—I think you should. Your instinct has been right with him all along." The old man scratched his bearded chin. "Besides, we haven't got a merlin that hasn't been spoiled by your sisters. They're either too fat, because the silly chits *will* come tidbit them all the time, or too skittish to fly this close to spring." He growled and ground his teeth. "How I'm supposed to keep them in condition to fly and eager to hunt when they're always sneaking bits of chicken heart to them, I'll never know."

She nodded, pleased that he agreed with her judgment, and sighed over her sisters. "I wish someone would give them larks in a cage, or starlings, or something," she replied in answer to his plaint. "They keep thinking the merlins are pets. If mother would let them, they'd have the poor things on perches in the solar and try to stuff them with sugar plums."

"Then screech and faint when they got footed

for their foolishness," Heinrich agreed sourly, then brightened. "Ah, well, soon enough they'll find some other foolishness—and you know, it might be worth my time to catch some young starlings this spring, and give a handsome little male to each one of them!"

Honoria laughed at his changed expression. "That's one of your better thoughts, master falconer! Call them 'dragonfly-falcons' or some other nonsense, or have some of the boys teach them to whistle a roundelay, and they'll be as happy as children with a bright bauble."

"Chances are, they won't even manage to sicken the poor creatures with all their treats," Heinrich replied with content, so pleased with himself that once again, Honoria had to hide her smile. "Never have seen a bird so hard to kill as a starling."

Honoria left him making plans, and went back out into the brilliant sunlight pouring down into the stable yard. She noted little things that probably would have escaped her sisters; the rooks beginning the first courting dances up on the roof tiles, the restive curvetting of a stallion being held for a knight to mount. Spring was coming, and no matter the snow still lying heavily in the fields. Soon it would be time to decide which birds would be intermewed through the summer molt, and which would be released in time to find mates and build nests. Soon there would be nothing to occupy Honoria's time but proper "maidenly" pursuits—

until summer came, and Heinrich found falcon aeries and hawk nests to pick this years' eyases from.

If they could be reached, that is, and if the parent birds didn't defend them too fiercely to be worth the price. *Better two eyes and no eyas,* was Heinrich's philosophy, and Honòria agreed, even as she yearned for a downy eyas to feed and warm. The helpless young babies, with big heads too heavy for their tiny necks, brought out a maternal warmth in her that she took care never to let anyone but Heinrich see.

"Lady Honoria—" The soft, diffident voice broke her out of her thoughts, and she stopped as a very young knight, still in his "maiden" year, approached her. He was new to the court, golden-haired with brilliant blue eyes, and she had to search her memory for a moment before she found his name.

"Sir Gunther?" she replied politely, as he waited for her to respond.

"Lady Honoria, I wondered if—would you permit—that is—" He flushed, and she repressed a sigh. *Oh, Blessed Virgin, another one! Why do they persist in finding me attractive, when that is the last thing I try to be?* But a cynical voice answered the question readily enough. *It's not the lady they find attractive, it's the rank.*

Meanwhile, Sir Gunther managed to find his voice and a few more words. "I am Bern's cousin, and my aunt—that is—"

That put a very different complexion on

things, and Honoria lost her annoyance with
him. "She wants you to keep an eye on him."
Honoria chuckled deep in her throat, relieved
that this time she wasn't going to have to fend
off another would-be admirer. "Would you care
to come along on his hunt tomorrow? Then
you'll be able to tell his mother, and his father,
too, what a fine falconer he's becoming." She
raised an eyebrow at him. "Master Heinrich and
I both believe he's ready to hunt with a peregrine, and we mean to take him up to a game-
hawk in the autumn, one he'll catch and train
himself."

Sir Gunther looked surprised and gratified;
Honoria now saw how like his younger cousin
he was, with the same guileless eyes, rough-
hewn features, and intelligent expression, the
same unruly blond hair. This was the muscular
body that Bern would one day grow into, and
she felt a little elated, and a little sad as she saw
Bern's future in his cousin's face.

"Thank you, Lady Honoria—I hadn't expected that honor," he replied, surprising her
with the honesty she sensed beneath his words.
"I only wanted to learn from his teacher if the
student was progressing. To learn he is doing
so well—that will please his father and mother
very much. And I, I am very happy for him."

He flushed again, and added, "When I was a
squire, the falconry master was as irritable as
one of his goshawks, and my knight never cared
to learn much beyond how to cast a bird up and

how not to flush the prey too early; he left all else to his hired falconers. I am glad Bern has better teachers."

Honoria wanted to laugh, but retained a serious expression, sensing that a laugh would probably hurt this young fellow's feelings past repair. "In that case, I invite you to share your cousin's lessons, provided you pledge me not to be shocked at my unmaidenly joy in the sport."

He hesitated, making Honoria wonder if she had already shocked him, then said, with a little bow of respect, "Your kindness to one of indifferent rank, my lady, only makes me determined that there can be nothing unmaidenly about you, only good will and a true, brave heart. I would gladly join my cousin in his lessons, and I give you my thanks again."

Well! That is the prettiest speech I've ever heard, especially from someone who isn't trying to win my hand! she thought with a sense of shock. From his words, there was no doubt that he must be the younger son of someone no higher in rank than landed knight; he would have no land of his own, nothing but his title and whatever small help his parents could give him. That alone would keep him from turning into a hopeful suitor; he hadn't a hope in the world of aspiring as high as the Crown Prince's eldest daughter. His best chance at fortune was to serve someone like her father, and hope that faithful service or an advantageous marriage would lead to a small manor or minor keep one day. If it did not—he would live and die a bachelor knight, always in the service of some greater lord until he was no longer fit to fight—assuming he survived that long.

"And I thank you, for providing me with a second congenial hunting companion and a willing pupil," she replied warmly, then laughed, now that the laugher would no longer hurt his feelings. "Do believe me, Sir Gunther, there is nothing that pleases the fanatic more than the opportunity to make another such! I look forward to your company at sunrise at the mews on the morrow."

Taking that for the dismissal it was, he bowed himself out of her presence, leaving her feeling far happier and contented with her lot than she had in many a day.

Such high feelings couldn't be maintained, of course, and as soon as she entered the royal suites, a page came to spoil them immediately. "Lady Honoria," the boy said, with a solemn bow all out of keeping with his tender years. "Your father the Prince and your mother the Princess request your presence immediately, in their private chambers.

Translation: Mother and Father are about to lecture me again, she thought bitterly, as her fine feelings flew away. As she handed the boy her cloak to take to her women, she smoothed her skirts and tried to think how she could have outraged their sensibilities this time. *I didn't— despite my lecture to Bern—make in to Valeria on*

*my belly. I didn't kirtle my skirts above my knees.
I'm not wearing breeches beneath my habit, though
without a doubt they'd be warmer than my stockings.
I went to mass before we went out hunting, and I
intend to do the same tomorrow. I haven't cut my
hair since the last time Mother caught me at it.* She
sighed, as she hurried up the stairs to the royal
chambers. There was nothing she could think of,
but without a doubt, there must be *something*
they were annoyed with her about.

She paused for a moment on the landing to
smooth the woolen skirts of her habit with a
nervous gesture, took a deep breath to compose
herself, then stepped into the first room of the
royal suite.

This was the most public of the royal chambers, and the one where the Prince and Princess
most often received visitors informally. Her
mother and father, seated side-by-side at a small
table covered with documents, had been talking
together in low voices, but they stopped as soon
as Honoria entered, turning as one to stare at
her.

Honoria looked into Prince Karl von Hansberg's face and saw her own disconcerting violet
eyes, her own high cheekbones and finely
etched eyebrows, but the face was square-jawed
and unashamedly masculine with no hint of
femininity. From her father, too, came the color
of her hair, a deep sable-black. Sulamith von
Hansberg had contributed her expressive mouth
and the heart shape of her face to her daughter,

and the fine figure that all of her daughters had inherited, but her eyes were an odd and un-canny color of pale gray-blue, and her hair an uncompromising blonde.

Honoria made a brief curtsy, and approached the heavily built wooden table as if there was nothing whatsoever in her mind but greeting her parents. "Bern and I had fine hunting, Fa-ther," she said with forced cheer. "He is learn-ing his craft swiftly. Heinrich and I believe we should take him straight to a game-hawk and skip merlins altogether this season. I venture to say that at the rate he's learning, your squire will be ready for knighthood before he has more than three hairs on his chin."

The Crown Prince had to smile at that, despite the lines of concern about his eyes and the faint crease between his brows. "I am pleased to hear you recommend him as highly as his other mas-ters, daughter," he replied, as the Princess com-pressed her lips in silent disapproval. "But I did not ask you here to discuss my squire. Please—" he gestured to a low-backed chair placed slightly to the side of the table. "Sit."

Oh, dear. She took the chair and sank into it with a further lowering of spirits.

"Honoria. . . ." Her father paused for a mo-ment, looking not at her, but at the documents before him, as if searching them for the words he needed. "Honoria, I have gotten a very gen-erous marriage proposal for your youngest sis-ter, Theresa. I intend to accept it; the betrothal ceremony will take place after Eastertide, and the wedding next year."

For a moment, Honoria could feel nothing but a rush of relief. *Not me! Thank you, Jesu, it was not for me!* Not that her father would force her, for he had pledged never to do so, but rejecting yet another proposal would result in weeks of tears, recriminations, and attempts to change her mind. Sulamith took her daughter's refusal to wed as a personal affront and an unmitigated disaster.

But her father wasn't done, not by any stretch of the imagination. "Honoria," he continued, earnestly, "*All* of your sisters are betrothed now. You are the only one of my daughters un-pledged. It isn't fitting that they be wedded be-fore your future is decided. It goes against all custom, and the Court will be appalled."

I want my future to be just as my past has been! "But it is not counter to law, Father," Honoria replied, as firmly as she dared. "The law says nothing of what order the daughters must be wed in, and customs are wont to change. The Court will manage to survive being appalled, I am sure."

The Princess made a choking sound, and put a silken kerchief to her lips.

"Honoria, we have been patient, your mother and I," her father said, for the first time with a hint of annoyance in his voice, and a stubborn expression on his face that Honoria recognized. He probably recognized it, too, because she was, doubtless, wearing it herself. In a battle of wills between Honoria and the Prince of Hansberg, the Prince had all the advantages. "I think we have been patient long enough. It is time for you to make a decision: I will not permit custom to be outraged, and my family to become the source of court gossip from here to the Rhine. I swore I would never force you to wed, and I never shall—but I *can* and *will* give you a choice and insist that you make it."

Honoria felt cold at her heart, as if she had suddenly gotten a lump of stone there instead of a warm and beating organ, and clenched her hands in her lap to still their shaking. She knew the look her father was wearing; he was the sole authority in this corner of the Empire, the Crown Prince, and he could not be persuaded in this mood, for he felt he was making a decision for the good of Family and Principality.

"I will even give you time to make that decision," he continued implacably, as the cold seeped from Honoria's heart into the rest of her body. "It is only proper for the length of a year fall between Theresa's betrothal and her marriage, for she is still barely twelve summers old. I would not send her to her bridegroom before that time, and no one would fault me for being too reluctant a father to release my daughter before then. But the rest of your sisters are fully ready to be wed, indeed are quite impatient to become brides, and I intend either a triple, or quadruple marriage take place so that all my daughters may be satisfied at once. Therefore, I give you until autumn to decide: either to wed, or to enter the Church."

The ax had fallen, and Honoria restrained the impulse that urged her hands toward her throat, to see if her head still remained on her neck. Now she knew why her mother so often made that choking sound when she was overcome with emotion. "And just who am I to wed, if you are not to be forsworn, Father?" she asked dryly, wondering how she managed to sound calm and sane even as she spoke the words. "I assume you have some ready candidate standing by. How is it that this does not negate your promise to me?"

"That is *your* choice, Honoria." This time it was her mother who spoke, her voice tight with anger. The Princess had never understood her eldest daughter, and saw Honoria's refusal to wed as a personal affront. "You have had several proposals; pick one of them. Pick one of your father's nobles, Pick a simple knight, for Jesu's sake! But pick *someone*, or pick the Church. That is more choice than any maiden has ever had since the world began!" She looked for a moment as if she had a great deal more to say, but something changed her mind as her husband patted her hand absently, and she fell silent.

"Remember Prince Siegfried—when you attended his birthday fête with your brother—"

her father began. "You said you found Siegfried congenial—"

"Prince Siegfried wedded Queen Odette just before his coronation," Honoria replied calmly, and with irrefutable logic. "The invitation to the wedding came before Christmastide; I sent a pair of merlins as my gift. Besides, he never had any intention of asking for any of us, that was plain from the moment we arrived."

That wasn't quite true, but Honoria had known before the birthday feast that Siegfried had found his bride—and it wasn't one of the six invited as his guests. Several of the other girls had been surprised, but not Honoria.

"I only meant that there has been, in the past, at least one possible suitor you found acceptable," the Princess continued, as if she had not interrupted, though the Princess made a hard, thin line of her lips. "What about his friend, Count Benno? You had good things to say about him! Should I send an invitation to him to pay court to you?"

Benno, who was too afraid of Freya even to stand near her? Oh, indeed. But at least here, again, she had a perfectly reasonable answer for him. "Count Benno is said to be courting King Siegfried's sorceress, Odile. I do not think it would be a good idea to interfere in that situation. It is not wise to anger a magician."

"No, indeed—" It was the Prince's turn to blanch at the thought. There were far, far too many examples of what happened when one did anger a sorcerer, examples proving that death was *not* the worst fate in the world. For that matter, one didn't even need to anger a sorcerer to suffer damage; one only needed to be in the way, as Queen Clothilde had discovered a split second before a large piece of her palace fell on her.

The Princess broke in angrily. "Siegfried, Benno, what does it matter? Make a choice, daughter! You have a wealth of young men to choose from, or, if you choose to take vows, the certainty of becoming an Abbess before your hair turns silver! Just *choose*."

Honoria stood up, prodded to anger that matched her mother's; she felt her face flush, and she clenched her fists at her side. This was so entirely *unfair*! "Yes, and this is a hair-splitting *choice* to give me, that skirts the vow that you would not force me to wed against my will! Either I must be walled up in a cloister, or I must tie myself to a man who may take as much of my freedom as any Holy Order would!"

Her father, ever the peacemaker, stood up as well, making soothing motions with his hands. "Honoria, I will honor *any* choice of man you make, no matter how lowly born. You have the time; *find* a husband who is exactly to your liking. Wed old Heinrich, if you will, for surely *there* is a man to match your mind!"

Honoria choked back a hysterical laugh at the idea of proposing marriage to Heinrich; her mother just choked. *Jesu! I can just imagine Hein-*

rich's face! It would almost be worth it, just for the sight! And as for Mother's face if I agreed to the notion—the temptation is almost too much!

Having cooled the anger of both women, the Prince sat back down. "I do not expect you to wed Heinrich, unless that truly is your will, Honoria. I only suggest it as an example, that you may choose anyone. If you take a man of lower birth than yours, you are like to find that he is so bemused by his elevation and grateful to you for it, that you are free to act as you choose."

Or more like to find myself beaten into submission. But her father was right, it was more likely that she could continue the life she'd enjoyed until now if she chose a man beneath her. He might even be willing to be led by her. . . .

Until I am with child, that is, she thought bleakly, following the path of logic to its end. *How much hunting may I do heavy with babe? And that assumes I shall survive motherhood. There is more to marriage than the simple acquisition of a husband, and how am I to keep him from my bed when he demands his rights there?*

But the other prospect, of taking Holy Vows, was even less appealing. *A year as a novice, another as a postulant, and how long as a sister before I have the right to fly a bird again? And even then, by canon law it can be nothing more than a merlin, and only if the Mother Superior deems it allowable. I would not dare flaunt the law until I became Abbess,*

*and how long would that take? Nuns live forever, it
seems, and Holy Mothers longer than that!*

"I have only one request, child," the Prince
said plaintively into the silence. "Should you
choose a peasant, *at least* let it be a man who
has performed such a deed of valor that I may
knight him."

The Princess choked again, her face entirely
hidden in her silk kerchief. *Evidently Mother does
not approve of Father's liberal-mindedness.*

Honoria clenched her teeth, but steeled herself
to make a civil reply. "Then I will obey your
orders, Father, hard though it goes with me. I
will not have it said that I did not know my
duty."

She rose from her chair, made the briefest of
curtsies, and left the room. She went straight
to the stables, so blind with mingled anger and
despair that she hardly knew where she was
going and did not remember asking for her
horse, nor mounting it. She only came to herself
again when she was on the road, away from the
palace, galloping her hunter as recklessly as any
of the young knights she had mentally chided
for the same reckless behavior this morning.

As soon as she realized what she was doing,
she reined the gelding in; this was no surface to
gallop on, and it was not the fault of the horse
that this had happened. "Sorry, Odo," she told
him, patting his neck as she pulled him to a
sedate walk, and relieved to see that he was no
more than damp. "It would be a worse ending

to a bad situation if I made you break a leg with
my carelessness."

She did not have the same feeling for horses
that she had for the birds, but she still felt more
of a kinship with any four-footed creature than
she did with their masters. "It is too bad that I
cannot have a would-be husband gelded," she
said aloud, since there was no one to hear her
make such shocking statements. "Then I could
wed with no fear of losing my freedom."

There, after all, was the rub—the loss of freedom to do exactly as she wished, within bounds
that were reasonable, and without having to
consider the desires or well-being of anyone except herself. Yes, she had taken responsibility
for young Bern's education, but she had done
that because she *wished* to, and because she was
willing to accept the constraints that came with
it. The Church would impose its rules on her—
rules so restrictive that she did not even for a
moment consider taking vows. *Sweet Jesu, in my
novice and postulant years, I would not even be able
to see the sky except when I passed from cloister to
chapel and back!* The very notion of such con-
finement gave her horrors—like the nightmare
in which she found herself close-confined in a
tiny room, with no doors and no windows.

So the only other choice was marriage. Which
was no choice at all.

Hot tears coursed down her cheeks, and with
no one to see or comment on them, she let them;
she didn't even bother wiping them away. Let

the chill breeze dry them on her cheeks and leave them chapped and unsightly; why should she make herself look attractive to a would-be husband she didn't want? That they were tears as much of anger as of sorrow didn't really matter at this point, for there was nothing she could do to change the cause of either.

She could only ride, ride until she regained control of herself, until the ache in her stomach eased and the burning resentment subsided a little, until solitude and the spring sunshine helped her find her composure again. Only then did she turn Odo and ride back to the palace.

She spent the afternoon in complete and defiant rebellion; not merely wearing her oldest and shabbiest clothing, but instead of wearing a gown, donning her brother's outgrown breeches and hose, tunic and leather vest. The last time she had dared to wear this combination, the Princess had spent an entire day closeted in her bedroom having hysterics, and another day alternately lecturing Honoria and weeping over her.

But there was no other set of clothing so suited to the dirty, ugly work of cleaning the mews and all her hawk furniture of the inevitable grime of a full season of successful hunting.

She didn't actually clean the entire mews, only the stalls of her particular birds: Victor, Valeria, and Melisande, her lovely peregrines; Freya, her remarkable goshawk; Regina, the stately gyrfalcon; Ares and Athena, high-strung merlins; and Johanna, her temperamental kestrel. Kestrels were also known as "tower-falcons," and were particularly suited for an afternoon of exciting flying when there was no real need to supplement the pantry. Fearless and fiery, they wrought great havoc among the sparrows who nested in each and every available chink of tower walls, and were useful for thinning the little pests out.

That made eight stalls to clean out; the usual way was to move each bird in turn to the weathering yard, rake the gravel of the stall until there was no sign of feathers, furs, mutes or castings, sweep out the feathers, fur and castings she'd raked out of the gravel, then scrape down the walls and the slats of the windows until they were clean as well. All the old perches and blocks would come out, to be returned to the equipment room for refurbishing, and she would replace them with new perches and a new, clean block from Heinrich's stores. It was vital to the hawk's health to perform this chore before the weather really warmed; infection, particularly bumble-foot, was a real danger if the stall wasn't cleaned of winter's detritus. It was easy to overlook a bit of food cached somewhere, or scraps of flesh mingled with the gravel, but once warm weather arrived, those were potential sources of foul smells and fever.

In Heinrich's estimation, a good falconer never left this to an underling unless he was so pressed by his other duties for time that he could not manage to squeeze in the few hours that it required. Much could be intuited of the health of one's bird from the state of her stall, and the remains of past dinners—eaten and un-eaten—and the products of digestion—cast from both ends. A *truly* good falconer also went into the stall several times a day during the molt, and gathered up primaries, secondaries, and tail feathers as they were shed. Not for frivolous use like hat trimming, but in case the bird broke one of those all-important feathers in the course of hunting; one of the old ones could be spliced, or "imped," to the stub of the broken one.

A hawk's weapon is her talons, but her life is her feathers. That was what Heinrich said, and it was true that a falcon could not hunt successfully without her full complement of primary feathers. A hawk was a little sturdier, however; because of the nature of the way she hunted among the trees and brush, and those wide wings, she could tolerate loss of a primary or two with no significant loss of hunting ability.

Perhaps that's another reason why I enjoy hunting Freya, Honoria thought, as she cleaned the last stall of all—the goshawk's. *She isn't so fragile.*

She installed the iron bow-perch wrapped with heavy rope in the center of the stall, replacing the old one that she had pulled up and carried out. Hawks used bow-perches, shaped like a strung hunting bow, rather than block-perches, which were short, round columns of wood with spikes on the bottom to push into the ground. Bow-perches replicated the hawk's chosen tree limbs and the rope wrapped tightly around them gave the talons purchase and grip, while the block-perches with leather tops simulated the rock ledges and protruding boulders of a falcon's cliff. With a sense of weary satisfaction, she pushed the spikes on either end of the bow deeply into the gravel and down to the earth beneath it with her foot, setting it securely so that it wouldn't wobble when Freya pushed off or landed on it. Then she went out into the last light of sunset to bring Freya out of the weathering yard, an area enclosed by a sturdy fence, where hawks and falcons could be tethered by their leashes to a perch and left to sunbathe or observe what went on around them. They needed to spend at least part of each day in the sun for the sake of their health, and if they didn't get it in hunting, they had to be out in the yard.

She took up the gos with no fear that Freya would bate; as always, the goshawk stepped up onto the gloved hand pushed against the back of her legs with perfect manners. Honoria pushed her free hand up under the soft breast feathers and scratched gently under Freya's wings; she could have sworn that the hawk sighed with pleasure at the caress.

She brought Freya into the mews and placed her on one of the wall-mounted perches mounted in the corners at breast height, rather than on the more exposed bow-perch in the middle. She knew Freya's habits after two years of working with her, and knew that the gos preferred a higher, more enclosed perch for sleeping.

Freya stepped down onto the perch with the same calm demeanor that she had shown in the yard. Honoria looked deeply into her strange, red eyes, and wondered how they managed to appear so thoughtful, when every other gos she'd ever seen looked angry, half-crazed, or both. The red or yellow-red color of an accipitor's eyes added to that impression of insanity or fury, of course; the huge, darker eyes of a falcon looked positively innocent and endearing by comparison. But Freya had never been the same as other goshawks, not since the moment the net had snapped down over her.

"Oh, Freya," Honoria sighed out loud, as the gos scratched her head with a foot, then stretched out right leg and right wing at the same time. "How I wish I could trade places with you. Even kept in a mews, you have more freedom than I."

She had never made so fervent a wish, or so sincere. But she hardly expected the gos to reply.

"Are you quite certain you mean that, my dear?"

The voice startled her; she glanced all around to see who could have come into the mews unnoticed, but there was no one there.

"Of course there's no one there; I was the one talking to you."

The voice was female, and entirely unfamiliar; it was with a sense of dislocation and entire disbelief that Honoria turned back to look at her goshawk.

Freya watched her with her head turned entirely upside-down; the position a raptor took when she wanted to get a really good look at something (not potential prey) that interested her.

"I must be going mad," she said, half to herself. "They've finally driven me mad."

"I assure you, you are as sane as I am." The hawk righted her head and opened her beak, like a human laughing silently. *"You are certainly aware that I'm abnormally sane for a goshawk, so that means both of us are clear-headed."*

At Prince Siegfried's fete, Honoria had brushed up against magic at work, powerful magic; she had seen it with her own eyes. Perhaps that made her readier to believe that magic *could* be at work here, magic or a miracle or both, and less inclined to run screaming of demons to the Royal Priest. "Why are you talking to me?" she breathed, drawing nearer to the bird, hardly daring to think she'd get a reply.

"You're taking this all very well, my dear. It's making things much easier that you're being so calm."

"Why shouldn't I be calm?" Honoria retorted. "It isn't going to *help* me to run away hysterically, not when you've just offered me a way to escape! But why? And why now?"

"Because you wished to trade places with me." Freya shook her head violently to dislodge a bit of fluff. *"You can, you know. Trade places with me, that is. But you'd better be certain that it's what you really want, because you'll be a goshawk for a very long time."*

"How long?" Honoria didn't question the truth of the promise; if she was dreaming all this, she'd awaken soon enough, and if there was any chance at all this was *real*, she was not going to chance losing this unlooked-for gift of Heaven! If Honoria had been granted a true miracle, surely *this* was the one she could have chosen!

"Thirty years. That's the duration of the spell. Then you either find someone who wishes she could trade places with you, and says so aloud, or you die a goshawk, and the spell dies with you." Freya cocked her head to one side. *"Actually, any time during the thirty years, you can try to find someone to trade, but the spell will only work on Walpurgis Night—May Eve. In the thirtieth year, it will work for the three days of every full moon."*

This was awfully detailed information for a hawk to be carrying around! "How do you know that?"

"Would you go light a lantern?" Freya said instead. *"It's getting too dark in here to stay awake properly."*

Hawks tended to fall asleep as soon as darkness fell, and Honoria did not wish the possible bearer of salvation to doze off. As Honoria hur-

ried out to the equipment room to fetch a lantern and light it at the one always kept burning
there, she realized that she wasn't actually hearing a *voice* when Freya spoke. She returned with
more questions—which Freya answered before
she even entered the stall.

*"I'm hearing your thoughts, of course, silly
goose."* The hawk was clearly amused. *"It comes
as part of the spell. Very convenient, knowing what's
happening even when you're hooded."*

Honoria brought the lantern into the stall and
set it carefully on the gravel; Freya, however,
was not going to wait for spoken questions.
Now that she'd started talking, it seemed that
she very much enjoyed having someone to
listen!

*"Let me tell you what you want to know, as
quickly as I can, before your parents send a page to
drag you in to dinner. I don't know who first set
this spell, but I know why—it was a girl who loved
freedom and falconry and hated the kind of life she
led as a human female. Like you, I suspect she must
have faced a coming situation that for her was un-
bearable. I think she might have found a powerful
sorcerer to change her shape for her, but she wanted
a chance to be a human again if she changed her
mind. So that was the 'escape' set into the spell—on
any Walpurgis Night, or on the night of every full
moon in the thirtieth year, if she wanted to resume
the life of a human woman, she needed to find a
human who wanted the same kind of freedom a hawk
has."* Freya gazed up at her with unblinking

eyes; shadows moved as the candle in the lantern flickers. *"Remember, before you say anything, what that also means. Freedom to starve or freeze to death in the winter, to be shot by a hunter or killed by an owl or an eagle, freedom to be crippled in an accident and die slowly and in great pain. There is an everyday price as well; you will have to hunt for your food unless you allow yourself to be taken by a falconer, and not all mews are as well-run as Heinrich's. You will have to protect yourself from other predators, and endure the long cold and scant food every winter. Unless you find it, you will have no shelter for the worst weather, and no escape from the heat of high summer. For everything there is a cost— that's the cost of this trade. And the final cost, if you change your mind and can't find someone to trade with, you die at the end of thirty years, as a hawk, unshriven and unmourned."*

"I could die in two years in childbed," Honoria replied impatiently. "I could die tomorrow from a fall from my horse. What odds is it? Thirty years is as much as most *humans* get. If you can read my thoughts, you *know* the ultimatum my parents have presented me with."

"That was why I spoke." Again, the beak opened in a silent laugh. *"But I had already guessed you would be likely to make that wish the moment I decided to let you trap me. At least four girls before me have thought the bargain worth the risk; my predecessor told me everything I just told you. Thirty years ago, I was just like you, but with less choice of spouse. My parents chose a man for*

me—a feeble, sickly old man, quite old enough to be my grandfather, and entirely insistent that once I was his wife, I give up all my frivolous pursuits to make his life comfortable. I was intended, not to be the bearer of his children, but to be his nursemaid, constant companion, and silent helper, destined to see no more of the out-of-doors than I could through a window until he finally died. Which promised to take years, for he had already worn out two such wives with his care."

Honoria could imagine it all too easily, and shuddered. "I'd have thrown myself off the tower, first." ·

"Believe me, I considered it. It wasn't an intermewed gos that spoke to me, it was a free bird circling the tower, who came to land beside me to make her offer." Freya looked away for a moment. *"That might have been why I was so willing to accept it—having a goshawk land on the parapet next to you and begin a conversation in the moment of your greatest despair is magical enough to make one believe in anything."*

Honoria almost laughed. "I can see that. But what had *she* been flying from?"

"A family in disgrace; her choice had been to take vows, which her predecessor found perfectly acceptable, as she found caring for an old man an acceptable alternative to living out her last year of life as a gos. She, with twenty-nine years of freedom behind her, was willing to gamble on outliving him. I wasn't." If there was ever a shrug in someone's voice, there was one in Freya's. *"What one of us finds*

intolerable, another finds acceptable, you see, especially after having had a full measure of freedom already. But before you agree—you must carefully consider the bargain. You could have a perfectly reasonable life as someone's spouse, the lady to a young man who worships you at this very moment. I'm speaking specifically of Sir Gunther."

"What?" Honoria shook her head, thinking she hadn't heard correctly.

"Child, the silly boy is head-over-heels in love with you. He'd do and accept anything you asked him to! Well, almost anything; you'd still have to be a wife to him."

"Yes, and just how free would I be producing babe after babe like a milch cow?" Honoria snapped. "I don't care if he's in love with me, I certainly don't love him, and that would be the *only* thing that would reconcile me to wedding *anyone!*" She shuddered, thinking of all the women she'd seen, suffering through childbirth and dying of it. The only difference between a lady and a peasant was that the lady wouldn't be worn out with work *and* bearing babies year after year—a lady could hand the babies over to nursemaids once they were born. But there were at least six months of every year when she would be forbidden to ride, hunt, walk for miles—all things Honoria loved.

The hawk sighed. *"You see what I mean? Wedding a handsome fellow like Gunther is perfectly acceptable to me, but not to you. That's why I chose you and let you catch me. I failed twice before; the girls gave in and married the lad their parents chose. They never said* I'd *give anything to trade places with you. You, on the other hand . . . well, you've got more spirit and more determination than they did. And I am very fond of Gunther. He's been making calf's-eyes at you ever since he arrived. I think he's been in love with you for the last year, though he's far too aware of his lowly status to ever betray himself to you."* Amusement tinged the hawk's thoughts. *"You aren't the only one to come to the mews and pour out sorrows to a bird; I've heard as many sad tales from him as I have from you. The fact that I'm your bird made it all the more romantic in his eyes, I suppose."*

"You've tried this twice before?" To her mind, that was far more important than Gunther's misplaced affections. Evidently, although this gift had literally dropped into her lap from Honoria's point of view, from Freya's, it had not come easily. Somehow that made it easier to believe in.

"Twice before, yes, but don't think you're my only chance." The hawk snapped her beak. *"If you don't free me, I can free myself, and will, and I still have eleven months of my last year to find someone else."*

But Honoria's mind was already leaping ahead. "It's three days until the first night of the full moon—how do we do this thing?"

"It's absurdly simple; we go where the moonlight falls on both of us, and truly desire with all our hearts to exchange places. That's all." The hawk

ducked her head. *"Well, not* quite *all. You'll have to get used to the hawk's body, and that won't be easy, but I can help you there. I won't set you free until you think you're ready."*

Honoria snorted in a way that would have made her mother blanch. "I'm ready *now*," she said. "Just wait and see."

After all, I've flown hawks and falcons most of my life, she thought. *I know everything there is to know about them. How hard can it be to become one?*

Three days later, just after sunset, Honoria slipped out of the palace and into the mews, still wearing the gown she'd worn to dinner, but with a gauntlet protecting her hand. She didn't risk taking a lantern, but went straight to Freya's stall, making plenty of noise in walking so that the bird would hear her coming.

"Here I am," she whispered, letting herself into the stall, and peering through the gloom for the bird.

"And I'm on the bow-perch," came the reply. *"Are you still quite sure you want to do this?"*

"Never more certain than now," Honoria replied firmly, stooping down to put her gauntlet under the bird, and feeling her step up onto it. She automatically took up the jesses as well, then started to release them.

"No, hold onto the jesses; the exchange is going to be a bit of a shock. You're better off to hold tightly, as if you expected me to bate, so that when you become me, you'll be the one held securely." That only

comforted her more; it didn't seem that Freya intended to deceive her in any way.

"The moon will rise soon after sunset," Honoria told her, as she used her free hand to feel along the wall to keep from walking into it in the dark. "I think it should be safe enough to just go out into the stable yard."

"Good." The hawk's talons relaxed a little as Honoria reached the door of the mews and stepped outside. The stable yard was deserted, with everyone inside the palace, at duties, or eating. As they waited for the moon to show itself above the outer walls, Honoria wondered what it was going to be like to see the world with a hawk's eyes.

The barest sliver of silver slid into view, and Honoria, remembering what Freya had told her, began to wish with all her heart and mind that *she* could be the hawk she held, that *she* could be the one to soar on wide wings, and look down on the poor, land-bound humans below, that—

A fist of darkness closed around her and squeezed all the breath out of her, squeezed hard enough to shatter every bone in her body. She tried to scream, and couldn't. Then she *could,* and her voice echoed maddeningly in the dark void all around her.

I can't see! I can't see! Desperately, she flailed around to try and touch the mews wall, and instead, found herself falling, then something grabbed at both her ankles and jerked at her—

Blind, terrified, and swinging upside-down from her ankles, Honoria flailed her arms wildly and gasped for breath.

"Gently, child, gently—you've just bated off the fist, I've got you by the jesses!" The voice was strange, full of harmonics and resonances Honoria had never heard in a human voice before, but there was no doubt of the amusement in it. "You're a hawk now, dear—you can't see, because hawks *don't* see well at night."

With a supreme effort of will, Honoria stopped thrashing; a giant hand supported her beneath her breastbone and placed her upright. Reflexively, her feet clenched the surface below her with desperate strength. She turned her head wildly around, and made out nothing more than a huge shadow beside her, vaguely human-shaped, an enormous space that could have been the stable yard, and black walls with a dim sphere rising above them. For her, there was no more light than on a night with a bare quarter-moon.

"Dear, *please* relax your grip—you can crush a rabbit's skull with those talons, and you're not far from piercing my hand!"

Sorry. With another effort of will, Honoria somehow told her feet to let go a little, and the voice sighed. "I have a great deal of advantage over you, I'm afraid. I still remember what it was like to be a human, but you have *never* been a hawk before. I did warn you it was going to be a shock."

Honoria bobbed her head, and the voice chuckled. "Let me get you back into the mews and on your perch—oh, and get you some light. We need to make some plans.

Plans? What for? She felt her bearer start to move, and her body made clumsy little adjustments to the movement. When the woman finally brought her into some light, the lantern in the mews workroom, it was with great relief that Honoria *saw* that the exchange had, indeed, taken place. The person beside her was—herself; odd from this perspective, and strangely colored. *Can a hawk see colors that a human can't?* She certainly didn't recall her face being so bluish. Nor so—gentle.

The woman lit a lantern and brought it with her; for her part, Honoria now experienced something else to unsettle her. From her point of view, she was balanced on a very small "platform," the platform was moving, and it was an awfully long way to the ground!

"Relax. Don't think about it. Your feet know what to do," the woman assured her. "If you relax, your feet will actually lock in place. That's why it's so hard to pry a hawk's talons off of something."

By this time, they had reached Freya's stall; the woman stooped down to the bow-perch near the floor. Instead of putting the perch behind her legs, she showed it to Honoria, who gingerly loosed one foot, transferred her grip from the glove to the perch, then did the same with the other foot. It was very good to feel the rough rope under her feet, and the firm iron beneath it.

The woman sat down on the gravel facing Honoria, with no more care for the gown than Honoria would have shown. "By now you've surely realized that you don't know how to do *anything* as a hawk. You can't even walk yet, much less fly or hunt. We have to have an excuse for *why* you're in this state, or Heinrich is going to think something very peculiar is going on. We don't want that; we particularly don't want him thinking that you have to be destroyed."

Immediately, Honoria realized that she was right, and felt incredibly stupid that *she* hadn't figured that out for herself.

"Don't feel stupid, you've never done this before," the woman said with a laugh. "I have; it's part of the bargain for the last one transformed to help the next one. I think what we should do is this—when I come into the mews tomorrow, you drop off the perch onto the ground, just as if you'd been struck down."

I can certainly do that, anyway, Honoria thought ruefully.

"I'll act as if you've had a fit, and call Heinrich. Goshhawks *do* have fits, sometimes; you flop around and shiver, to make it look realistic. I'll insist on nursing you myself, and take you up to the bedchamber. And by the way, thank you for taking me all over the palace yesterday, otherwise I'd have to find someone to show me the way tonight without arousing more suspicion!" The woman who had been Freya was enjoying herself immensely, from the sound of her voice. And now that she was getting used to things, Honoria was beginning to enjoy herself, too.

"At any rate, I'll keep you up there in a basket by the fire for a couple of days, then bring you back down to the mews—recovered from the fit, but not what it did to you, do you see? We'll have the reason why you have to learn how to fly and hunt all over again." Now, instead of amusement, Honoria heard sympathy, and saw it in the woman's eyes as well. "I promised you that I would see you through all of this, and it won't be as hard as you think." She reached her hand forward, and scratched under Honoria's wings—Honoria was astonished at how good it felt. "I'd better get back before I'm missed. Remember what to do in the morning."

She left and took the light with her, but as she had promised, the more Honoria relaxed, the steadier she felt on her perch. In a far shorter time than she would have thought, she was asleep.

It was in sleep that she learned the last of the spell-gifts; all of the memories of flight and hunt as experienced by all the women to wear this body. These were purely *hawk* dreams, no thoughts from the women intruded. Flying dreams kept her enraptured all night long, as she read the wind, the updrafts and crosswinds, and angled her wings to take proper advantage of them. She felt the adjustments of each feather as she guided her path; reached with feet instead of hands when she meant to grasp, adjusted her body moment by moment as a branch or glove moved under her. She understood what it meant to pursue quarry, and to wrench herself around in mid-stoop to adjust for the evasive gyrations of her prey. And when dawn arrived, and with it wakefulness, for a moment she despaired of actually *mastering* all of it.

But soon after dawn, Freya arrived, and their ruse took shape without a hitch. Heinrich held her quivering body and peered at her with a frown of anxiety as he examined her, but showed no sign of guessing that her fit was only feigned.

"Warmth's the best cure, if there's a cure to be had, my lady," he said, finally, shaking his head in despair. "I cannot promise a cure, though. She's bad, very bad; I've seen fits like this take a hawk off."

"If warmth and nursing care are what she needs, I'll see to it myself, Heinrich," the woman said firmly, and took Honoria back from the falconry master. "Can you please see to the rest of my birds? I—" her voice broke a little, and Honoria marveled at her ability to feign upset. "She's always been so special—"

"Have no fear, I'll see to your birds, and to young Bern and Gunther as well; do you concentrate on her." Heinrich, greatly daring,

reached out and patted her arm awkwardly.
"Now, you take her up, and put her by the fire.
If anyone can bring her back, it'll be you."

Cradling Honoria like a baby, the woman carried her off, her body shaking with suppressed
laughter. It was only when Honoria was tucked
comfortably into a basket beside the fire in what
had been her old bedchamber that the woman
gave vent to that laughter.

"Oh, that was well done, child!" she chuckled.
"I could not have managed that 'fit' better
myself!"

*It's a lot easier to flop around than try and manage
anything like control at this point,* Honoria thought
wryly, wondering if the woman could hear her
thoughts as she had heard Freya's.

"Don't worry; you'll have control soon
enough," Freya soothed. "If you slept last night,
you found out that you've got the memories of
your predecessors in your dreams. The best
thing you can do at the moment is sleep as
much as you can. With every dream, you'll have
better control over your body, and in two days
you'll be able to manage the same kind of short
flights as a brancher."

If a hawk could have groaned, Honoria would
have; this was certainly *not* what she had imag-
ined her life as a hawk would be!

Freya *tsk*ed, and wagged a finger at her. "Patience and practice, my child! You'll need plenty
of both! Now sleep, while *I* get used to being a
woman again." Another chuckle as she stood

up. "This little bout of nursing and isolation is going to serve both of us well, I think." Honoria looked up, as Freya took off the coif she had always worn, and frowned at the uneven mass of her hair. "What did you do to yourself? Hack this off with a hunting knife?"

Well, yes. Honoria gave her the same defiant look she'd given her mother at the time. *It was in the way.*

Freya shook her head and smiled. "Well, I think this exchange is going to have an entirely unexpected and gratifying result for your parents."

Which is?

"Your mother will probably *not* die of apoplectic embarrassment after all."

For two days, Freya pretended to nurse Honoria, banishing all maidservants from the room on the grounds that her goshawk needed absolute quiet. Meals came up on trays, and Freya reacquainted herself with eating human-style, as Honoria learned to hold meat in her talons and tear at it like a hawk. There wasn't a great deal of "taste" in her tongue; most of it came from the back of the tongue and the throat, and not nearly as much as with a human. To her surprise, for she had expected feeding to revolt her, she found the taste of hot, fresh-killed flesh intoxicated her. Longer-dead meat was good, but not as pleasurable. And she didn't at all mind eating the bits of fur and bone she knew she had to have to keep healthy; it didn't taste of much, and the texture wasn't in her throat long enough to bother her. It was a little odd to feel the sense of "fullness" from just below her throat, in her crop rather than her stomach, but she got used to that as well. What was harder to get used to was not being able to smell anything; her nostrils only felt the chill of the air that came into them.

"I'd forgotten how many scents there were in the world," Freya said, burying her face in a bouquet of flowers "someone" had left anonymously on the tray. She looked like a cat drunk on catnip. "Oh, how I love the early spring flowers!"

Honoria turned her head upside down to look more closely at the flowers; there were more colors there than she remembered seeing in flowers, and she was coming to the conclusion that a hawk *did* see more colors than a human.

The hawk's acuity of vision came as something of a shock, too; it was one thing to be aware that a hawk had particularly sharp sight, it was quite another to experience it. She saw every thread in a gown from across the room, every vein in the petals of a tiny spring blossom, every shadowed crevice in every stone of the window frame. Movement in particular caught her attention; there was a mouse hole just under the great wardrobe chest in the corner, and every so often, a mouse would venture to stick a whisker just outside it. Presumably the mice smelled *her*, and instinct warned them that there was something in the room that would gladly eat them. But every time there was a hint of movement under the wardrobe, Honoria's attention snapped to it.

Both of them practiced walking; Honoria practiced both the dignified stalk and the ungainly waddle-hop with half-spread wings. Freya practiced the management of gowns with trailing hems. Both of them were doing better than they had thought they would.

Freya was also doing something else; she was changing the way she—or rather Honoria—had always looked. All of the gowns came out of the wardrobe; those that needed mending or cleaning were left out with the empty trays for the servants to fix. She took scissors and evened off her hair, then—slowly and clumsily at first, but with greater and greater deftness as time went on—she arranged it in various styles, trying out which ones suited the relatively short hair. Even trimmed, it still fell to the bottom of her shoulder blades, although most grown women boasted plaits that descended to the floor.

You look very nice, Honoria observed absently, as Freya walked gracefully back and forth across the floor, practicing the willowy glide that the Crown Princess had mastered so well. *Nicer than I ever did. Where did that gown come from?*

"It was in the back of your wardrobe; don't you remember wearing it?" The gown in question was of heavy damask with a train; tight in the arms, fitted to the waist, then spreading out like the bell of a flower. The color was unusual; a faded rose. Freya wore a belt of silver links in the form of flowers, and a necklace of carved pink quartz beads.

Not really, Honoria said truthfully. *It might have been the one I wore to Siegfried's birthday feast; what with all that went on, gowns were the last thing on my mind.*

"Well, it's very becoming. There are a dozen brand-new gowns in your wardrobe that I don't ever remember seeing you wear." Freya took off the jewelry, then pulled the gown over her head, folding it and putting it away with care in the wardrobe chest. Clad only in a shift, and barefoot, she selected another, one that Honoria *did* remember. Her mother insisted on calling it a "riding habit," but it was far too encumbering for anyone to ride in, and she'd only worn it once.

Mother sent me off with an entire new set of clothing; that's part of it. The habit, cut very like the gown but with a sleeveless surcoat to go over it, was of deep blue lambswool, a very fine, soft fabric. The surcoat, in a lighter blue, had been embroidered with a fanciful heraldic hawk on the breast, and trimmed in squirrel fur. Both had far too much skirt for Honoria's way of thinking.

Freya put her hair up in two coiled braids, crossing over the top of her head, and pinned the merest scrap of a veil over them. She turned to face Honoria, holding out her arms. "Well, I'm ready to face the world. Are you?"

Why not? Honoria hopped up onto the seat of a chair with the help of her wings, then onto the back. *I want to learn to fly!*

"And I want to see your mother's face when I come to dinner like this!" Freya giggled, then pulled on a brand-new, blue-dyed hawking glove that matched the gown, one Honoria remembered receiving, but also remembered rejecting in favor of her old, well-worn, and supple favorite.

Freya held out her arm, and Honoria leaped from the back of the chair, crossing the room in clumsy wingbeats, and landing without mishap on the glove. "I'm not going to hold your jesses; you aren't going to bate, and if for some reason you startle, I want you to learn to land on the ground."

Fair enough: I hate dangling by my ankles anyway. Honoria relaxed her feet, then set them, then relaxed her legs, feeling her feet literally lock into position on the glove. Freya had been right; when at rest, a hawk's talons locked so securely in whatever grip she was using that it was nearly impossible to pry them off.

As Freya bore her down the stairs, skirts held gracefully in one hand, hawk balanced on the other, Honoria laughed to herself at the looks on the faces of those they passed. They would look, not recognize Freya at first, then stare blankly as they realized who it was but could not reconcile that knowledge with what they saw.

It was the same all the way across the stable yard to the mews, with one exception. Sir Gunther was beside the mews door, as if he had been waiting for someone—and when he saw Freya, he jumped to his feet and hurried over, face flushed.

"Is—my lady, is your hawk well?" he stammered, and Honoria, looking carefully at him for the first time, knew in an instant that Freya had been right. He *was* in love with her. He didn't even look at Honoria when he asked about the hawk, only at Freya.

"Yes, and no, I am afraid," Freya said, with a careful shading of concern in her voice. "She has recovered from whatever struck her down, but now she is like the youngest brancher, almost an eyas in her tameness. I fear she will have to learn her skills all over again."

"Then if I can be of any service at all, *please*, let me help!" Gunther was so pathetically eager that Honoria felt an unaccustomed sympathy for him. Of course, it was easy for her to feel sympathy for him; *she* wasn't the object of his devotions anymore.

"You can be of very great help, Sir Gunther!" Freya said sincerely, looking directly into his eyes. "Especially since Bern has duties elsewhere, and retraining a hawk in this way is tedious work, requiring much patience."

"Then you have all of my help that you need,

my lady!" Gunther took the hand that Freya held out to him and kissed it, then accompanied her into the mews.

Freya explained the hawk's "ailment" to Heinrich, who shook his head but admitted that he had heard of such a thing. "And the best thing to do for her, my lady, is to train her exactly as you plan," he agreed. "God and Saint Francis be praised, that she came through it no more harmed than that!"

So Honoria was taken with great ceremony to Freya's stall, newly cleaned *again*, lest there have been some contagion there, and left on the bow-perch with a fine pigeon. Sir Gunther escorted Freya away, with such solicitude that *she* might have been the one who'd been "ill."

Over the course of the next weeks, as spring finally came to the principality, and the countryside blossomed in earnest, Freya took Honoria out every day and assiduously worked with her. First came flights to the fist from Sir Gunther's or Bern's glove to Freya's—though Honoria only pretended to eat the tidbit Freya held. Little by little the distance between Freya and her helper increased, until Honoria made it swiftly and surely across the length of the stable yard.

Then they moved their training out into the open. A leash tied to Honoria's jesses and tied in turn to a creance "prevented" her from flying off, and she went from fist, to perch, and back again. This was to give her practice in landing on something other than a glove; it was surprising how hard it was at first to grasp that tiny perch with outstretched talons. Then, when Freya was "sure that the hawk would come back to the fist," the creance and leash came off, and Honoria was free to learn to land in trees.

It wasn't as easy as it had always looked.

the first time she tried, she missed the branch she'd been aiming for, and crashed into the boughs. The second time she was more careful, but unfortunately chose a branch too slender for her weight, and found herself hanging upside down for a moment. It took experience to learn how to choose the right branches, and to seize them correctly, and Honoria had never until now appreciated the sheer *work* it took to be a bird!

But the work had only begun, for now Freya taught her to hunt. They began with a lure of rabbit fur dragged through the grass; they went on to the same lure, but with Freya, Gunther, or Bern doing their best to keep it away from her. Then Gunther or Bern went out into the fields, and came back with her first live prey. They brought her young rabbits, just weaned and on their own, and not yet used to outwitting hawks. Even so, the rabbits escaped her, time and time again, as she wound up exhausted, panting, and gazing after them in frustration and fury, her talons full of grass and a little fur.

Then, one afternoon—success at last.

She pursued the escaping rabbit as it twisted and turned, doubled back, while her blood raced and a wild emotion she could not have named filled her and gave her a sudden burst of energy—and struck, and finally, her talons sank into flesh for the first time.

The rabbit screamed, and she reacted to the sound by lashing out with her beak and biting it, hard, where the skull met the backbone. It went limp; she hesitated for a mere second, then let her body do what it wanted to, and found herself beak-deep in hot, red, living blood, a taste that filled her with incredible euphoria and intoxication. She tore into the soft underbelly of the rabbit, as footsteps approached.

"Aren't you going to stop her? She's breaking in," Gunther said, worried.

"No—because I'm not going to keep her," Freya replied. "She's worked so hard to live, and now she's working so hard to learn, I'd like to reward her. I always intended to turn her free someday, and once she can hunt on her own, I think I ought to. Breaking into the quarry isn't a vice in a wild hawk."

"No, it isn't," Gunther agreed. At that point, since it was clear that Freya wasn't going to take this *delicious* meal away from her, Honoria ignored them in favor of stuffing her crop. She only stopped when she couldn't stuff in another morsel, and stepped off the carcass, which at this point wasn't much but bones. She had noticed how euphoric her birds got when she allowed them to break in and eat newly killed prey; now she knew why. She stropped her beak in the grass, then began fastidiously cleaning her talons. Freya waited politely until she'd finished, then offered her glove to step up on.

"Well, my dear, congratulations on your first kill," she said to Honoria, who blinked at her, overwhelmed by lethargy after her meal.

"My lady, you have accomplished a wonderful thing," Gunther said earnestly.

Freya blushed.

That made Honoria take notice; a blush, as she knew all too well, was not a reaction that one could control. Freya—blushing at a compliment from Sir Gunther? What had been going on while she was in the mews?

She kept her questions to herself for the moment, merely observing as the two of them took her back to her stall. Gunther was just as much in love with Freya, but *Freya,* although she managed to keep a collected exterior, was not as indifferent to Gunther as Honoria had supposed.

Only when she was alone with Freya in the mews did Honoria "think out loud" as she had learned to do when she wanted Freya to hear and understand her.

So—how long have you been infatuated with our friend? she asked, amused. She was even more amused when Freya blushed a deep crimson.

"Long enough," Freya murmured uncomfortably. "I don't suppose he still comes out here to pour his heart out to you?"

Not that I've noticed—but why don't you tell him that you're allowed to wed anyone you choose? Why don't you at least tell Father that he's the one you want? It seemed incomprehensible that Freya hadn't made any efforts in that direction, but evidently, she hadn't.

"I—I'd like him to at least say something, first," Freya sighed. "What if he's changed his mind? What if it's just a temporary infatuation?"

What if pigs fly? demanded Honoria. Freya only shook her head.

It wasn't the first time that Honoria had noted how illogical people in love were. But when Freya left, she resolved to take matters into her own hands—well, talons—as soon as ever she could.

From that moment on she had two tasks: first, to master the skills she would need for freedom and independence, and second, to see to it that Sir Gunther declared himself before she won that independence.

Every chance she saw to bring the two physically closer together, she took. She'd work a jess off and drop it in such a way that they both reached for it at the same time. She'd make a flyover so close to one or the other that the involuntary flinch drove them into physical contact with each other. She even stole things and made them chase her to retrieve them. Each time, she thought surely that Gunther would speak.

But he never quite managed to get up the courage. It was very frustrating.

Her quest to master flying and hunting skills,

however, progressed with great success. She
graduated from baby rabbits to adults, from
adult rabbits to hares, and from hares to far
more difficult winged prey. The goshawk was
so named because the breed was routinely used
to hunt geese, formidable foes for a bird of prey.
With their strong wings, they could break a goshawk's leg or wing, their clawed feet could open
terrible wounds, and they could take out an eye
with a blow from their beaks. They outweighed
a goshawk by a considerable amount as well,
and most of that weight was muscle.

Honoria had to work up to geese, therefore.
She began with partridge, then mastered the
teal, and by autumn, routinely took ducks. And
while she worked to conquer flying prey, she
learned when it was prudent to pursue prey into
cover, afoot. Only a goshawk would dare something so outlandish, but occasionally it was a
good idea when she knew that the prey couldn't
escape from the cover. When she'd been the falconer and not the bird, Freya had occasionally
gone into a thicket after a rabbit or a partridge;
there would be a violent commotion followed
by a death cry, and the gos would emerge, backward, dragging the bird in her beak. She usually
had broken feathers to show for the exercise,
and it wasn't something to do lightly, but if prey
was scarce, she knew she'd better learn to hunt
in that odd way *now*, when a mistake would be
less costly with lighter consequences.

The day came when Honoria finally took her

first goose, in a perfect kill; in the air over land rather than water, so she didn't make her kill only to lose it. As she stood on the body, watching as Freya and Gunther walked toward her, she knew that this had been the signal Freya was waiting for.

"I think she's ready, Sir Gunther," Freya said quietly. "Look at her! She's gained back all that she lost, and more."

She wasn't looking at Gunther, who appeared to Honoria like a man who had just heard his own death sentence.

Of course he had; there would be no more excuse to spend countless hours in Freya's company, "helping" her with the hawk. As lowly as his rank was, he would not dare to approach her anyplace else. He didn't even have the excuse of sharing Bern's lessons in falconry, as Heinrich had taken those over so that Freya could spend all her time with Honoria.

Something drastic had to be done, and Honoria was just the hawk to do it.

As they neared, she crouched; when they froze, as a good falconer would, to keep from frightening the bird off her kill, she sprang into the air, and struck without mercy.

With both feet fisted, striking as a peregrine would rather than a gos, she hit Gunther in the head hard enough to knock him off his feet. As he dropped to the ground, dazed, Freya leaped to his side, and Honoria returned to her kill.

"Gunther! Dear Jesu, are you all right?" She

gathered Gunther's head to her breast in a most poetic and romantic—and completely un-planned—manner, frantic with fear, searching for bloody gashes in his scalp beneath his long hair. Which of course would not be there; that was why Honoria had fisted her feet. "Did she hurt you, beloved? Oh my love, please, has she hurt you?"

Sir Gunther gazed up at her for a moment, more stunned by her words than by the blow Honoria had given him. Then, with the most comical mixture of hope and horror on his face that Honoria had ever seen, he struggled to his feet. As Freya rose, terribly confused now, he dropped to his knees before her, groveling, lifting the hem of her skirt and kissing it.

Oh, blessed Virgin Mary—this lad has listened to far too many romantic tales!

"My lady—dearest lady—you mustn't say such things—" he babbled. "I dare not—I am beneath your notice, you must forget me—"

"Forget you!" Freya cried, dragging him up by main force. "Never!"

"My lady—my love—" Gunther was clearly in agony, and if Honoria hadn't felt so sorry for him, she'd have been doubled over in silent laughter.

He'd better find someone else to compose lover's speeches for him, she thought mirthfully.

"Oh, if *only* you were a poor knight's daughter!" he cried wildly, which was, of course, exactly the sort of thing that Freya had been waiting to hear. "I would carry you to the priest at this moment—"

He looked down at her, and Freya's face, shining with bliss, made him forget whatever else he was trying to say.

"You will have to wait until spring, my dearest love," she said softly. "For Father has given me leave to wed where my heart is, so long as I wed along with my sisters and their betrotheds. And my heart—" She placed her palm on his chest, just above the place where his heart beat so wildly Honoria could hear it from where she stood. "—my heart is *here.*"

Very nice speech, for a former hawk, Honoria snickered. As the two began an impassioned embrace, forgetting about anything but each other (including Honoria), she began picking at her jesses and the bracelets that held them to her ankles. She'd begun weakening them some time ago, since they weren't actually being used for anything, and it didn't take very long for a beak designed to tear through tough skin to make short work of the leather bands around her ankles. She stepped neatly out of them, and looked up at the lovers.

Gunther gazed into Freya's eyes as he held her in his arms. "I dreamed so often of this moment. I can scarce believe that this moment is *not* a dream—"

A much better speech, sir knight. And I believe I will take that as my parting line. Honoria pushed off from her prey for the second time, rising strongly and gracefully into the sky. *You may keep the goose, dearest friend and teacher*, she thought back at Freya. *Take it home and let it serve at your betrothal feast. I have somewhere I must go now. . . .*

And into freedom she soared, flying high on strong, wide wings.

Science Fiction Anthologies

☐ **ALIEN ABDUCTIONS**
   Martin H. Greenberg and Larry Segriff, editors 0-88677-856-5—$6.99
Prepare yourself for a close encounter with these eleven original tales of
alien experiences and their aftermath. By authors such as Alan Dean Foster,
Michelle West, Ed Gorman, Peter Crowther, and Lawrence Watt-Evans.

☐ **FUTURE CRIMES**
   Martin H. Greenberg and John Helfers, editors 0-88677-854-9—$6.99
Techno thieves. Virtual vandals. Cybersleuths. And a best-selling lineup
of suspects: Alan Dean Foster, Barbara Paul, Craig Shaw Gardner, Ron
Goulart, and Peter Crowther, among others, to explore the future of crime
in a brand-new collection of high-tech mystery.

☐ **MOON SHOTS**
   Peter Crowther, editor   0-88677-848-4—$6.99
July 20, 1969: a date that will live in history! In honor of the destiny-
altering mission to the Moon, these original tales were created by some
of today's finest SF writers, such as Ben Bova, Gene Wolfe, Brian Aldiss,
Alan Dean Foster, and Stephen Baxter.

☐ **MY FAVORITE SCIENCE FICTION STORY**
   Martin H. Greenberg, editor   0-88677-830-1—$6.99
Here is a truly unique volume, comprised of seminal science fiction stories
specifically chosen by some of today's top science fiction names. With stories
by Sturgeon, Kornbluth, Waldrop, and Zelazny, among others, chosen by such
modern-day masters as Clarke, McCaffrey, Turtledove, Bujold, and Willis.

Prices slightly higher in Canada   **DAW: 104**

Payable in U.S. funds only. No cash/COD accepted. Postage & handling: U.S./CAN. $2.75 for one
book, $1.00 for each additional, not to exceed $6.75; Int'l $5.00 for one book, $1.00 each additional.
We accept Visa, Amex, MC ($10.00 min.), checks ($15.00 fee for returned checks) and money
orders. Call 800-788-6262 or 201-933-9292, fax 201-896-8569; refer to ad #104.

Penguin Putnam Inc.   Bill my: ☐Visa ☐MasterCard ☐Amex_____(expires)
P.O. Box 12289, Dept. B   Card#_____
Newark, NJ 07101-5289

Please allow 4-6 weeks for delivery.   Signature_____
Foreign and Canadian delivery 6-8 weeks.

Bill to:

Name_____

Address_____City_____

State/ZIP_____

Daytime Phone #_____

Ship to:

Name_____ Book Total $_____

Address_____ Applicable Sales Tax $_____

City_____ Postage & Handling $_____

State/Zip_____ Total Amount Due $_____

This offer subject to change without notice.

Don't miss out on the action in these titles featuring
THE EXECUTIONER®, ABLE TEAM® and PHOENIX FORCE®!

The Executioner®

Nonstop action, as Mack Bolan represents ultimate justice, within or beyond the law.

#61184	DEATH WARRANT	$3.50	☐
#61185	SUDDEN FURY	$3.50	☐
#61188	WAR PAINT	$3.50 U.S.	☐
		$3.99 CAN.	☐
#61189	WELLFIRE	$3.50 U.S.	☐
		$3.99 CAN.	☐
#61190	KILLING RANGE	$3.50 U.S.	☐
		$3.99 CAN.	☐
#61191	EXTREME FORCE	$3.50 U.S.	☐
		$3.99 CAN.	☐
#61193	HOSTILE ACTION	$3.50 U.S.	☐
		$3.99 CAN.	☐

(limited quantities available on certain titles)

TOTAL AMOUNT	$
POSTAGE & HANDLING	$
($1.00 for one book, 50¢ for each additional)	
APPLICABLE TAXES*	$ _____
TOTAL PAYABLE	$ _____
(check or money order—please do not send cash)	

To order, complete this form and send it, along with a check or money order for the total above, payable to Gold Eagle Books, to: **In the U.S.:** 3010 Walden Avenue, P.O. Box 9077, Buffalo, NY 14269-9077; **In Canada:** P.O. Box 636, Fort Erie, Ontario, L2A 5X3.

Name:_____

Address:_____ City:_____

State/Prov.:_____ Zip/Postal Code: _____

*New York residents remit applicable sales taxes.
Canadian residents remit applicable GST and provincial taxes.

GEBACK10